LONG LOST

DAVID MORRELL

WARNER BOOKS

An AOL Time Warner Company

WARNER BOOKS EDITION

Copyright © 2002 by David Morrell

Cover design by Jesse Sanchez
Cover photos by Herman Estevez

Warner Books, Inc.
1271 Avenue of the Americas
New York, NY 10020

Visit our Web site at www.twbookmark.com.

An AOL Time Warner Company

Printed in the United States of America

Originally published in hardcover by Warner Books
First International Paperback Printing: October 2002
First U.S Paperback Printing: April 2003

10 9 8 7 6 5 4 3 2 1

POWERHOUSE PRAISE FOR DAVID MORRELL AND *LONG LOST*

"Everything [David Morrell] writes has a you-are-there quality, and that, coupled with his ability to propel characters through a scene, makes reading him like attending a private screening."
—*Washington Post Book World*

"Morrell, an absolute master of the thriller, plays by his own rules and leaves you dazzled."
—**Dean Koontz, bestselling author of *Sole Survivor***

"Surprising and savvy . . . good storytelling, neatly plotted, and admirably paced . . . Morrell's best in years."
—*Kirkus Reviews*

"David Morrell is a master of suspense. He wields it like a stiletto—knows just where to stick it and how to turn it."
—**Michael Connelly, author of *City of Bones***

"Another winner . . . maintains the suspense until the last page."
—*Library Journal*

"Scary. . . . Morrell has always had the ability to put the reader right in the middle of the action, and he does it again here in riveting fashion."
—*Booklist*

"David Morrell is a dynamite storyteller."
—*Winston-Salem Journal*

Please turn to the back of this book for a preview of David Morrell's new novel, *The Protector*.

ALSO BY DAVID MORRELL

FICTION

First Blood (1972)
Testament (1975)
Last Reveille (1977)
The Totem (1979)
Blood Oath (1982)
The Brotherhood of the Rose (1984)
The Fraternity of the Stone (1985)
The League of Night and Fog (1987)
The Fifth Profession (1990)
The Covenant of the Flame (1991)
Assumed Identity (1993)
Desperate Measures (1994)
The Totem (Complete and Unaltered) (1994)
Extreme Denial (1996)
Double Image (1998)
Black Evening (1999)
Burnt Sienna (2000)

NONFICTION

John Barth: An Introduction (1976)
Fireflies (1988)
American Fiction, American Myth
(Essays by Philip Young)
edited by David Morrell and Sandra Spanier (2000)
Lessons from a Lifetime of Writing:
A Novelist Looks at His Craft (2002)

To Jeffrey Weiner:
master of accounts.
A long time ago, you made a promise and you kept it.
Thanks for helping keep distractions from my door
and giving me more time to write.

To the legion of the lost ones,
to the cohort of the damned.
　　　　　—Rudyard Kipling

LONG
LOST

Part One

1

When I was a boy, my kid brother disappeared. Vanished off the face of the earth. His name was Petey, and he was bicycling home from an after-school baseball game. Not that he'd been playing. The game was for older guys like me, which is to say that I was all of thirteen and Petey was only nine. He thought the world of me; he always wanted to tag along. But the rest of the guys complained that he was in the way, so I told Petey to "bug off, go home." I still remember the hurt look he gave me before he got on his bike and pedaled away, a skinny little kid with a brush cut, glasses, braces on his teeth, and freckles, wearing a droopy T-shirt, baggy jeans, and sneakers — the last I saw of him. That was a quarter of a century ago. Yesterday.

By the time supper was ready and Petey hadn't shown up, my mother phoned his friends in the neighborhood, but they hadn't seen him. Twenty minutes later, my father called the police. His worst fear (until that moment at least) was that Petey had been hit by a car, but the police dispatcher said that there hadn't been any accidents involving a youngster on a bicycle. The dispatcher promised to call back if he heard anything and, meanwhile, to have patrol cars looking for him.

My father couldn't bear waiting. He had me show him the likely route Petey would have taken between the playground and home. We drove this way and that. By then it was dusk, and we almost passed the bicycle before I spotted one of its red reflectors glinting from the last of the sunset. The bike had been shoved between bushes in a vacant lot. Petey's baseball glove was under it. We searched the lot. We shouted Petey's name. We asked people who lived on the street if they'd seen a boy who matched Petey's description. We didn't learn anything. As my father sped back home, the skin on his face got so tight that his cheekbones stood out. He kept murmuring to himself, "Oh Jesus."

All I could hope was that Petey had stayed away because he was mad at me for sending him home from the baseball game. I fantasized that he'd show up just before bedtime and say, "Now aren't you sorry? Maybe you want me around more than you guess." In fact, I *was* sorry, because I couldn't fool myself into believing that Petey had shoved his bike between those bushes — he loved that bike. Why would he have dropped his baseball glove? Something *bad* had happened to him, but it never would have happened if I hadn't told him to get lost.

My mom became hysterical. My dad called the police again. A detective soon arrived, and the next day, a search was organized. The newspaper (this happened in a town called Woodford, just outside Columbus, Ohio) was filled with the story. My parents went on television and radio, begging whoever had kidnapped Petey to return him. Nothing did any good.

I can't begin to describe the pain and ruin that Petey's disappearance caused. My mother needed pills to steady her nerves. Lots of times in the night, I heard her sobbing. I couldn't stop feeling guilty for making Petey leave the baseball game. Every time I heard our front door creak open, I prayed it was him coming home at last. My father started drinking and lost his job. He and Mom argued. A month after he moved out, he was killed when his car veered off a highway, flipped several times, and crashed onto its roof. There wasn't any life insurance. My mother had to sell the house. We moved to a small apartment and then went to live with my mom's parents in Columbus. I spent a lot of time worrying about how Petey would find us if he returned to the house.

He haunted me. I grew older, finished college, married, had a son, and enjoyed a successful career. But in my mind Petey never aged. He was still that skinny nine-year-old giving me a hurt look, then bicycling away. I never stopped missing him. If a farmer had plowed up the skeleton of a little boy and those remains had somehow been identified as Petey's, I'd have mourned bitterly for my kid brother, but at least there would have been some finality. I needed desperately to know what had happened.

I'm an architect. For a while, I was with a big firm in Philadelphia, but my best designs were too unorthodox for them, so I finally started my own business. I also decided it would be exciting to change locales — not just move to another East Coast city but move from the East Coast altogether. My wife surprised me by liking the idea even more than I did. I won't go into all the reasons we chose Denver — the lure of the mountains, the myth of the West. The main thing is, we settled there, and almost from the start, my designs were in demand.

Two of my office buildings are situated next to city parks. They not only blend with but also reflect their surroundings; their glass and tile walls act like huge mirrors that capture the images of the ponds, trees, and grassland near them, one with nature. My houses are what I was especially proud of, though. Many of my clients lived near megadollar resorts like Aspen and Vail, but they respected the mountains and didn't want to be conspicuous. They preferred to be with nature without intruding upon it. I understood. The houses I designed blended so much that you couldn't see them until you were practically at their entrances. Trees and ridges concealed them. Streams flowed under them. Flat stretches of rock were decks. Boulders were steps. Cliffs were walls.

It's ironic that structures designed to be inconspicuous attracted so much attention. My clients, despite their claims about wanting to be invisible, couldn't resist showing off their new homes. *House Beautiful* and *Architectural Digest* did articles about them, although the photographs of the exteriors seemed more like nature shots than pictures of homes. The local CBS TV station taped a two-minute spot for the ten o'clock news. The reporter, dressed as a hiker, challenged her viewers to a game: "Can you see a house among these ridges and trees?" She was standing ten feet from a wall, but only when she pointed it out did the viewer realize how thoroughly the house was camouflaged. That report was noticed by CBS headquarters in New York, and a few weeks later, I was being interviewed for a *ten*-minute segment on the *CBS Sunday Morning* show.

I keep asking myself why I agreed. Lord knows, I didn't need any more publicity to get business. So if it wasn't for economic reasons, it must have been because of vanity. Maybe I wanted my son to see me on television. In fact, both he and my wife appeared briefly in a shot where we walked past what the reporter called one of my "chameleon" houses. I wish we'd *all* been chameleons.

2

A man called my name. "Brad!"

That was three days after the *CBS Sunday Morning* show. Wednesday. Early June. A bright, gorgeous day. I'd been in meetings all morning, and the rumblings in my stomach reminded me that I'd missed lunch. I could have sent my secretary to get me a sandwich, but what she was doing was a lot more important than running an errand for me. Besides, I felt like going outside and enjoying the sun. Downtown Denver is a model of urban planning — spacious and welcoming, with buildings low enough to let in the light. My destination was a deli across the street, Bagels and More, nothing on my mind but a corned-beef sandwich, when I heard my name being called.

"Brad!"

At first, I thought it was one of my staff trying to catch my attention about something I'd forgotten. But when I turned, I didn't recognize the man hurrying toward me. He was in his mid-thirties, rough-looking, with a dirty tan and matted long hair. For a moment, I thought he might be a construction worker I'd met on one of my projects. His clothes certainly looked the part: scuffed work boots, dusty jeans, and a wrinkled denim shirt with its sleeves rolled up. But I've got a good memory for faces, and I was sure I'd have remembered the two-inch scar on his chin.

"Brad! My God, I can't believe it!" The man dropped a battered knapsack to the sidewalk. "After all these years! Christ Almighty!"

I must have looked baffled. I like to think people enjoy my company, but very few have ever been so enthusiastic about seeing me. Apparently we had once known each other, although I hadn't the vaguest idea who the guy was.

His broad grin revealed a chipped front tooth. "You don't recognize me? Come on, *I'd* have recognized *you* anywhere! I did on television! It's me!"

My brain was working slowly, trying to search my memory. "I'm afraid I don't —"

"Peter! Your *brother*!"

Now everything became totally clear. My brain worked very fast.

The man reached out. "It's so damned good to see you!"

"Keep your hands away from me, you son of a bitch."

"What?" The man looked shocked.

"Come any closer, I'll call the police. If you think you're going to get money from —"

"Brad, what are you talking about?"

"You watched the *CBS Sunday* program, didn't you?"

"Yes, but —"

"You made a mistake, you bastard. It isn't going to work."

On TV, the reporter had mentioned Petey's disappearance. The day after the show, six different men had called my office, claiming to be Petey. "Your long-lost brother," each of them cheerily said. The first call had excited me, but after a few minutes' conversation, I realized that the guy hadn't the faintest idea about how Petey had disappeared or where it had happened or what our home life had been like. The next two callers had been even worse liars. They all wanted money. I told my secretary not to put through any more calls from anyone who claimed to be my brother. The next three con men lied to her, pretending to have legitimate business, tricking her into transferring the call. The moment they started their spiel, I slammed down the phone. The day after that, my secretary managed to intercept eight more calls from men who claimed to be Petey.

Now they were showing up in person.

"Stay the hell away from me." Too impatient to go down to the traffic light, I turned sharply, found a break in traffic, and headed across the street.

"Brad! For God's sake, listen!" the man yelled. "It really is *me*!"

My back stiffened with anger as I kept walking.

"What do I have to do to make you believe me?" the man shouted.

I reached the street's center line, waiting impatiently for another break in traffic.

"When they grabbed me, I was riding home on my bicycle!" the man yelled.

Furious, I spun. "The reporter mentioned that on television! Get away from me before I beat the shit out of you."

"Brad, you'd have a harder time outfighting me than when we were kids. The bike was blue."

That last statement almost didn't register, I was so angry. Then the image of Petey's blue bike hit me.

"*That* wasn't mentioned on television," the man said.

"It was in the newspaper at the time. All you needed to do was phone the Woodford library and ask the reference department to check the issues of the local newspaper for that month and year. It wouldn't have been hard to get details about Petey's disappearance."

"*My* disappearance," the man said.

On each side, cars beeped in warning as they sped past.

"We shared the same room," the man said. "Was *that* ever printed?"

I frowned, uneasy.

"We slept in bunk beds," the man said, raising his voice. "I had the top. I had a model of a helicopter hanging from a cord attached to the ceiling just above me. I liked to take it down and spin the blades."

My frown deepened.

"Dad had the tip of the little finger on his left hand cut off in an accident at the furniture factory. He loved to fish. The summer before I disappeared, he took you and me camping out here in Colorado. Mom wouldn't go. She was afraid of being outdoors because of her allergy to bee stings. Even the sight of a bee threw her into a panic."

Memories flooded through me. There was no way this stranger could have learned any of those details just by checking old newspapers. None of that information had ever been printed.

"Petey?"

"We had a goldfish in our room. But neither of us liked to clean the bowl. One day we came home from school, and the bedroom stank. The fish was dead. We put the fish in a matchbox and had a funeral in the backyard. When we came back to where we'd buried it, we found a hole where the neighbor's cat had dug up the fish."

"Petey." As I started back toward him, I almost got hit by a car. "Jesus, it *is* you."

"We once broke a window playing catch in the house. Dad grounded us for a week."

This time, *I* was the one reaching out. I've never hugged anybody harder. He smelled of spearmint gum and cigarette smoke. His arms were tremendously strong. "Petey." I could barely get the words out. "Whatever happened to you?"

3

Pedaling home. Angry. Feelings hurt. A car coming next to him, moving slowly, keeping pace with him. A woman in the front passenger seat rolling down her window, asking directions to the interstate. Telling her. The woman not seeming to listen. The sour-looking man at the steering wheel not seeming to care, either. The woman asking, "Do you believe in God?" What kind of question? The woman asking, "Do you believe in the end of the world?" The car veering in front of him. Scared. Hopping the bicycle onto the sidewalk. The woman jumping from the car, chasing him. A sneaker slipping off a pedal. A vacant lot. Bushes. The woman grabbing him. The man unlocking the trunk, throwing him in. The trunk lid banging shut. Darkness. Screaming. Pounding. Not enough air. Passing out.

Petey described it to me as we faced each other in an isolated booth at the rear of the deli I'd been headed toward.

"You never should have made me leave that baseball game," he said.

"I know that." My voice broke. "God, don't I know it."

"The woman was older than Mom. She had crow's-feet around her eyes. Gray roots in her hair. Pinched lips. Awful thin . . . Stooped shoulders . . . Floppy arms. Reminded me of a bird, but she sure was strong. The man had dirty long hair and hadn't shaved. He wore coveralls and smelled of chewing tobacco."

"What did they want with you? Were you . . ." I couldn't make myself use the word *molested*.

Petey looked away. "They drove me to a farm in West Virginia."

"Just across the border? You were that close?"

"Near a town called Redemption. Sick joke, huh? Really, that's what it was called, although I didn't find out the name for quite a while. They kept me a prisoner, until I escaped. When I was sixteen."

"Sixteen? But all this time? Why didn't you come to us?"

"I thought about it." Petey looked uncomfortable. "I just couldn't make myself." He pulled a pack of cigarettes from his shirt pocket.

But as he lit a match, a waitress stopped at our table. "I'm sorry, sir. Smoking isn't permitted in here."

Petey's craggy features hardened. "Fine."

"Can I take your orders?"

"You're good at giving them."

"What?"

"Corned beef," I told the waitress, breaking the tension.

Petey impatiently shoved his cigarettes back into his pocket. "A couple of Buds."

As she left, I glanced around, assuring myself that no customers were close enough to hear what we were saying.

"What did you mean, you couldn't make yourself come to us?"

"The man kept telling me Mom and Dad would never take me back."

"What?"

"Not after what he did to . . . He said Mom and Dad would be disgusted, they'd . . ."

"Disown you? They wouldn't have." I felt tight with sadness.

"I understand that now. But when I escaped . . . let's just say I wasn't myself. Where they kept me a prisoner was an underground room."

"Jesus."

"I didn't see the light of day for seven years." His cheek muscles hardened. "Not that I knew how much time had passed. When I got out, it took me quite a while to figure what was what."

"But what have you been doing?"

Petey looked tortured. "Roaming around. Working construction jobs. Driving trucks. A little of everything. Just after my twenty-first birthday, I happened to be driving a rig to Columbus. I worked up the nerve to go to Woodford and take a look at our place."

"The house had been sold by then."

"So I found out."

"And Dad had died."

"I found that out, too. Nobody remembered where Mrs. Denning and her son Brad had moved."

"We were in Columbus with Mom's parents."

"So close." Petey shook his head in despair. "I didn't know Mom's maiden name, so I couldn't track her through her parents."

"But the police could have helped you find us."

"Not without asking me a lot of questions I didn't want to answer."

"They'd have arrested the man and woman who kidnapped you."

"What good would that have done *me*? There'd have been a trial. I'd have had to testify. The story would have been in all the newspapers." He gestured helplessly. "I felt so . . ."

"It's over now. Try to put it behind you. None of it was your fault."

"I *still* feel . . ." Petey struggled with the next word, then stopped when the waitress brought our beers. He took a long swallow from his bottle and changed the subject. "What about Mom?"

The question caught me by surprise. "Mom?"

"Yeah, how's she doing?"

I needed a moment before I could make myself answer. "She died last year."

". . . Oh." Petey's voice dropped.

"Cancer."

"Uh." It was a quiet exhale. At the same time, it was almost as if he'd been punched. He stared at his beer bottle, but his painful gaze was on something far away.

4

Kate's normally attractive features looked strained when I walked into the kitchen. She was pacing, talking on the phone, tugging an anxious hand through her long blond hair. Then she saw me, and her shoulders sagged with relief. "He just walked in. I'll call you back."

I smiled as she hung up the phone.

"Where have you been? Everybody's been worried," Kate said.

"Worried?"

"You had several important meetings this afternoon, but you never showed up. Your office was afraid you'd been in an accident or —"

"Everything's great. I lost track of the time."

"— been mugged or —"

"*Better* than great."

"— had a heart attack or —"

"I've got wonderful news."

"— or God knows what. You're always Mr. Dependable.

Now it's almost six, and you didn't call to let me know you were okay, and . . . Do I smell alcohol on your breath? Have you been drinking?"

"You bet." I smiled more broadly.

"During the day? Ignoring appointments with clients? What's gotten into you?"

"I told you, I have wonderful news."

"*What* news?"

"Petey showed up."

Kate's blue eyes looked confused, as if I was speaking gibberish. "Who's . . ." At once, she got it. "Good Lord, you don't mean . . . your brother."

"Exactly."

"But . . . but you told me you assumed he was dead."

"I was wrong."

"You're positive it's him?"

"You bet. He told me things only Petey could know. It *has* to be him."

"And he's really here? In Denver?"

"Closer than that. He's on the front porch."

"What? You left him *outside*?"

"I didn't want to spring him on you. I wanted to prepare you." I explained what had happened. "I'll fill in the details when there's time. The main thing to know is, he's been through an awful lot."

"Then he shouldn't be cooling his heels on the porch. For heaven's sake, get him."

Just then, Jason came in from the backyard. He was eleven but small for his age, so that he looked a lot like Petey had when he'd disappeared. Braces, freckles, glasses, thin. "What's all the noise about? You guys having an argument?"

"The opposite," Kate said.

"What's up?"

Looking at Jason's glasses, I was reminded that *Petey* had needed glasses, too. But the man outside wasn't wearing any. I suddenly felt as if I had needles in my stomach. Had I been conned?

Kate crouched before Jason. "Do you remember we told you that your father had a brother?"

"Sure. Dad talked about him on that TV show."

"He disappeared when he was a boy," Kate said.

Jason nodded uneasily. "I had a nightmare about it."

"Well, you don't have to have nightmares about it anymore," Kate said. "Guess what? He came back today. You're going to meet him."

"Yeah?" Jason brightened. "When?"

"Just as soon as we open the front door."

I tried to say something to Kate, to express my sudden misgivings, but she was already heading down the hallway toward the front door. The next thing, she had it open, and I don't know what she expected, but I doubt that the scruffy-looking man out there matched her idealized image of the long-lost brother. He turned from where he'd been smoking a cigarette, admiring the treed area in front of the house. His knapsack was next to him.

"Petey?" Kate asked.

He shifted from one work boot to the other, ill at ease. "These days, I think 'Peter' sounds a little more grown-up."

"Please, come in."

"Thanks." He looked down at his half-smoked cigarette, glanced at the interior of the house, pinched off the glowing tip, then put the remnant in his shirt pocket.

"I hope you can stay for supper," Kate said.

"I don't want to put you out any."

"Nonsense. We'd love to have you."

"To tell the truth, I'd appreciate it. I can't remember when I last had a home-cooked meal."

"This is Jason." Kate gestured proudly toward our son.

"Hi, Jace." The man shook hands with him. "Do you like to play baseball?"

"Yeah," Jason said, "but I'm not very good at it."

"Reminds me of myself at your age. Tell you what. After supper, we'll play catch. How does that sound?"

"Great."

"Well, let's not keep you standing on the porch. Come in," Kate said. "I'll get you something to drink."

"A beer if you've got it." The man who said he was Petey started to follow Kate inside.

But before he crossed the threshold, I had to know. "Are you wearing contact lenses?"

"No." The man frowned in confusion. "What makes you ask?"

"You needed glasses when you were a kid."

"Still do." The man reached into his knapsack and pulled out a small case, opening it, showing a pair of spectacles, one lens of which was broken. "This happened yesterday morning. But I can get around all right. As you know, I need glasses just for distance. Was that a little test or something?"

Emotion made my throat ache. "Petey . . . welcome home."

5

"This is the best pot roast I ever tasted, Mrs. Denning."

"Please, you're part of the family. Call me Kate."

"And these mashed potatoes are out of this world."

"I'm afraid I cheated and used butter. Now our cholesterol counts will be shot to hell."

"I never pay attention to stuff like that. As long as it's food, it's welcome." When Petey smiled, his chipped front tooth was visible.

Jason couldn't help staring at it.

"You want to know how I got this?" Petey gestured toward the tooth.

"Jason, you're being rude," Kate said.

"Not at all." Petey chuckled. "He's just curious, the same as I was when I was a kid. Jace, last summer I was on a roofing project in Colorado Springs. I fell off a ladder. That's also how I got this scar on my chin. Good thing I was close to the ground when I fell. I could have broken my neck."

"Is that where you live now?" I asked. "In Colorado Springs?"

"Lord no. I don't live anywhere."

I stopped chewing.

"But everybody lives somewhere," Kate said.

"Not me."

Jason looked puzzled. "But where do you sleep?"

"Wherever I happen to be, there's always someplace to bed down."

"That seems . . ." Kate shook her head.

"What?"

"Awfully lonely. No friends. Nothing to call your own."

"I guess it depends on what you're used to. People have a habit of letting me down." Petey didn't look at me, but I couldn't help taking his comment personally. "And as for owning things, well, everything of any importance to me is in my knapsack. If I can't carry it, I figure it holds me back."

"King of the road," I said.

"Exactly. You see" — Petey leaned toward Jason, propping his elbows on the table — "I roam around a lot, depending on where the work is and how the weather feels. Each day's a new adventure. I never know what to expect. Like last Sunday, I happened to be in Butte, Montana, eating breakfast in a diner that had a television. I don't normally look at television and I don't have any use for those Sunday-morning talk shows, but this one caught my attention. Something about the voice of the guy being interviewed. I looked up from my eggs and sausage, and Lord, the guy on TV sure made me think of somebody — but not from recently. A long time ago. I kept waiting for the announcer to say who the guy was. Then he didn't need to — because the announcer mentioned that the guy's kid brother had disappeared while bicycling home from a baseball game when they were youngsters. Of course, the guy on television was your father."

Petey turned to me. "As I got older, I thought more and more about looking you up, Brad, but I had no idea where you'd gone. When the announcer said you lived in Denver, I set down my knife and fork and started for here at once. Took me all Sunday, Monday, and Tuesday. Mind you, I tried phoning along the road, but your home number isn't listed. As for your *business* number, well, your secretary wouldn't put me through."

"Because of all those crank calls I told you about on the way over here." I felt guilty, as if he thought I'd intentionally rejected him.

"Three days to drive from Montana? You must have had car trouble," Kate said.

Petey shook his head from side to side. "A car's just something else that would own me. I hitchhiked."

"*Hitchhiked?*" Kate asked in surprise. "Why didn't you take a bus?"

"Well, there are two good reasons. The first is, in my experience, people who ride buses tend to have the same boring stories, but any driver with the courage to pick up a hitchhiker is definitely someone worth talking to."

The way he said that made us chuckle.

"If it turns out they're *not* interesting, I can always say, 'Let me off in the next town.' Then I take my chances with another car. Each ride's a small adventure." Petey's eyes crinkled with amusement.

"And what's the second reason for not taking the bus?" I asked.

The amusement faded. "Work's been a little scarce lately. I didn't have the money for the ticket."

"That's going to change," I said. "I know where there's plenty of work on construction projects — if you want it."

"I sure do."

"I can give you some pocket money in the meantime."

"Hey, I didn't come here for handouts," Petey said.

"I know that. But what'll you do for cash until then?"

Petey didn't have an answer.

"Come on," I said. "Accept a gift."

"I guess I could use some cash to rent a motel room."

"No way," Kate said. "You're not renting any motel room."

"You're spending the night with us."

6

Petey threw a baseball to Jason, who was usually awkward, but this time he caught the ball perfectly and grinned.

"Look, Dad! Look at what Uncle Peter taught me!"

"You're doing great. Maybe your uncle ought to think about becoming a coach."

Petey shrugged. "Just some tricks I picked up on the road, from Friday nights when I ended up at baseball parks in various towns. All you have to remember, Jace, is to keep your eye on the ball instead of on your glove. And make sure your glove is ready to snap shut."

Kate appeared at the back door, her blond hair silhouetted by the kitchen light. "It's time for bed, Little Leaguer."

"Aw, do I have to, Mom?"

"I've already let you stay up a half hour longer than usual. Tomorrow's a school day."

Disappointed, Jason turned to his uncle.

"Don't look at me for help," Petey said. "What your mother says goes."

"Thanks for the lesson, Uncle Peter. Now maybe the other kids'll let me play on the team."

"Well, if they don't, you let me know, and I'll go down to the ballpark to have a word with them." Petey mussed Jason's sandy hair and nudged him toward the house. "You better not keep your mother waiting."

"See you in the morning."

"You bet."

"I'm glad you found us, Uncle Peter."

"Me, too." Petey's voice was unsteady. "Me, too."

Jason went inside, and my brother turned to me. "Nice boy."

"Yes, we're very proud of him."

The setting sun cast a crimson glow over the back-yard's trees.

"And Kate's . . ."

"Wonderful," I said. "It was my lucky day when I met her."

"There's no getting around it. You've done great for yourself. Look at this house."

I felt embarrassed to have so much. "My staff teases me about it. As you saw from the TV show, my specialty is designing buildings that are almost invisible in their environment. But when we first came to town, this big old Victorian seemed to have our name on it. Of course, all the trees in the front and back conceal it pretty well."

"It feels solid." Petey glanced down at his calloused hands. "Funny how things worked out. Well . . ." He roused himself and grinned. "Coaching's thirsty work. I could use another beer."

"Be right back."

When I returned with the beers (inside, Kate had raised her eyebrows, not used to seeing me drink so much), I also had something in a shopping bag.

"What's that?" Petey wondered.

"Something I've been keeping for you."

"I can't imagine what you'd —"

"I'm afraid it's too small for you to use if you want to play catch with Jason another time," I said.

Petey shook his head in confusion.

"Recognize this?" I reached in the bag and pulled out the battered baseball glove that I'd found under Petey's bike so long ago.

"My God."

"I kept it all these years. I never let it out of my room. I used to hold it next to me when I went to bed, and I'd try to imagine where you were and what you were doing and . . ." I forced the words out. ". . . if you were still alive."

"A lot of times, I wished I *wasn't* alive."

"Don't think about that. The past doesn't matter now. We're together again, Petey. *That's* what matters. God, I've missed you." I handed him the glove, although I couldn't see him very well — my eyes were misted.

7

"So what do you think of him?" I asked Kate, keeping my voice low as I turned off the light and got under the covers. Petey's room was at the opposite end of the hall. He wouldn't be able to hear us. Even so, I felt self-conscious talking about him.

Lying next to me in the darkness, Kate didn't answer for a moment. "He's had a hard life."

"That's for sure. And yet he seems to enjoy it."

"A virtue of necessity."

"I suppose. All the same . . ."

"What are you thinking?" Kate asked.

"Well, if he didn't like it, he could always have lived another way."

"How?"

"I guess he could have gone to school and entered a profession."

"Maybe have become an architect, like you?"

I shrugged. "Maybe. It wouldn't have been out of the

question. I've seen a couple of stories on the news about twins separated at birth and reunited as adults. They discover they have the same job, the same hobbies, wives who look the same and have the same personality."

"I'm not sure I like being linked with someone's hobby. Besides, you and your brother aren't twins."

"Granted. Even so, you know what I mean. Petey could have ended up like me, but he chose not to."

"You really think people have that much choice in their lives? You told me you never would have become an architect if it hadn't been for a geometry teacher you really liked in high school."

Wistful, I stared at moonlight streaming through our bedroom window. "Yeah, I sure was weird — the only kid in high school who liked geometry. To me, that teacher made the subject fascinating. He told me what I had to do, where to go to college and all, if I wanted to be an architect."

"Well, I seriously doubt that your brother had a geometry teacher. Did he even go to high school?" Kate asked.

"Somebody must have taught him *something*. He's awfully well spoken. I haven't heard a foul word from him."

Kate turned to face me, propping herself on an elbow. "Look, I'm willing to do all I can to help. If he wants to stay here for a while until he decides what to do next, that's fine with me."

"I was hoping you'd feel that way." I leaned over and kissed her. "Thanks."

"Is that the best way you can think of to thank me?" she asked.

I kissed her again, this time deeply.

"Far more sincere." She drew a hand up my leg.

"Mmm." It was the last sound for a while. The presence of a stranger in the house made us more self-conscious about being overheard. When we climaxed, our kiss was so deep that we swallowed each other's moans.

We lay silently, coming back to ourselves.

"If we get more sincere than that, I'll need to be resuscitated," I murmured.

"Mouth-to-mouth?"

"Brings me to life every time." Getting up to go to the bathroom, I glanced out the window. In the darkness, peering down toward the backyard, I saw something I didn't expect.

"What are you looking at?" Kate asked.

"Petey."

"What?"

"I can see him in the moonlight. He's down there in a lounge chair."

"Asleep?" Kate asked.

"No, he's smoking, staring up at the stars."

"Given everything that's happened, he probably couldn't sleep."

"I know how he feels."

"I'll tell you one thing," Kate said. "Anyone who's polite enough not to smoke in the house is welcome."

8

Although Petey had said that he enjoyed his life on the road, I was determined to make sure he enjoyed it even more by paying attention to a few basic matters: his appearance, for example. That chipped front tooth made a terrible first impression. I had a suspicion that Petey had been losing work because contractors he approached to hire him felt he looked like a troublemaker. So, the next morning, I phoned our family dentist, explained the situation, and got him to agree (for double his usual fee) to give up his lunch hour.

"Dentist?" Petey told me. "Hell no. I'm not going to any dentist."

"Just to smooth out that chip in your tooth. It's not going to hurt."

"No way. I haven't been to a dentist since I needed a back tooth taken out six years ago."

"*Six years ago?* Good God. All the more reason for

you to have a checkup." I didn't tell him that the hygien-
ist had agreed to give up *her* lunch hour, too.

Before that, I phoned several barbershops, until I found
one that wasn't busy. Long hair — my own's hardly what
you'd call short — doesn't have to look tangled and scruffy.
After the barbershop, we bought some clothes. Not that I
deluded myself into thinking that Petey could use dress
slacks and a sport coat, but some new jeans and a nice-
looking shirt wouldn't do any harm. After that, a shoe store:
new work boots and sneakers.

"I can't accept all this," Petey said.

"I'm glad to do it. If you want, we'll call it a loan.
Sometime, when you're flush, you can pay me back."

Then it was time for the dentist. Afterward, Petey's
teeth looked great, although he had several cavities, the
dentist said. They'd be taken care of when Petey went
back in a couple of weeks. Petey's hair looked stylishly
windblown. I was almost tempted to ask a plastic surgeon
if anything could be done about the scar on Petey's chin.
No matter, a little maintenance had accomplished a lot. He
looked like he'd just gotten dressed after playing tennis.

"Hungry?"

"Always," Petey said.

"Yeah, I get the impression you've been missing a few
meals lately. You could use about ten more pounds. Do
you like Italian food?"

"You mean spaghetti and meatballs?"

"Sort of. But where we're going, spaghetti's called
pasta, and the dishes have names like chicken marsala."

"Hold on a second."

"After lunch, I'm going to take you to see a man about
a job."

"Brad . . . Stop. . . . Hold it."

"Why? What's wrong?"

"Don't you have work to do?" Petey asked. "You took yesterday afternoon off. This morning, you didn't go to work, either. Kate said you had appointments, meetings."

"None of it's as important as you."

"But you can't run a business that way, not and spend money on me the way you are. We have a lot to catch up on, but we don't have to do it all at once."

Petey's worried expression started me laughing. "You think I'm getting carried away?"

"Just a little."

"Then what do you suggest?"

"Go to work. There's a park across the street. I'd like to hang out there for a while. Get my mind straight. All these changes. I'll meet you at home for supper."

"That's really what you want?" I asked.

"You've done enough for me."

"But how will you get home?"

"Hitchhike," Petey said.

"What if you don't get a ride?"

"Don't worry. I've got a knack for it." Petey's teeth looked great when he grinned.

"I have a better idea," I said. "Use my car. You can pick me up at the end of the day."

"Can't. I don't have a driver's license."

"That's something else we'll take care of."

"Tomorrow," Petey said.

"We're going to see about getting your glasses fixed, too."

"Right," Petey said. "Tomorrow."

9

Petey and Jason were cutting the lawn when I got home. The power mower was awkward for Jason, so Petey was walking beside him, helping him make the turns.

"Hey, look at me, Dad!" Jason yelled to be heard above the motor's roar.

I raised my thumb enthusiastically.

They stopped beside me.

"Can you control it, Jace?" Petey asked.

"I'm pretty sure."

"Then it's all yours. I'll be over here talking to your dad."

Jason nodded, concentrating on keeping the mower in a straight line. Its roar diminished as he navigated among trees toward the far side of the yard.

Petey motioned me toward the porch steps, where he picked up a bottle of beer. "I might've created a monster. If he gets any better at this, you're going to have to raise his allowance."

"It's the first time he's shown an interest. Could be you've hit on something," I said. "Normally, a lawn service does this for me, but it'd be good for him to help a little and learn some responsibility."

"Can't be too young to learn responsibility." Petey took a drink of his beer.

"Listen, I appreciate the effort, but you didn't have to mow the grass," I said.

"No big deal. It looked a little long. I want to do my share."

"Honestly, it isn't necessary. I'm just glad to have you here. Anyway, since you'll be working next week, take it easy for now."

Petey cocked his head. "Working next week?"

"Yeah, I made some calls. I got you a job."

"You *did*? Great!"

"On a building I designed."

"Couldn't be better."

"Uncle Peter!" Jason yelled in panic. At the end of a row, the boy struggled to turn the mower. It veered toward a shrub.

"Hang on!" Petey ran to help him.

10

"No need to help with the dishes," Kate said.

"It's the least I can do." Petey dried another pot. "I can't remember when I had a tastier beef stew."

"We don't normally eat this much red meat," she said. "I'm trying to put some weight on you."

"The lemon pie was spectacular."

Jason eyed a second piece. "Yeah, we hardly ever get desserts in the middle of the week."

"Well, you worked hard mowing the lawn," Kate said. "You deserve a treat."

Sitting at the end of the table, I couldn't help smiling. The reality that Petey was actually over there by the sink, reaching to dry another pot, still overwhelmed me.

"Anyway," he said, returning to an earlier topic, "it doesn't surprise me that you moved here to Denver."

"Oh?"

"That camping trip you and I and Dad went on. Remember?" Petey asked.

"I sure do."

"Out here to Colorado. What a good time. Of course, the long drive from Ohio was a pain. If it hadn't been for the comic books Dad kept buying us along the highway . . . Once we got here, the effort sure was worth it. Camping, hiking, rock climbing, and fishing, Dad showing us what to do."

"The first fish you ever caught, you were so excited that you reeled in before you hooked it good," I said. "It jumped back into the lake."

"You remember that much?"

"I thought about that trip a lot over the years. A month after we got back, school started, and . . ." I couldn't make myself refer to Petey's disappearance. "For a lot of years, it was the last good summer of my life."

"Mine, too." Petey looked down. A long second later, he shrugged off his regret and picked up the last pot. "Anyway, what I'm getting at is, maybe you came out here because in the back of your mind you wanted to return to that summer."

"Camping?" Jason broke the somber mood.

We looked at him. He'd been silent for a while, eating his second piece of pie.

"Dad promised to take me, but we never did," Jason said.

I felt embarrassed. "We went on plenty of hikes."

"But we never used tents."

"Are you telling me you've never actually gone camping?" Petey asked.

Jason nodded, then corrected himself. "Except, I once slept in a tent in Tom Burbick's backyard."

"Doesn't count," Petey said. "You've gotta be where you hear the lions and tigers and bears."

"Lions and tigers?" Jason frowned, looking vulnerable behind his glasses.

"It's a joke." Kate rumpled his hair.

She left some soapsuds. He swatted at them. "Mom!"

"But that might not be a bad idea." She looked at Petey and me. "A camping trip. The two of you can pick up where you left off. Jump over the years. I know it's been hard for you, Peter, but now the good times are starting again."

"I think you're right, Kate," Petey said. "I can feel them."

"What about *me*?" Jason asked. "Can't *I* come?"

"We'll *all* go," Petey said.

"Sorry. Not me, gentlemen." Kate held up her hands. "Saturday, I'm scheduled to give a seminar." Kate was a stress-management counselor; her specialty was advising corporations whose employees were burned out because of downsizing. "Besides, sleeping in the woods isn't high on my list."

"Just like Mom." Petey turned to me. "Remember?"

"Yeah, just like Mom."

"Except your mother," Kate said, "was afraid of bees, whereas in my case it's a matter of natural selection."

"Natural selection?" I asked, puzzled.

"You guys are a lot better equipped to crawl out of a tent at night and pee in the woods."

11

"I've been meaning to ask you something."

Petey quit studying the map and looked at me. "About what?"

It was almost eleven o'clock: a radiant Saturday morning. My Ford Expedition was loaded with all kinds of camping equipment. We'd followed Interstate 70 west out of Denver and were now well into the mountains, although Jason wasn't appreciating their snowcaps. He was dozing in a sleeping bag on the backseat.

"After you . . ." I had trouble continuing. "It suddenly occurs to me that you might not want to talk about it."

"There's only one way to find out."

"After you got away from . . ."

"Say it. The sick bastards who kidnapped me. It's a fact. You don't need to tap-dance around the subject."

"You were sixteen when you escaped. You've talked about roaming the country, working on construction jobs or whatever. But you never mentioned anything about school. When you disappeared, you were in the fourth grade, but you've obviously had more education than that. Who taught you?"

"Oh, I had plenty of education in politeness," Petey said bitterly. "The man and woman who kept me in that underground room insisted on a lot of 'Yes, sir, yes, ma'am, please and thank you.' If I ever forgot, they punched my face to remind me." The sinews in his neck tightened into ropes.

"I'm sorry. I wish I hadn't raised the subject," I said.

"It's fine. There's no point in hiding from the past. It'll only catch up in other ways." Petey's gaze hardened. He took a deep breath, subduing his emotions. "Anyhow, in terms of education, I have better memories. As I wandered from town to town, I learned that an easy way to get a free meal was to show up at church socials after Sunday-morning services. Of course, I had to sit through the services in order to get the free meals. But most times, I didn't mind—the services were peaceful. After so many years of not reading, I'd sort of forgotten how to do it. When members of this or that congregation realized that I couldn't read the Bible, they took steps to make sure I learned my ABC's and, more important, the Good Book. There were always teachers in the congregations. After work some evenings, I'd get private classes at a church in whatever town I happened to be in. There are a lot of decent folks out there."

"I'm glad to hear it."

"Hear what, Dad?" Jason asked sleepily from the backseat, where he'd woken up.

"Just that there are decent people in the world."

"Didn't you know that?"

"Sometimes I wondered. You and your uncle better concentrate on the map. Our turnoff isn't far ahead."

12

___

We were looking for a place called Breakhorse Ridge. It's odd how some names stay in my memory. Twenty-five years earlier, that was where Dad had taken Petey and me on our camping trip. Somebody at the furniture factory where Dad was the foreman had once lived in Colorado and had described to Dad how beautiful the Breakhorse Ridge area was. So Dad, who'd already committed to taking us camping in Colorado, had decided that would be our destination. But back then, all during the long drive, I'd had a horrifying mental image of somebody breaking horses in half. Not knowing anything about how cowboys "broke" wild horses so people could ride them, I'd been afraid of what we were going to see. Dad finally got me to tell him what was bothering me. After he explained, my fear turned to curiosity. But when we arrived, there weren't any horses or cowboys, just a few old wooden corrals, and a meadow leading down to a lake and an aspen forest with mountains above it.

I never forgot the name. But as Petey, Jason, and I had made plans, I couldn't find the place on a map. I finally had to phone the headquarters for park services in Colorado. A ranger had faxed me a section of a much more detailed map than I was using, showing me the route to Breakhorse Ridge. I'd spread my general map on the dining room table, put the fax over the section we were interested in, and shown Petey and Jason where we were going.

Now we were almost there, turning to the right onto Highway 9, heading north into the Arapaho National Forest.

"It gets tricky from here on, guys. Keep comparing the map to what's around us," I said.

Jason crawled into the front, and Petey buckled his seat belt over both of them.

"What are we searching for?" Jason asked.

"This squiggly line." Petey showed him the fax. "It'll be a narrow dirt road on the right. With all these pine trees, we'll have to watch closely. It'll be hard to spot."

I steered around a curve. The trees got thicker. Even so, I thought I saw a break in them on the right. But I didn't say anything, wanting Jason to make the discovery. Petey must have read my mind. I saw him look up from the map and focus his eyes as if he'd noticed the break, but he didn't say anything, either.

I drove closer.

The break became a little more distinct.

"There!" Jason pointed. "I see it!"

"Good job," Petey said.

"For sure," I added. "I almost went past it."

I steered to the right and entered a bumpy dirt lane.

Scrub grass grew between its wheel ruts. Bushes squeezed its sides. Pine branches formed a canopy.

"Gosh, do you think we'll get stuck?" Jason leaned forward with concern.

"Not with this four-wheel drive," Petey said. "It'd take a lot worse terrain than this to put us in trouble. Even if it snowed, we wouldn't have to worry."

"Snowed?" Jason frowned. "In June?"

"Sure," Petey said. "This time of year, you can still get a storm in the mountains." The trees became sparse. "See those peaks ahead and how much snow they still have? Up here, the sun hasn't gotten hot enough to melt it yet."

Taking sharp angles, the lane zigzagged higher. The slope below us became dizzyingly steep. The bumps were so severe that only those cowboys who'd ridden bucking wild horses here years earlier could have enjoyed the ride.

"Who do you suppose built this road?" Jason asked. "It looks awfully old."

"The forest service maybe," I said. "Or maybe loggers or ranchers before this area became part of the national forest system. I remember our dad saying that in the old days cattlemen kept small herds here to feed prospectors in mining towns."

"Prospectors? *Gold?*" Jason asked.

"And silver. A long time ago. Most of the towns are abandoned now."

"*Ghost* towns," Petey said.

"Gosh," Jason said.

"Or else the towns became ski resorts," I said, hoping to subdue Jason's imagination so Petey and I wouldn't be wakened by his nightmares about ghosts.

The road crested the slope and took us into a bright meadow, the new grass waving in a gentle breeze.

"It's the way I remember it when Dad drove us here," I told Petey.

"After all these years," Petey said in awe.

"Are we there yet?" Jason asked.

The age-old question from kids. I imagined that Petey or I had asked our dad the same thing. We looked at each other and couldn't keep from laughing.

"What's so funny?" Jason asked.

"Nothing," Petey said. "No, we're not there yet."

13

It took another half hour. The meadow gave way to more pine trees and a slope steeper than the first one, the zigzag angles sharper. We crested a bumpy rise, and I stopped suddenly, staring down toward where the barely detectable road descended into a gentle grassy bowl. Sunlight glinted off a picture-book lake, aspens beyond it, then pine trees, then mountains towering above.

"Yes," I said, my chest tight. "Just as I remember."

"It hasn't changed," Petey said.

On the right, old corrals were the only variation in the meadow. Their gray weathered posts and railings had long ago collapsed into rotting piles. We drove past them, nearing the lake. There weren't any other cars. In fact, I couldn't find an indication that anyone had been around in a very long time.

We stopped fifty feet from the lake, where I recalled Dad stopping. When we got out of the car, I savored the fresh, pleasantly cool air.

"Look at this old campfire, Dad!"

Petey and he were on the right side of the car. I looked over toward a scorched circle of rocks that had charred hunks of wood in the middle.

"Old is right," Petey said. "I bet it hasn't been used in years." He looked at me. "I wonder if this is the same place you and I and Dad built *our* campfire?"

"It's nice to think so."

Jason brimmed with energy. "Where are we going to put up the tent?"

"How about over there?" I pointed to the right of the old campfire site. "I think that's where Petey and I helped Dad put up our tent."

"Can *I* help, Dad?"

"Of course," Petey said.

There was a moment after I lifted the back hatch and we unloaded our gear when the déjà vu I'd been feeling reached an overwhelming intensity. Everything seemed realer than real. I looked over at Jason and Petey as they pulled the collapsed tent from its nylon sack and tried to figure how to put it together. Jason's glasses and freckles, his sandy hair at the edge of his baseball cap, his baggy jeans and loose-fitting shirt, made him look so much like Petey had looked as a boy that I shivered.

Jason noticed. "What's the matter, Dad?"

"Nothing. This breeze is a little cold is all. I'm going to put on my windbreaker. You want yours?"

"Naw, I'm fine."

"Big brother," Petey called. "You're the expert in how buildings are put together. Do you think you can show us how to put this damned *tent* together?"

The three of us needed an hour to get the job done.

14

By then, it was almost 1:30. Kate had packed a lunch in a cooler: chicken, beef, and peanut butter sandwiches, along with soft drinks, apples, and little packages of potato chips. Jason didn't touch the apples. Otherwise, he wolfed everything down, the same as Petey and I did. We saw fish splashing in the lake but decided to get our poles out later. For now, there was plenty to do, exploring. We put our lunch trash in a bag, locked it in the car, and set out, hiking to the left around the lake.

"I remember there was a cave up there." I pointed above the aspens. "And lots of places to climb."

Petey yelled to Jason, who was running ahead of us. "Do you like to climb?"

"I don't know!" Jason turned to look at us, continuing to run. "I've never done it!"

"You're going to love it!"

The lake was about a hundred yards across. We reached the other side and found a stream that fed into it. The stream was swift from the spring snowmelt, too wide to cross, so we followed its cascading path up through the aspens, the roar of the water sometimes so loud that we couldn't hear one another.

Even though we were three thousand feet higher than the altitude of five thousand feet we were used to in Denver, the thin mountain air didn't slow us. If anything, it was invigorating. It was like inhaling vitamins. Stretching my legs to climb over fallen trees or to clamber on and off boulders, I felt such pleasure from my body that I criticized myself for not having taken time from work to do this earlier.

Across the stream, above us, a deer moved, its brown silhouette stiffening at our approach, then bounding gracefully away through the white trunks of the aspens. With the noise from the stream, it couldn't have heard us coming, I thought. It must have smelled us. Then another silhouette stiffened and bounded away. A third. Even with the noise from the stream, I heard their hooves thunder.

Soon we reached where the stream cascaded from a high, narrow draw that was too dangerous to go into. We angled to the left, following a steep upward trail that had hoof marks on it. The trail veered farther to the left, maintaining a consistent level along a wooded slope, so predictable that when a sunlit outcrop above us attracted our attention, we decided to explore. Getting to it was more difficult than it appeared. At one time or another, both Petey and I slipped on loose rocks underfoot. We'd have rolled to the bottom, scraping our arms and legs, maybe even breaking something, if we hadn't managed to clutch exposed tree roots. By contrast, Jason scurried up like a mountain goat.

Breathing hoarsely, Petey and I crawled over the rim and found Jason waiting for us on a wide slab of rock that provided a view of the stream below us and the chasm through which it churned. Two hundred feet above it, we were far enough from the roar for me not to need to shout when I warned Jason, "Stay away from the edge."

"I will," he promised. "But, gosh, this is totally neat, Dad."

"Beats watching television, huh?" Petey said.

Jason thought about it. His face assumed an expression of "I wouldn't go *that* far."

Petey laughed.

"Where's that cave you mentioned?" Jason asked.

"I'm having trouble remembering," I said. "Somewhere on this side of the stream is all I know for sure."

"Can we look for it?"

"Absolutely. After we take a break."

I settled onto the stone slab, unhooked my canteen from my belt, and took a long swallow of slightly warm, slightly metallic-tasting, incredibly delicious water. The park ranger I'd spoken to on the telephone had emphasized that we needed to take canteens with us and knapsacks containing trail food, a compass and a topographical map (neither of which I knew how to use), a first-aid kit, and a rain slicker in case the weather turned bad. "Dress in layers," she'd advised. "Keep a dry jacket in your knapsack." I'd already put on my denim windbreaker before we left the car. Now the hike had so warmed me that I took off the jacket and stuffed it into the knapsack.

"Anybody want some peanuts and raisins?" I asked.

"I'm still full from lunch," Petey said.

Jason looked uncomfortable.

"What's the matter?" I asked.

"I have to . . ."

It took me a moment to understand. "Pee?"

Jason nodded, bashful.

"Go around that boulder over there," I told him.

Hesitant, he disappeared behind it.

My parental obligations taken care of for the moment, I stepped forward to admire the chasm. The stream tumbled down a series of low waterfalls. Spray hovered over it. How had Jason described the view? "Neat"? He was right. This *was* totally neat.

Behind me, he suddenly shouted, "Dad!"

Something slammed my back with such force that it took my breath away. I hurtled into space.

15

The drop sucked more of my breath away. The little that was left jolted from my mouth when I struck loose stones. Avalanching with them, rolling sideways, I groaned. Abruptly, I hurtled into the air again, plummeting farther, my stomach squeezing toward my throat. I jerked to an agonizing stop, my left arm stretching as if it were about to be ripped from its socket. My arm slipped free of something. I dropped again and hit something hard. Cold mist swallowed me. Darkness swirled.

When my eyelids slowly opened, black turned to gray, but the swirling continued. Pain awoke throughout my body. Delirious, I took a long time to realize that the gray swirling around me was vapor thrown up from the cascading stream. The roar aggravated my dizziness.

I felt that I was breathing through a cold, wet washcloth. Gradually, I understood that my left arm was across my nose and mouth. My shirtsleeve was soaked from the vapor that the thundering stream tossed into the air. Then

I trembled, seeing that my sleeve was wet from something besides the mist. Blood. My arm was gashed.

Alarm shot through me. I fought to raise my head, and discovered that I was on my back on a ledge. Below was a fall of what I judged to be 150 feet. A series of outcrops led sharply down to the roaring stream.

Jesus, what had happened?

I peered up. The vapor made it difficult for me to see the top of the cliff. Nonetheless, through the haze, I could distinguish a long slope of loose stones below the rim. The slope had saved my life. If I'd fallen directly to where I now lay, my injuries would have been catastrophic. Instead, I'd rolled down the slope, painfully reducing the length of the fall. But beneath the slope of loose stones, there had been a ledge over which I'd tumbled to the ledge I'd landed on, and the distance between them was about twenty feet. A potentially lethal drop. Why wasn't I dead?

My knapsack dangled above me. It was caught on a sharp branch of a stunted pine tree that had managed to grow from the side of the cliff. I remembered stuffing my windbreaker into the knapsack and hanging the knapsack over my left shoulder before I'd walked over to peer into the chasm. The branch had snagged the knapsack. The sharp pain in my left shoulder indicated the force with which I'd been jerked to a stop. My arm had slipped free from the strap. I'd fallen a body length to this ledge. Luck was all that had saved me.

Every movement excruciating, I strained to sit up. My mind tilted, as if ball bearings rolled from the front of my skull to the back. For a moment, I feared that I'd vomit.

"Jason!" I tried to yell. "Petey!"

But the words were like stones in my throat.

"Jason!" I tried harder. "Petey!"

The roar of the stream overpowered my voice.

Don't panic, I fought to assure myself. It doesn't matter if they can't hear me. They know where I am. They'll help me.

My God, I hope they don't try to climb down, I suddenly thought.

"Jason! Petey! Stay where you are! You'll fall and get killed!"

My voice cracked, making my words a hoarse whisper.

Straining to see through the haze, I hoped to catch a glimpse of Jason and Petey peering over the rim to try to find me. No sign of them. Maybe they're trying to get a better vantage point, I thought. Or maybe they're hurrying back to the mouth of the chasm, hoping to reach me from below.

I prayed that they'd be careful, that Jason wouldn't take foolish chances, that Petey would make sure he didn't. Trembling, I parted the rip in my sleeve. Wiping away the blood, I saw a gash five inches long between my elbow and my wrist. Blood immediately welled up, obscuring the wound. It dripped from my arm, pooling on the ledge.

Bile shot into my mouth.

Do something, I thought. I can't just sit here and let myself bleed to death.

My knapsack seemed to float above me. I stretched my good arm but couldn't reach it. In greater pain, I mustered the strength to try to stand.

The first-aid kit in the knapsack, I thought.

My legs gave out. I clawed at a niche and barely avoided toppling into the chasm. Despite the cold from the stream, I sweated. Shock made me tremble as I grabbed for a higher niche and wavered to my feet. For a moment, I saw specks in front of my eyes. Then my vision cleared, and I stared up toward the knapsack. Despairingly, it seemed as high as ever. My injured left arm dangled at my side. I extended my right arm upward. *Another six inches*. All I need is six inches more, I thought.

Pressing my chest against the cliff, standing on tiptoes, wincing from new throbbing pain in my hips, my sides, and my ribs, I stretched as high as I could, then breathed out in triumph as I touched the knapsack's strap.

Vapor from the stream had slicked the nylon. I lost my grip but instantly pawed for the strap again, pushing my tiptoes to their limits, this time clutching with all my strength. I tugged the knapsack to the side, toward the chasm, working to free it from the stout branch it had snagged on. I tugged once, twice, and suddenly felt weightless as the knapsack jerked free.

Falling, I dove toward the ledge. I screamed as my injured arm landed, but I couldn't let myself react. I had to concentrate solely on my good arm hanging over the ledge, the knapsack dangling from my fingers.

Cautiously, I rolled onto my back and placed the knapsack on my chest. The temptation to rest was canceled by the increased flow of blood from my arm. Nauseated, I opened the knapsack, pawed past my windbreaker and rain slicker, pushed the Ziploc bags of trail food aside, and found the plastic case of the first-aid kit.

I clumsily pried it open, dismayed to find only Band-Aids and two-inch-square pads along with scissors, antiseptic swabs, antibiotic cream, and a plastic bottle of Tylenol. None of that was going to stop the bleeding.

A tourniquet, I thought. I'll use my belt. I'll tighten it around my arm and . . .

But even as I unbuckled my belt, I remembered something I'd read about tourniquets being dangerous, about the risk of blood clots and gangrene if the tourniquet wasn't loosened at proper intervals.

What difference does it make? I thought. I'll bleed to death before I die from gangrene.

A pressure bandage. Whatever I'd read about tourniquets had warned that a pressure bandage was the safe way to stop bleeding, something that put pressure on the wound without cutting off the flow of blood. But where was I going to find something like that?

The bleeding worsened.

Perhaps because I was light-headed, I took more time than I should have to remember something else that might be in the knapsack. Once when Kate had been on a college trip to Paris, she'd sprained an ankle and had limped painfully from drugstore to drugstore, trying to find an Ace bandage, the wide, long elastic material you wrap around a sprain to give the injured area some support. Since then, whenever she traveled, she made sure to carry one in her luggage, and she always took care to pack one for me.

More dizzy, I used my right hand to search through the knapsack. Where *is* it? I thought. It isn't like Kate not to have packed one.

Damn it, this time she hadn't.

Desperate, I was about to dump everything out, when I noticed a bulge at the side of the knapsack. Struggling to clear my mind, I freed a zipper on a pouch and almost wept when I found a folded elastic bandage.

Working awkwardly with one hand, sometimes using my teeth to open packets, I cleaned the gash with antiseptic swabs, spread antibiotic ointment over it, and pressed several two-inch pads onto it. Blood soaked them. Hurrying, I wrapped the elastic bandage around my left forearm. Keeping it tight, circling layer upon layer, I saw blood tint each layer.

I urgently wrapped more layers, applying more pressure, worried about how little of the bandage remained. I prayed that the blood wouldn't soak all the way through. Two more layers. One. I secured the end with two barbed clips that came with the bandage. Then I stared at the bandage, shivering, concentrating to see if blood would soak through. For a moment, I feared that the pale brown of the bandage would become pink, about to turn red. I held my breath, exhaling only when a small area of pink didn't spread.

My watch's crystal was shattered, the hands frozen at ten after two. I had no idea how long I'd been on the ledge, but when I peered up through the vapor from the stream, the sun seemed to have shifted farther west than I would have expected from the brief time since I'd fallen. Evidently I'd been unconscious longer than it seemed.

I stared up at the rim but still didn't see Petey and Jason. Give them time, I thought.

The trouble was, if I didn't get off the ledge soon, I was going to be in a lot worse trouble.

I wasn't an outdoorsman—I'd certainly proven that. But it wasn't possible to live in a mountain state like Colorado without seeing stories in the newspaper or on the TV news about the dangers of hypothermia. Hikers would go into the mountains, wearing only shorts and T-shirts. A sudden storm would soak them. If the temperature dropped, if the hikers were more than three hours from warm clothes and hot fluids to raise their rapidly dropping core temperature, they died from exposure.

Lying on the damp, chill ledge, I shivered. My hands and feet felt numb. If I don't get off this ledge soon, I thought, it won't matter that I stopped the bleeding. Hypothermia will kill me.

I tried to calculate how to climb up the almost sheer face to the next ledge and then up the slope of loose stones to the rim. I knew that my injured arm wouldn't support me. The only other way to get off the ledge was . . .

I stared down, trying to judge how the cliff led to the stream. It was a steep slope of outcrops, the ledge below me five feet away, the one after that twice as far. I didn't want to think about the obstacles farther down.

But the sun was already past the rim of the cliff. The bottom of the chasm was in shadow. Even though it was only late afternoon, darkness would come soon. The nearby mountains would block the sun earlier than I was used to. Once it was dark, I couldn't hope to be rescued until morning.

By then, I'd be dead.

The pain of movement was excruciating as I eased the knapsack onto my back, lay on my stomach, and squirmed over the edge. I dangled as far as my good arm would allow, then dropped.

The shock of landing jolted me to the bone. I almost

fainted. Crawling over the side of the next outcrop, I ripped my shirt and scraped my chest. My lacerated knees showed through my torn jeans. Straining to control my emotions, I kept struggling downward. A few spots that looked impossible from above turned out to be deceptive, boulders acting like steps. Other spots that looked easy were terrifyingly difficult.

Throughout, the light faded. As the stream's roar grew closer, I descended with greater caution. Testing my footing, I almost fell when a boulder dislodged under my weight and rumbled to the bottom. While the dusk thickened, so did the vapor from the stream, beading my face, soaking my clothes, making me shiver harder. I remembered reading that victims of hypothermia become stupefied near the end, unaware of what's around them. I fought to keep my thoughts clear.

As it was, I struggled to the bottom before I realized it, nearly stepping into the raging current, so deadened by its thunder that I hadn't been aware how close I was. Lurching back, I almost twisted my ankle. Unnerved by the surreal contrast between the blue sky above the chasm and the gathering dusk within it, I shifted along the roiling water with delicate care. Spray drenched me. As the chasm sloped toward its murky exit, I worried that I'd break a leg within sight of my escape. I made my way over slick rocks, gripping boulders for support, my mind and body so numbed that it took me a minute to understand that the object I leaned against was an aspen tree, not a boulder, that sunlight was angling toward me, that I'd left the chasm a while ago and now was stumbling through a forest.

It's almost over, I told myself. All I need to do is follow the stream through the trees to the lake. As my steps quickened, I imagined unlocking the car. I anticipated the relief of crawling in and starting the engine, of turning on the heater and feeling hot air blow over me as I changed into warm clothes from my suitcase.

"Jason! Petey!"

I lurched from the aspens to the edge of the lake and squinted through dimming sunlight toward the opposite side.

My stomach sank when I saw that the car wasn't there.

Easily explained. Petey and Jason went for help, I thought. They'll be back soon. All I have to do is crawl into the tent and try to get warm.

The tent was also gone.

"No!" The veins in my neck threatened to burst, but I couldn't stop screaming. "*Noooo!*"

16

Denial's an amazing emotion. During my descent, suspicions had nagged at me, but I'd managed to suppress them, too preoccupied with staying alive. Now I still kept trying to tell myself that I was wrong. After all, six hours previously, the possibility that my brother would push me off a cliff would have been unthinkable, especially given the load of guilt that I'd been carrying around.

My God, what had Petey done with Jason?

Furious, shivering so hard that my teeth clicked together, I yanked off my wet shirt, pulled my denim jacket from the knapsack, and quickly put it over my bare skin. The jacket was damp from having been near the stream, but it felt luxurious compared to what I'd been wearing.

It wasn't going to be enough. I had to get a fire started, had to dry my jeans and socks and shoes. After opening a pouch on my knapsack and confirming that a metal container of matchbooks was as waterproof as the camping-equipment clerk had promised, I went to the aspens to get wood.

A breeze made my wet jeans cold and penetrated my jacket. I hugged myself, trying to generate warmth, but trembled worse than ever. Not knowing what I was doing, I imitated the campfire arrangement on the other side of the lake and put rocks in a circle in a clearing. I placed some twigs and dead leaves in the middle, set some broken sticks over them, and struck a match, but my hand shook so severely that as I brought the match toward the leaves, the flame went out. I tried again, desperate to keep my hand still, concentrating to control my arm muscles, and this time the flame touched the leaves, smoke rising, fire crackling.

A terrible thirst overtook me, but when I reached for the canteen on my belt, it wasn't there. I was dismayed not only that I'd lost it but that I hadn't noticed until now. My tongue was so pasty that it stuck to the roof of my mouth. The roar of the nearby stream tempted me to go to it and scoop water from my hands to my mouth, but I had no idea what kind of bacteria might be in it. I didn't dare risk getting sick. Vomiting or diarrhea would dehydrate me more than I already was.

All the while, sunset dimmed. I needed to pile up all the branches I could. As the last of the sun dipped below the mountains, I worked with greater urgency, dragging back large fallen limbs. Too soon, darkness enveloped me.

But it wasn't as black as my thoughts. Jason. *Had Petey hurt him?* Please, God, protect my son. *Please.*

The word became my mantra as the night's chill made me huddle closer to the fire. I was caught between the need to get warm and the fear of depleting my fuel supply before the night was over. I picked up the shirt I'd taken off. Holding it to the fire, turning it often, I feared that I'd burn it before I dried it. Although parts of it were in rags, it would provide an extra layer. Hating to expose my chest and back to the cold, I quickly removed my jacket and put on the shirt, then got into the jacket again. I took the rain slicker from my knapsack and put that on as well, pulling its hood over my head, anything to provide more insulation. My hands felt stung by the cold. Rubbing them over the fire, I blamed myself for not having been smart enough to bring gloves.

Hell, if I'd been smart, I never would have invited Petey into my home. But as hard as I tried to find some warning signs from the previous few days, I couldn't think of any.

You bastard! I inwardly screamed, then regretted the word, hating myself for insulting my parents. Every curse I could think of somehow involved them, but what had happened wasn't their fault. It was mine.

The weather forecaster had predicted a low of forty degrees Fahrenheit. If I fell asleep and the flames died, my body might get so cold that I'd never wake up. I thought of the warm sleeping bags that had been in the car. I imagined zipping into one of them and . . .

Awakening with a start, I found myself lying on the cold grass next to the barely glowing embers of the fire. Terrified, I tried to make my right hand work, groped for a handful of twigs, used a stick to poke them into the ash-covered coals, and watched the twigs burst into flame. Clumsy, I added larger pieces, my numbness slowly leaving me, but not the terror of dying from exposure. Dry-mouthed, I tried to chew peanuts and raisins. Praying for Jason helped energize my mind. Guarding the fire, I brooded about Petey.

Hated him.

And stayed awake.

17

At first, the feeling was so soft that I thought I imagined it, an invisible cool feather tickling my face in the darkness. Then I heard a subtle hissing on the hot rocks around the fire. In my confusion, it reminded me of the hiss from our coffeemaker whenever a few drops fell from the unit's spout and landed on the burner. At once, the flurries became a little stronger, the breeze that brought them turning colder.

I straightened from the stupor I'd been in, the gray of false dawn hinting at what swirled around me. My first alarmed instinct was to pile more wood on the fire, but as snow sizzled louder on the hot stones, the sun tried to struggle above the eastern peak, providing sufficient light for me to see the white on the grass around me. Dark clouds hung low. Despite the extra wood I'd thrown on the fire, the flames lessened. Smoke rose.

Panicked, I put on my knapsack. As Petey had told Jason when we'd left the highway, early June wasn't too late for snow in the mountains. On TV, the forecasters sometimes cautioned people that at high altitude, the weather could change for the worse without warning. But that hadn't been predicted, and I'd figured that with the car and the tent, there wasn't anything to worry about. Now I cursed myself for not making better plans.

The highway was a half hour away by car. Frowning at the thickening, angrier clouds, I tried to calculate how far I'd have to go on foot. The road into the mountains had been so bad, the terrain so rough, that most of the time I hadn't been able to drive more than twenty miles an hour. That meant the highway was about ten miles off. But with my ankle hurting, ten miles might take me five or six hours on foot. In clothes too flimsy for the cold. Besides, as the flurries intensified, preventing me from seeing the lake, I realized that I probably wouldn't be able to find my way to the highway, that I'd risk wandering in circles until I dropped. Of course, if I'd known how to use the compass the camping-equipment clerk had sold me, my chances might have been different. But regret wasn't a survival emotion. Fear for Jason was. Rage at Petey was.

Thinking of Jason, I was suddenly reminded of the last time I'd seen him. The shelf of rock. "Where's that cave you mentioned?" he'd asked.

The cave.

If I could find it before the storm got worse . . .

Fighting for strength, I lurched into the trees. Abruptly, visibility lessened, and I stumbled to the right toward the stream, not to drink from it but to use it as a guide. A white veil enveloped me as I followed the churning water up through the trees. The flakes became thicker. The snow on the ground covered my tennis shoes.

My tennis shoes. I'd bought a compass, which I didn't know how to use, and yet I hadn't taken the camping-equipment clerk's advice to buy sturdy hiking boots. They weren't necessary, I'd told him. We weren't going to be doing anything heavy-duty.

My feet started to lose sensation. Limping, I worked my way along a slope, worrying that a rock beneath the snow would shift and cause me to fall. Could I rely on my memory of where the cave was? For all I knew, it was on the opposite side of the stream, and it was merely a crevice in a cliff, which, as a thirteen-year-old boy, I had thought was huge.

The slope reached a steep ridge that went to the left. While I plodded along it, the aspens became pine trees. Branches jabbed at my arms and scratched my face. As the snow gusted thicker, I feared that I'd stumble past the cave and never see it. In the summer, hikers would find my body, or what was left of it after the forest scavengers had feasted on it.

I'm an architect, not a survival expert, I thought. I could hardly feel my hands. Why the hell hadn't I put gloves in my knapsack? I was so stupid, I *deserved* to die.

Trying to avoid a pine branch, I lost my footing, fell, and almost banged my head against a boulder on my right. Stupid. Deserve to . . .

18

Architect.

The vague thought nudged my dimming consciousness.

Know how to . . .

Slowly, the thought insisted, making me turn toward the boulder my head had nearly struck.

Build things.

When I struggled to my feet, I discovered that the boulder was as high as my chest. A second boulder, five feet to the left, was slightly less high. The boulders lay against a cliff, which formed a rear wall.

Build things, I repeated.

I stumbled to the pine branch I'd tried to avoid, put all my weight into it, and felt a surge of hope when a *snap* intruded on the smothering stillness. Working as hard as I could, I dragged the branch through the snow to the boulders and hefted it on top, bracing it across them.

Staggering, I repeated the process several times, overlaying the needles, trying to form a roof.

The cold made my hands ache so much that tears streamed from my eyes, freezing on my cheeks, but I didn't have time to stick my hands, raw and bloody, under my rain slicker to try to warm them against my chest. There was too much to do. I used football-size rocks to weigh down the edges of the branches.

Delirious, I kicked the snow from the ground between the boulders, adding it to the drift outside the shelter. I stuck two needled branches at the shelter's entrance, forming a further windbreak. No matter how pained my hands were, I couldn't stop. I had to get dead twigs, leaves, and sticks, piling them at the back of the shelter.

I'd left a small hole at the back, where the boulders touched the cliff, hoping that smoke would escape through it. Away from the wind and the falling snow, I felt less assaulted by the cold. But my hands were like paws as I clumsily made a small pile of leaves and twigs, then fumbled to open the container of matches and pull out a book of them. I could hardly peel off one of the matches. My fingers didn't seem to belong to me. The match kept falling. It was finally so damaged that I had to peel off a second match, and this one, blessedly, caught fire when I struck it. It fell from my hands onto the clump of leaves and twigs, remained burning, and started a small fire. Smoke rose. I held my breath to keep from coughing. Pushed by heat, the smoke drifted toward the hole in the back.

My throat was so dry that it swelled shut, restricting the passage of air to my lungs. Desperate for something to drink, I reached my unfeeling right hand outside and fumbled to raise snow to my mouth. Instantly, I regretted it. The melting snow made my lips and tongue more numb than they already were. Shivering, I felt a deeper cold. I dimly remembered TV news reports that warned hikers caught in a blizzard not to eat snow as a way of getting moisture. They'd use so much body heat melting the snow in their mouths that they had a greater risk of dying from hypothermia.

The small amount of water from the melted snow hadn't done any good. Almost instantly, my lips became dry again. My swollen tongue seemed to fill my mouth. It was a measure of how dazed I'd become that I stared blearily down at the metal container of matches for a long time before my muddled thoughts cleared and I realized what I had to do. Shaking, I put the matches in the first-aid kit. I picked up their metal container, reached outside into the wind, packed the container with snow, and set it near the fire.

Slowly, the crystals melted. Worried about burning my hand, I put my shirtsleeve over my fingers before I gripped the hot container and pulled it away from the fire. It was only half an inch thick and two inches square, but it might as well have been a sixteen-ounce glass, so irresistible was the tiny amount of water in it. I forced myself to let it cool.

Finally, I couldn't be patient any longer. I used my sleeve to raise the container. I brought it close to my lips, blew on it, then gulped the warm, bitter water. My parched mouth absorbed it before I could swallow. I reached greedily outside and packed it with more snow. The lingering heat in the metal reduced the snow to water without my needing to set the container near the fire.

Again, I gulped it. Again, the water never got near my throat. I refilled the container, placed it near the fire, and put a few more sticks on the flames.

That became my pattern. When my mouth and throat were moist enough, I pulled a plastic bag of peanuts and raisins from my knapsack, chewing each mouthful thoroughly, making them last. Worrying about Jason, hating Petey, I stared at the fire.

19

I vaguely remember going out to clear a drift from the smoke hole and to find more fuel. Otherwise, everything blurred. A couple of times when I woke, the flames had died out. On those occasions, all that kept me from freezing to death was the heat that the boulders had absorbed.

When I noticed that the pressure bandage around my left forearm was completely pink from the bleeding under it, I didn't react with dismay—the arm seemed to belong to someone else. Even when I saw sunlight beyond the branches and drifts at the entrance to my shelter, I felt oddly apart from it. Eventually, I discovered that an entire day had passed, but while I was trapped in the shelter, time hardly moved.

Probably I'd have lain in a stupor until energy totally failed me, if it hadn't been for water dripping through the roof. The cold drops struck my eyelids, shocking me. The sunlight was painfully bright. I moved my head. The drops fell into my mouth, tasting vaguely of turpentine from the resin on the pine branches. I gagged and spat the water out, sitting up to reach a dry spot.

More drops splashed around me, raising smoke from the almost-dead fire. Coughing, I grabbed my knapsack and stumbled outside, kneeing through the branches and drifts at the entrance. The heat of the sun was luxurious. Snow fell from trees. Rivulets started to form. Standing in the melting snow, my feet and shins became wet again, but it was a different kind of wet, the sun warming me, so that I didn't shiver. From the sun's angle in the east, I judged that the time was midmorning. As much as my body didn't want to move, I knew that if I didn't take advantage of the improved weather, I might never have another chance.

I took a long look back at the shelter. It was loose and flimsy, as if a child had put it together, and yet I'd never been prouder of anything I'd designed.

I started down. Light reflecting off the snow lanced my eyes. By the time the sun was directly overhead, much of the snow had melted, the ground turning to mud as I crossed the first meadow. Still, the road remained hidden, and with little to guide me, all I could do was keep heading downward, aiming toward breaks in the trees where the road possibly went through them.

I don't remember reaching Highway 9, or collapsing there, or being found by a passing motorist. Apparently, that was at sunset. I woke up in a small medical clinic in a town called Frisco.

By then, a state trooper had been summoned. He leaned over the bed and wanted to know what had happened to me. I later found out that it took him twenty minutes to get a coherent account from me. I kept screaming for Jason, as if my son was within arm's reach and I could help him.

The doctor stitched my left forearm. He disinfected and bandaged my hands, which he was worried might have frostbite.

The state trooper returned from talking on the phone. "Mr. Denning, the Denver police sent a patrol car to your house. The lights were off. No one answered the doorbell. When they aimed a flashlight through a garage window, they saw your Ford Expedition."

"In the garage? That doesn't make sense. Why would Petey have gone back to the house?" The awful implication hit me. "*Jesus.*"

I tried to scramble out of bed. It took both the doctor and the state trooper to stop me.

"The officers broke a window and entered your house. They searched it thoroughly. It's deserted. Mr. Denning, do you have any other vehicles?"

"What difference does . . ." My head pounded. "My wife has a Volvo."

"It isn't in the garage."

That didn't make sense, either. "The bastard must have taken it. Why? *And where are my wife and son?*" The increasingly troubled look on the trooper's face made me realize that he hadn't told me everything.

"The master bedroom and your son's room had been ransacked," the trooper said.

"*What?*"

"Drawers had been pulled out, clothes scattered. It looked to the Denver officers as if somebody tore through those bedrooms in an awful hurry."

I screamed.

Part Two

1

No matter how desperately I wanted to get home, the doctor refused to release me until the next morning. The state trooper drove me back to Denver. My right wrist ached from the IV the doctor had given me. After two days without food, I should have been ravenous, but the shock of my emotions killed my appetite. I had to force myself to chew slowly on a banana and take small sips from a bottle of orange juice.

When we turned onto my street, I saw the maple trees in front of our Victorian, a van and a station wagon in our driveway, and a Denver police car at the curb. Farther along were other cars and two trucks from local TV stations.

Getting out of the cruiser, I recognized the female television reporter who stalked toward me, armed with a microphone, a cameraman behind her. Her male equivalent from a rival station wasn't far behind. Reporters scrambled from the other cars.

"How the hell did they find out?" I asked.

"Get in the house."

Holding out his arms, the state trooper formed a barrier while I limped across the lawn. The pants and shirt the doctor had lent me (my own had been rags) hung loosely on me, increasing my sense of frailty. I managed to get inside and shut the door, blocking the noise of the reporters shouting my name. But other voices replaced them. A police officer, several men in sport coats, and others holding lab equipment stood in the living room, talking to one another.

One of the men, heavyset, with a mustache, noticed me in the foyer and came over. "Mr. Denning?"

The motion of nodding made me dizzy.

"I'm Lieutenant Webber. This is Sergeant Pendleton." He indicated a younger, thinner man, clean-shaven.

"We checked the attic, the basement, and the trees in back. There's no sign of your wife and son," Pendleton said.

For a moment, I didn't understand what the detective was talking about. The officers who'd entered the house the previous night had said that Kate and Jason weren't home. If Petey had taken them in Kate's Volvo, why would the police now have checked the attic and the . . . I felt sick when I realized that they'd been searching for well-hidden corpses.

"You don't look so good, Mr. Denning. You'd better sit down." Webber guided me into the living room, where the other men shifted to the side. "I'll get you some water."

Despite the fluids the doctor had given me, I still felt parched. When the detective came back with a full glass, I had a moment's disorientation, as if this were *his* home and I were a guest. I held the glass awkwardly between my bandaged hands and took a swallow. My stomach protested. I managed to ask, "You've no idea where my wife and son are?"

"Not yet," Webber said. "The state police relayed what you told them, but we need to ask you some questions." He looked at the scrapes on my face. "Do you feel strong enough to answer them?"

"The sooner I do, the sooner I'll get my family back."

A look passed between them, which I understood only later—they weren't as confident as I was that I'd get my family back.

"It would help if . . ." Pendleton glanced at where my fingertips projected from the bandages on my hands. "We need to take your prints."

"Take my . . . But why would . . ."

"So we can separate yours from the man who kidnapped your family. Which bedroom was his?"

"Go to the left at the top of the stairs." I felt out of breath. "The room's at the end of the hall. On the right."

"That's the one with the baseball glove on the bed," Webber told a technician.

"*Baseball glove?*" I tensed. "*On his bed?*"

Pendleton frowned. "Yes. Is that important?"

"The glove was Petey's a long time ago."

"I don't understand."

"He's saying he doesn't want the damned thing anymore. Because he's got something better."

"Slow down, Mr. Denning. We're not following you."

As a technician pressed my fingertips on an inky pad and then onto a sheet of paper that had a place for each digit, I tried as hard as I could to make them understand.

2

"Long-lost brother?"

"God help me, yes."

"But how did you know he really *was* your brother?"

"He told me things only my brother could have known."

The detectives gave each other that look again.

"What's wrong?"

"Just a thought," Webber said. "Maybe you heard what you wanted to hear. Some con men are good at making general statements sound specific. The people they're trying to fool fill in the gaps."

"*No.* I tested him. He got every detail right."

"They can be awfully clever."

"But it doesn't make sense. A con man's motive would have been robbery. All he'd have needed to do was wait until Kate and I went to work and Jason was at school. He'd have had all day to loot the house. He wouldn't have needed to try to kill me. That was *personal*. That was Petey getting even!"

Pendleton made a calming gesture. "We're just trying to get a sense of the man we're after."

"For God's sake, a con man wouldn't be stupid enough to add murder and kidnapping to a burglary charge."

"Unless he enjoyed violence."

The direct look Webber gave me was dizzying in its effect. All along, I'd worked to assure myself that Jason and Kate were alive. Now, for the first time, I admitted to myself that Jason might be dead in the mountains, that Kate's body might be lying in a ditch somewhere.

I almost threw up.

Pendleton seemed to sense my panicked thoughts. His tone suggested an attempt to distract me. "You don't happen to have a photograph of him, do you?"

"No."

"With the excitement of the homecoming, you didn't take any pictures?"

"*No.*" I wanted to scream. If only I hadn't let a stranger into my house . . .

But he isn't a stranger, I tried to tell myself.

What the hell's the matter with you? I thought. After twenty-five years, Petey *is* a stranger!

"Mr. Denning?"

I looked over at Pendleton, realizing that he'd said my name several times in an effort to get my attention.

"If you're able, we'd like you to walk through the house and tell us if anything's missing."

"Whatever I have to do."

They handed me latex gloves and put on their own. Unsteady, I began in the downstairs rooms, and immediately I noticed that the silverware Kate had inherited from her grandmother was no longer on the sideboard in the dining room. A silver tea set was missing also. In the TV room, the DVD and videotape players were gone, along with an expensive audio/video receiver.

"He'd probably have taken the TV, too," I said bitterly, "except that it's forty-six inches and wouldn't fit in the Volvo. I don't understand why he didn't keep the Expedition. It's got more room. He could have stolen more things."

Webber looked uncomfortable. "We'll talk about it later. Finish checking the house."

The microwave and the Cuisinart food processor were missing from the kitchen. Numerous compact power tools were gone from the garage. My laptop computer wasn't in my office.

"What about firearms?" Pendleton asked. "Do you have any in the house? Did he take them?"

"No guns."

"Not even a hunting rifle?"

"No. I'm not a hunter."

I made my way upstairs and froze at the entrance to Jason's room, seeing his drawers pulled out, his clothes scattered on the floor. It took all my willpower to step inside and look around.

"My son saves his loose change in a jar on his desk," I said.

It wasn't there.

I had an even harder time going into the chaos of the master bedroom. Stepping over some of Kate's dresses on the floor, I stared toward the back of the walk-in closet. "Four suitcases are gone."

As the implication hit me, my knees weakened so much that I had to lean against the doorjamb.

I'd assumed that Petey had ransacked the bureaus and closets because he was in a rush to find things to steal. Now, daring to hope, I took a closer look and realized that Kate's and Jason's clothes weren't just scattered—some of them were missing.

"If they're dead, he wouldn't have packed clothes for them," I told the detectives. "They're alive. They've got to be alive."

In a daze, I followed Webber's instructions and kept looking. Some of *my* clothes were gone, too. My emergency stash of five hundred dollars was no longer at the back of my underwear drawer. Kate's jewel box was missing, along with a gold Rolex that I wore on special occasions. None of it mattered; only Kate and Jason did.

Throughout, the technicians kept photographing the chaos in the bedrooms and checking for fingerprints. To get out of their way, the detectives took me downstairs. Again I had the sense that the house no longer belonged to me.

"Why the Volvo?" I managed to ask. My voice seemed to come from far away. "You said we'd talk about why he took it. The Expedition would have allowed him to steal more things."

"Yes." Pendleton spoke reluctantly. "But the Volvo has something that the four-wheel-drive vehicle doesn't."

"I don't know what you mean."

"A trunk."

"A . . ." Understanding forced me to sit.

"Maybe it isn't a good idea to go into the details."

"Tell me." My bandaged hands ached as I clutched the sides of the leather chair. "I need to know."

Webber glanced away, as if he couldn't bear to see my eyes. "The way it looks, he came back here with your son and then subdued your wife. We have to assume they were bound and gagged."

A rope seemed to cut into my wrists.

"He wouldn't have risked driving with them scrunched down in the backseat. Sooner or later, someone would have noticed," Pendleton said.

"So he put them in the . . ."

"With the garage door closed, nobody would have seen him do it."

"Jesus." Imagining the stench of gasoline and car exhaust, I felt nauseated. "How could they breathe?" I suddenly remembered Petey's haunted look when he'd described how the man and woman had forced *him* into a trunk.

A shrill beep startled me. Webber reached beneath his blazer and unhooked his cell phone from his belt. As he turned his back and walked toward the piano that Kate enjoyed playing, I barely heard his muted voice.

He put away the phone.

"Something?" I straightened, nervously hoping.

"The Volvo's been found. At a rest stop off Interstate Twenty-five."

"Kate and Jason? Are they—"

"Not with the car. He left the state. Wyoming troopers found the Volvo north of Casper."

"*Wyoming?*"

"For all he knew, he had plenty of time, and the Volvo wouldn't have been missed for several days," Webber said. "But suppose your wife was expected somewhere Saturday night, or suppose friends were going to arrive, and no matter what he did to persuade her, she wouldn't tell him about it?"

My skin turned cold at the thought of the pain Kate would have suffered.

"His best choice was to get your wife and son away before anyone suspected something was wrong," Webber said. "The nearest ATM for your bank has a record of a six-twenty-one P.M. withdrawal of five hundred dollars, the most that the machine is allowed to take from an account on any one day. The videotape shows a man making the withdrawal, but his head's bowed so his face is hidden."

Sweat chilled me when I realized that Petey had forced Kate to tell him our ATM number.

"It looks like he drove until nightfall, then used the cover of darkness to carjack another vehicle at the rest stop outside Casper. The likely target would have been someone traveling alone, but the driver wasn't found near the rest stop, so we assume that he or she is in the car with your wife and son. Until the driver's reported missing, we won't know what kind of car to search for."

"Three people trying to breathe in a trunk? Jesus."

Something in the detectives' eyes made me guess what they were thinking. As dangerous as Petey was, it might be only *two* people trying to breathe. He might not have let the driver live.

"Wyoming? But why in hell would he have gone to Wyoming?" At once, I remembered something Petey had said. "Montana."

"You sound like that means something to you," Pendleton said. "What are you getting at?"

"Montana's north of Wyoming."

They looked at me as if I was babbling.

"No, listen to me. My brother said that when he saw me on the *CBS Sunday Morning* show, he was having breakfast in Montana. In a diner in Butte. Maybe that's why he's heading north. Maybe something in Montana's drawing him back."

For the first time, Webber was animated. "Good." He hurriedly pulled out his phone. "I'll send descriptions of this guy, your wife, and your son to the Montana state police."

"We'll contact the Butte police department," Pendleton quickly added. "Maybe they know something about this guy. If he's been arrested, they'll have a photograph of him that we can circulate."

"Assuming he called himself Peter Denning up there." I stared dismally down at the floor.

"There are other ways to investigate. Kidnapping across state lines means the FBI will get involved. The feds will do their best to match the fingerprints we find with ones they have on file. If this guy ever used an alias, we have a good chance of learning what it is."

I tried hard to believe what they were saying.

"Have you a recent photograph of your wife and son?"

"On the mantel." I looked in that direction. The beaming faces of Kate and Jason made me heartsick. I'd taken the photograph myself. Normally, I hardly knew which button to press on a camera, but that day, I'd gotten lucky. We'd been to Copper Mountain skiing, although falling down was more what Kate and I had done. Jason had been a natural, however. He'd grinned all day. Despite our bruises, so had Kate and I. In the photo, Kate wore a red ski jacket, Jason a green one, the two of them holding their knitted ski caps, Kate's blond hair and Jason's sandy hair glinting in the sun, their cheeks glowing.

"We'll return it as soon as we have copies made," Pendleton said.

"Keep it as long as you have to." The truth was, I hated to part with it. The empty place on the mantel reinforced my hollowness. "Anything else—anything at all—just ask."

What they need more than anything, I thought, is for God to answer my prayers.

3

Throughout, the phone had rung frequently. I'd been vaguely aware that a policeman had answered it. Now he handed me a list of who'd called, mostly reporters wanting an interview—TV, radio. What had happened would be all over the state by evening.

"Jesus, Kate's parents." Hurrying, I left Webber and Pendleton in the living room. In the kitchen, my bandaged hand shook when I pressed numbers on the telephone.

"Hello?" an elderly man said.

"Ray . . ." I could hardly make my voice work. "Sit down. I'm afraid I've got bad news."

It made me sick to have to tell them, to hear their lives change in a minute. Neither of them was in good health. Even so, they immediately wanted to drive the three hundred miles from Durango through the mountains to Denver. I had a hard time convincing them to stay home. After all, what were they going to accomplish in Denver?

Kate's father was breathing so fast that he sounded like he was going to have a heart attack.

"Stay put," I said. "All we can do now is wait." I had a terrible mental image of Kate's father rushing to get to Denver, losing control of his car, and plummeting down a gorge. "You can wait just as easily at home. I'll let you know the instant I learn anything."

Setting down the phone, I took a deep breath, then noticed Webber and Pendleton at the entrance to the kitchen.

"What?" I asked.

"We just got a call from the Wyoming state police," Webber said.

I braced myself.

"A woman from Casper's been reported missing. Saturday evening, she was en route from visiting her sister in Sheridan, which is about a hundred and fifty miles north of where she lives."

"You think my brother carjacked her?"

"The timing fits. Just after dark, she would have approached the rest stop where the Wyoming state police found your wife's Volvo. If the woman had to use the rest room . . ."

Inwardly, I flinched as I imagined Petey coming at the woman and how terrified she must have been.

"She was driving a 1994 Chevy Caprice," Pendleton said. "Apart from the fact that she was driving alone, her abductor probably singled her out because that type of car has a large trunk. He kept heading north. The Wyoming police gave the license number to the police in Montana, who found the Caprice at a rest stop on Interstate Ninety near Billings."

"Were my wife and son . . ."

"With the Caprice? No."

Something about Pendleton's tone made me suspicious. "What about the woman who owned it?"

He didn't answer.

"Tell me."

Pendleton glanced at Webber, who nodded as if giving permission.

"Her body was in the trunk."

"Dear God." I didn't want to know, and yet I couldn't stop from asking, "What did Petey do to her?"

"Tied her hands and covered her mouth with duct tape. She"—Pendleton's voice dropped—"had asthma. She choked to death."

Thinking about the woman's desperate struggle to breathe, I could barely concentrate as Webber explained that Petey could have driven the Caprice from Casper, Wyoming, to Billings, Montana, that same night. He'd presumably carjacked another vehicle at the Billings rest stop. As the driver got out of the car to go to the bathroom, Petey would have lunged from the shadows.

I imagined how horrifying it would have been for Kate and Jason, pressed next to the dying woman in the dark, the air foul, feeling her thrash, hearing her muffled choking sounds, her frenzied movements, her strangled gasps slowing, getting weaker, stopping.

"It's never going to end," I managed to say.

"No, we could be close to boxing him in," Pendleton said. "You predicted right. He was headed to Montana. Probably back to Butte. Billings is on the interstate that leads there. The local police don't have any criminal record for someone named Peter Denning. But they're searching for a man who matches this guy's description, especially that scar on his chin. The driver of the most recent vehicle he carjacked will soon have somebody report him or her missing. Once the Butte police get the make and license number of the vehicle, they can narrow their search. Meanwhile, they're checking motels and any other places they can think of where your brother might be able to hide your wife and son. Butte's not a big city. Believe me, if he shows himself, he'll be spotted."

"But what if Petey senses the danger and leaves?"

"We thought of that. The Montana state police have unmarked cars along the interstate, watching for any white male in his thirties who's driving alone. As soon as the FBI processes his fingerprints, we'll have a better idea of who we're dealing with. The way he operates, he's had practice. He's probably got a criminal record, in which case the feds will come up with a recent mug shot we can distribute."

4

One of the callers on the list the policeman had handed me was from my office, so I had to phone and again explain what had happened. Saying it out loud reinforced the nightmare. Several times, I heard the buzz of call waiting. Twice, I switched to the incoming call in case it had something to do with Kate and Jason, but both times it was a journalist, and after that, I didn't pay attention to call waiting.

The moment I hung up, the phone rang again. We had caller ID, but most times I'd found it was useless, a lot of the calls listed as UNKNOWN CALLER or, in this case, BLOCKED NUMBER. But I answered anyhow, and of course, it was another journalist; after that, I let the policeman answer the phone.

When the lab crew finally left, Webber, Pendleton, and everybody else going with them, the house had never felt so empty. My footsteps echoed off the hardwood floors as I went upstairs. Fingerprint powder smudged furniture, and clothes remained on the bedroom floors. I sat on Jason's bed, inhaling his boy smell. I went into the master bedroom, picked up one of Kate's blouses, and pressed it to my face.

I have no idea how long I remained there. The phone rang again. Ignoring it, I went into the bathroom, took off my borrowed clothes, and tried to take a bath without getting my bandaged hands and my stitched left forearm wet. Dirt and dried blood floated from me. Steam rose, but instead of the water's heat, what I felt was spreading pain as the effect of the pills the doctor had given me began to wear off. The extent of my bruises was appalling. I did my best to shave, then put on fresh clothes, but I begrudged their comfort, telling myself that I didn't deserve it, given the hell that Kate and Jason would be going through.

The doorbell rang. Limping, I needed extra time to get downstairs. Meanwhile, the bell rang again and then again. If this is a reporter . . . , I thought. When I opened the door, I saw a straight-backed man in a dark suit, with polished shoes and short, neat, slightly graying hair. His lean face was all business.

"Mr. Denning?"

Behind him, out on the street, a camera crew started forward.

"I'm not giving interviews." I stepped back to close the door.

"No, you don't understand. I'm FBI Special Agent John Gader." The man showed his ID. "I kept phoning, but no one answered, so I took a chance and drove over."

"I was . . . I didn't . . . Please, come in."

As the reporters neared the house, I shut the door and locked it.

Gader opened his briefcase and took out several small electronic devices. "These are voice-activated tape recorders." He linked one to the living room phone. "Is there a phone in the kitchen?"

He installed a recorder there also. "We'll deal with the rest of the house later. I've already obtained a court order to have your phone tapped and all calls traced, but it never hurts to have a backup system. If the man who took your wife and son phones to demand a ransom, we'll have a recording of it here, as well as through our intercept at the phone company."

"There won't be a ransom demand."

"You never know."

"I *do* know. My brother doesn't want money. He wants my wife and my son."

"Your brother?" Gader sounded as if he knew only the general parameters of the case.

So, yet again, I explained what had happened. Gader pulled out a pocket-size tape recorder and took notes as a backup. He assured me that the Bureau would give my case its full attention. After he left, it was as if he'd never been present.

Emptiness again enveloped me.

This can't have happened, I thought, straining to convince myself. I'm having a nightmare. I'll wake up soon. Kate and Jason will be back. Everything'll be perfect, the way it was.

But when I woke in the night, pain racking my body, I reached next to me and was confronted by the emptiness on Kate's side of the bed.

Nothing had changed.

As the days stretched on, the Butte police failed to catch Petey or find any sign of Kate and Jason. The Montana state troopers finally stopped watching the interstate.

5

"He isn't your brother."

"*What?*"

"The man who took your wife and son isn't Peter Denning," Gader said as he stood at my front door. "His name's Lester Dant."

I felt as if I'd been shoved. "You mean Petey used the name Lester Dant as an alias?"

"No. The other way around."

"For God's sake, what are you talking about?"

"The prints the crime-scene crew found in your house belong to a man named Lester Dant." Gader stepped inside. "Here's the file we have on him. Background. Social Security number. Criminal record."

Bewildered, I sat in the living room and stared at the photograph that came with the documents. Complete with chipped tooth and scarred chin, Petey's face confronted me from a mug shot that had been taken in Butte.

But the file identified the man as Lester Dant. He'd

been born in Brockton, Indiana, a year before Petey was born. Over the years, he'd been arrested for, but never convicted of, auto theft, armed robbery, and manslaughter.

"Dant did time for extortion, drug dealing, and rape," Gader said. "It's a miracle he didn't kill you all in your sleep. See where the Butte police have a record on him? Lester Dant got in a bar fight and put a man in the emergency ward. He was released from jail a week before the *CBS Sunday Morning* broadcast you were on."

"But . . ." My sense of unreality intensified so much that the living room seemed to tilt. "How did he know so much about Petey?"

"They must have crossed paths," Gader said. "Maybe your brother saw the *CBS Sunday Morning* show and talked about it with some people he knew, including Dant. Later, in private, Dant got more specifics from him and decided to pay you a visit."

I raised my voice in dismay. "My brother hung around with people like *Dant*?"

"Maybe your brother had as rough a life as Dant claimed."

"But why in God's name didn't Petey come to see me himself?"

Gader stared at me, and I tensed with the realization that Dant might have killed Petey to prevent him from interfering.

"It doesn't make sense," I told Gader. "If Dant's this vicious, why would he have packed clothes for my son? Why would he have taken Jason along instead of . . ." The words caught in my throat.

"Killing him?" Gader looked uncomfortable. "I'm not sure that's a topic you want to get into."

"Let *me* decide that. *Answer me.*"

Gader exhaled slowly. "It's probable that Dant took your son to put pressure on your wife. By threatening to hurt Jason, he could force your wife to submit to him."

I felt as if I'd been struck in the face. "No."

"I'm sorry, Mr. Denning. You asked me to be candid."

"Petey . . . Lester Dant . . ."

"Fingerprints don't lie."

"There's got to be a mistake. What Petey told me about when we were kids and how he was abducted—"

"What *Dant* told you. He probably kept buying your brother drinks to keep him talking, supplying details."

"But it all felt so *real*. I'm sure he was telling the truth."

"Listen, some of these con men are good-enough actors, they could have won Academy Awards if they'd gone straight."

"It's just that . . ."

"Everything was a lie. The name of the town in West Virginia where he told you he was held prisoner."

"Redemption."

"There's no such place."

"What?"

"Other parts of his story don't hold together, either. He told you he got the scar on his chin last summer when he fell off a ladder on a roofing project in Colorado Springs."

"That's right."

"Well, our agents showed Dant's photograph to all the roofing contractors in that area. Nobody recognized him.

The same with the construction contractors. If somebody had gotten a two-inch gash on his face, they'd remember it, they say. It would have required stitches, but the hospitals in the area don't have any record of a construction worker coming in last summer with that kind of injury. However, the Colorado Springs police have a security-camera tape of a man who looks like Dant beating a clerk in a liquor store robbery. A police car chased his vehicle into the mountains. He may have gotten the injury to his face when his car skidded off a curve and tumbled into a draw. There was blood but no driver when officers climbed down to examine the wreckage."

Bitterness twisted my voice. "Yeah, Petey has a habit of vanishing."

"You mean Dant."

"Sure. . . . Dant."

"We'll get him," Gader said. "The money he took from you won't last long. Eventually he'll have to steal again. One mistake. That's all he has to make, and we'll get him."

"Eventually." The word that Gader had used stuck in my throat. I tried not to think about what was happening to Kate and Jason.

6

So a man who was my brother or who *wasn't* my brother but who was pretending to be him had abducted my family and torn my world apart. He'd covered his trail by fooling me and the police into thinking he was going to Butte, Montana. Then he'd vanished off the face of the earth. No other motorists were reported missing for that time period, which meant that the police didn't have a license number and a description of a carjacked vehicle to focus their search. There were numerous reports of stolen cars. Hundreds in Montana, Wyoming, and Colorado. Thousands nationwide. But when any of these were located, Petey (I still couldn't bring myself to call him Dant) was never linked to them. Perhaps he'd switched license plates with another vehicle. The owner of the other vehicle might have taken quite a while to notice that the plates had been switched, by which time Petey might have stolen another car or switched plates again. Or perhaps Petey had taken the money he got for the things he

stole from my house to buy an old car and then showed a
fake ID to register the car under an alias that the police
didn't know he had. Perhaps. Could have. Might have.

The local TV stations repeated the story. The networks
picked it up, especially CBS, which included excerpts
from the *Sunday Morning* segment that Kate, Jason, and
I had been in. They emphasized the sick twist that a man
who claimed to be my long-lost brother had vanished
again, this time with my family. I got calls from men who
claimed to have taken Kate and Jason. In graphic detail,
they described the torture they inflicted. The police
traced the calls, but nothing was learned, except that
some people love to aggravate the suffering of others.
Several of the callers were charged with obstructing the
investigation, but none ever went to jail.

Despair and lack of sleep gave me headaches. I went
through the motions of working, but my staff ran the
business. I spent most of my time in a trance. As the
search lost momentum, it became obvious that unless
Petey—again I tried to substitute Dant's name, but I
couldn't manage to do so—unless Petey stumbled into a
policeman, he was never going to be found, especially if
he grew a beard to cover the scar on his chin so his mug
shot would no longer resemble him.

Blurred photos of Kate and Jason appeared on milk
cartons and in mailers. *Have you seen this woman and
this boy?* the caption read. But if *I* couldn't recognize the
indistinct faces, I couldn't imagine anyone else being
able to. I'd never paid attention to the faces on those milk
cartons and those mailers when it was someone else's
wife or child who was missing. How could I hope that

anyone would pay attention when it was *my* wife and child who were missing?

Friends were supportive initially: phone calls of encouragement, invitations to dinner. But after a while, many wearied of my despair. Unable to come up with fresh expressions of sympathy, they kept their distance.

A few remained loyal, though, and it was from my next-door neighbor, Phil Barrow, that I learned how things could get worse. I was listlessly raking dead leaves in my front yard, vaguely aware that autumn had once been my favorite time of year, frost in the air, wood smoke, the rattle of dead leaves, and now it meant nothing, when I happened to look up and see Phil hug his sweater tighter to his chest, then step off the sidewalk and approach me.

"How are you doing, Brad?"

Kate had once told me that no matter how shitty either of us felt, we should always answer "Never better."

Phil's shoulders moved up and down as if from a bitter chuckle. "Yeah, I can see that. You've been raking that same pile of leaves for about an hour."

"Neatness counts."

Phil looked down at his hands. "I don't know if I should tell you this."

"Oh?" I felt a cold breeze.

"Marge says I shouldn't upset you, but I figure you've got enough trouble without getting *more* trouble from the people who are supposed to be helping you."

The breeze got colder. "What are you talking about?"

"An FBI agent came to see me at work yesterday."

"John Gader?"

"Yeah, that was his name. He asked me if you and

Kate got along. If there were a lot of family arguments. If you ever hit your son."

"*What?*"

"He wanted to know if you lost your temper when you drank. If you had a girlfriend."

"The FBI suspects *me*?"

7

"You son of a bitch."

Gader faltered when I stepped in front of his car in the parking garage of Denver's Federal Building. "Calm down."

"You think I killed my wife and son!"

"I gather that some of your friends told you I'd been asking them questions about you."

"Destroying my reputation is more like it!" Fists clenched, I stepped toward him.

"Take it easy," Gader said.

Its engine echoing, a car drove past in the garage, the driver frowning at us.

"This area has security cameras. It's patrolled," Gader said. "You don't even want to *think* about assaulting a federal agent on federal property."

"It'd be worth it!"

Gader held up his hands in surrender. "I'm not going to fight you. If you'll calm down and listen . . ."

Behind him, a door banged open. A guard stepped into the garage's harsh lights. His hand was on his holstered gun. "Is everything all right, Mr. Gader?"

"I'm not sure." Gader's lean face was stern. "*Is* everything all right, Mr. Denning?"

I squeezed my fists so tightly that my knuckles ached.

"If you go to prison, how's that going to help your wife and son?" Gader asked.

I trembled, feeling anger burn my face.

"Think about what your family needs," Gader said.

I relaxed my fists.

"It's going to be fine, Joe," Gader told the guard. "You can leave us now."

"I'll watch the monitor," the guard said.

"Good idea." Gader waited until the door rumbled shut.

"How could you possibly think I killed my wife and son?"

"It's a standard part of an investigation. When a family member's missing or killed, a lot of times the person responsible is another family member."

"Jesus, how could I have driven the Volvo to Wyoming, then stolen a car and abandoned it in Montana, and somehow have gotten back here to maroon myself in the mountains?"

"You could have if this guy Dant had been working for you."

The depth of Gader's suspicion shocked me. "*Why would I have asked Petey to do that?*"

"Dant. If you had money troubles and needed the payout from a life-insurance policy, or if you had a girlfriend who made your wife an inconvenience."

I clenched my fists again.

"But there weren't any unusual withdrawals from your bank accounts or your stock portfolio, and there wasn't a hint of scandal about your relations with your family. Besides, I couldn't figure out how you'd have crossed paths with Dant after he got out of jail in Butte and . . . Quit staring at me like that. The investigation wasn't going anywhere. I had to try a different approach."

"You son of a bitch, you made my friends think I'm responsible for my family's disappearance."

"It wasn't personal. I told you, I was following standard procedure. The point is, you came through the investigation perfectly. You're in the clear."

"Thanks. Thanks a fucking lot."

8

"You seem determined to avoid using Lester Dant's name," the psychiatrist said.

I didn't answer.

"The FBI did a thorough background check," the psychiatrist continued. "They proved that he's not your brother."

My chest was so tight that I could hardly get the words out. "They think Dant crossed paths with my brother and learned what had happened to him as a child. He decided to switch places with Petey, possibly killed him."

I stared out a window toward a pine tree.

"But you don't believe it," the psychiatrist said.

"I *can't*."

" 'Can't' ?" The psychiatrist evaluated the word.

The tightness spread to my throat. "If I accepted that Dant kidnapped my wife and son, I'd have to admit that, given his profile, he'd have done whatever he wanted to them and . . ." I couldn't bring myself to say "killed them." I kept staring through the window toward the pine tree. "But if Petey was using Dant as an alias . . ." My voice broke. "If *Petey* took them, there's a good chance they're still alive."

The psychiatrist sat forward. "Why do you think that?"

"I've tried to put myself in his place." The tree became a blur. "I've done my best to imagine what Petey must have felt when he came into my house. My loving family, my comfortable surroundings. Petey wouldn't have wanted merely to kill me for destroying his life. He'd have wanted *my* life, the one I'd made for myself."

I forced myself to continue. "I've analyzed the moment when Petey pushed me into the gorge. I've relived it again and again. I think Petey's plan was to wait until Jason wasn't around and then kill me, making it look like an accident. Then he intended to sympathize with Kate and Jason, to make himself indispensable, and eventually to take my place. The only problem was, Jason saw him push me."

I took a deep breath. "So the plan was ruined. What was Petey going to do? Kill Jason? Make *that* death look like an accident also? Try to take my place with Kate? No. Jason was an essential part of what Petey wanted. Not just my wife but my *family*. Obviously, he couldn't live in my house then, not without Jason telling the police what he'd seen. *But Petey could steal my family*. He could hide them someplace and screw my wife whenever he wanted. He could force my son to treat him like a father." I squeezed the words out. "At least they'd be *alive*. If Petey and Dant are the same person. If *Petey* took them. But if Dant's who the FBI claims he is, if he isn't

Petey, he probably killed Jason right away and hid his body in the mountains. Then he made the best of a failed plan by looting the house and forcing Kate to go someplace with him, probably the Montana mountains, where he could rape her as much as he wanted before he got bored with her and—" I stopped, unable to admit Kate might be dead.

The psychiatrist narrowed her eyes as if I'd just described hell. But whether it was the hell that Kate and Jason suffered or whether it was the hell of what she considered my delusional mind, I couldn't know.

9

As I swallowed another antidepression pill, I heard the doorbell ring. The FBI with news, I hoped.

But when I opened the door, I frowned at children in costumes on my porch. Trick-or-treaters. It was Halloween, but I hadn't been aware. I didn't have candy. Not that they cared. They stumbled back as if *I* was the one in a scary costume. When I tried to explain, they ran from the porch.

I closed the door and shut off the light. Peering out a darkened window, I saw other costumed children, and as I hoped, they passed the house. I couldn't help remembering that Halloween was one of Jason's favorite holidays. How he'd loved to dress up as a space monster or a mad scientist. How *I* had loved to go out with him. But that wasn't going to happen now. It made me angry that I'd frightened the children. Was my face that twisted with loss? Were my eyes that dark with insanity?

The vial of pills remained in my hand. Cursing, I

threw it across the living room. Depression gave way to fury. What was it that Petey had said when he'd first approached me and I'd thought that he was a fake, when I'd told him to get away before I beat the shit out of him? "Brad, you'd have a harder time outfighting me than when we were kids." We'll see, I thought. In that moment, as I heard someone on the street shout to warn children away from my porch, I vowed to stop waiting for the police and the FBI to do something. I had to stop hoping that something would happen.

I had to *make* something happen.

10

"A theory of substitution?" Gader asked.

"Yes." I was so distraught that I stood in front of his desk instead of sitting. "We know that Petey lied."

"Dant."

"But what if the reason he was so convincing is that he based his lies on the truth? He *was* in Butte and Colorado Springs at the times he said, after all. He just wasn't doing what he claimed."

"What's that got to do with this theory of—"

"You told me that West Virginia doesn't have a town called Redemption."

"That's correct."

"But what about the rest of the country? Is there a town called Redemption *anywhere*? Or what about towns in West Virginia whose names have a religious connotation similar to Redemption?"

Gader thought about it. "Possibly. It would help Dant to keep his stories straight."

"Could you check?"

Gader leaned back in his chair. His thin face looked even thinner from weariness. "I'll try. The Bureau has me working double time on . . ." He pointed toward a thick stack of documents on his desk. "What difference would it make? All that stuff Dant said about his past was a lie to make you sympathize with him."

"But what if it was only *partly* a lie?"

"It still won't help us find your wife and son. Every lead's been followed. The task force has been disbanded. All we can do is wait for Dant to surface."

"Petey." I strained to keep control. "Damn it, doesn't *anything* you learn about him take you one step closer to understanding his patterns and where he might go?"

"Sure," Gader said. "Of course." He stood and walked me to his frosted-glass door. "The theory of substitution," he said without conviction. "Certainly. I'll definitely do some checking. By all means, if you think of anything else, just let me know."

11

"Mr. Payne will see you now," the receptionist said.

I set down the three-month-old *Newsweek,* which might as well have been up-to-date, given how little I'd paid attention to what was happening in the world. Crossing the small waiting area, I entered an office that was spacious by comparison, although in my own company it would have been considered tiny.

It was austere: a wooden chair, a desk, a computer, another chair. And a fish tank into which a portly, bespectacled man tapped grains of food. His white hair contrasted with the healthy ruddiness of his cheeks. His sport coat was off. He wore yellow suspenders over a blue shirt.

"How are you this afternoon, Mr. Denning?"

"Not very good, I'm afraid. Otherwise, I wouldn't be here."

Payne nodded, his puffy chin bobbing slightly. "It's for sure nobody comes to me with happy news. I used to internalize it all. At the end of the day, I'd be a wreck. But then I remembered the fish tank in my dentist's office and how it calmed me before I went in to have my teeth drilled. These are just garden-variety goldfish. I don't know if they help my clients, but they do wonders for *me*. Would you believe that I used to be a hundred-and-forty-pound bundle of anxiety? But ever since I got these fish, I've"—he spread his arms to his girth—"blossomed."

I had to smile a little.

"That's the spirit, Mr. Denning." Payne set down the box of fish food and eased into the chair behind his desk. "Would you like some coffee? A soft drink?"

I shook my head no.

He laced his fingers over his ample stomach and gave me the most sympathetic look I'd ever experienced. "Then tell me how I can help you."

Haltingly, I explained about Kate and Jason.

Payne nodded. "I read about it in the newspapers and saw the stories on television. A terrible thing."

"My attorney says you're the best private investigator in Denver."

"Maybe he doesn't know a lot of private investigators."

"He says you used to be with the FBI. He says you tracked down a serial killer."

"That's right."

"He says you predicted where a team of interstate bank robbers was going to hit next."

"True."

"And *when* they were going to do it. He also says you blocked a domestic-terrorist attempt to—"

"But that was only on the weekends."

The joke caught me unprepared.

"Please. All that flattery just makes my cheeks get redder," Payne said. "I was part of a team. We each did our share."

"My attorney says that you did *more* than your share."

"Did he also tell you that it cost me my first marriage, not to mention a bullet in my knee that forced me to leave the Bureau? I finally got the wisdom to stop having undue expectations of myself. *You* shouldn't have undue expectations either, Mr. Denning. I'm good, but only because I often see patterns others don't. For something like this, it's important to your emotional health that you don't count on the impossible."

With nowhere else to turn, I swallowed my disappointment. "Fair enough."

"So let me ask you again: How do you think I can help you?"

"The FBI and the police have given up." I tried to keep my voice steady. "It's been six months. I heard somewhere that in missing persons' cases, the more time drags on, the less chance there is of finding the people who are missing." I could barely add, "Finding them alive at least."

"It depends. Every case is different. Statistics are a record of the past, not a prediction of the future."

"In other words, you've got an open mind. You're exactly the person I need. Name any fee you want. Money isn't an issue."

"Money isn't an issue with me, either. I charge the same fee to everyone," Payne said. "But what do you expect *I* can do that the police and the FBI couldn't?"

"At the moment, they're not doing anything."

"Possibly because there isn't anything to be learned."

"I refuse to believe that."

"Understandably." Payne spread his hands. "But you have to realize that I can't duplicate the resources available to the FBI."

"Of course not. You can listen to new ideas, though. You can . . . I don't think I've made myself clear. I don't want to hire you just to continue the investigation."

"Oh?" Payne looked mystified. "Then what *do* you want?"

"I want you to teach me so *I* can continue the investigation."

12

"I need a handgun," I said.

"What kind?" The clerk had a beard and a ponytail.

"Whatever's the most powerful and shoots the most bullets."

"Rounds," the clerk said.

"Excuse me?"

"They're not called bullets. They're called rounds. The bullet's the part that blows away from the casing and hits the target."

"Fine. Whatever shoots the most rounds."

"Is this for target shooting or home defense? The reason I ask is, some people believe a shotgun's the best way to deal with a burglar."

"How about one of those?"

"A revolver? It only shoots six. These semiautomatics shoot more. But you'll need to decide which caliber you want: nine-millimeter or forty-five."

"Which is the biggest?"

"The forty-five."

"I'll take it."

"Just so you know your options, biggest isn't always best. The forty-five holds seven rounds in the magazine and one in the firing chamber. But this nine-millimeter over here holds *ten* rounds in the magazine and one in the chamber. A lot of power with eight rounds, versus somewhat less power but *eleven* rounds."

"How much less power?"

"With the nine-millimeter? Let's put it this way, it gets the job done. Actually, the only reason the magazine in this nine-millimeter holds only ten rounds is that in the mid-1990s, Congress passed an anti–assault weapon law that limits the capacity of handgun magazines. But *before* the law . . ."

"Yes?"

"There's a gun show in town Saturday. I'll introduce you to a friend who's willing to sell a *pre*law Beretta nine-millimeter that holds *fifteen* rounds in the magazine and one in the chamber."

"That's a lot."

"You bet. Don't misunderstand. There's nothing illegal about him selling the weapon. The law only forbids manufacturing or importing magazines that hold more than ten rounds. But because my friend bought his before the law was enacted, it's legal. That model doesn't come on the market often, so I expect you'll have to pay extra."

"Naturally."

"But after that . . ." The clerk looked uncomfortable.

"After that?"

"No offense. You're obviously new to this. So you don't shoot your foot off, you might want to take some lessons."

13

In the darkness beyond my window, the first snow-storm of the season gusted, but I hardly paid attention, too busy using Internet addresses that Payne had given me: sites that he said the FBI favored for researching places. Next to my new laptop computer, I had dictionaries and thesauruses to help me find words associated with redemption. Most weren't promising. I couldn't imagine anyone calling a place Atonement, Propitiation, Mediation, Intercession, or Judgment, for example. As it turned out, a village in Utah *was* called Judgment.

On the wall to my right, I'd attached a large map of the United States. Periodically, I got up and stuck a labeled thumbtack where a place's name had a religious connotation. After several hours, there were tacks all over the country, but no pattern. None was in Montana. I was beginning to understand why Gader hadn't wanted to investigate my theory.

My discouragement increased when I suddenly realized how many places had been named after saints. More thumbtacks got added to the map. I soon didn't have any more.

14

"How does a person create a false identity?"

Payne considered my question while tapping fish food into the tank. His chair creaked when he settled his weight into it. "The way it used to be done, first you pick a city where you've never lived."

"Why?"

"To prevent your real identity and your assumed one from contaminating each other. If you were raised in Cleveland, you don't want the character you're creating to have come from there, too. Otherwise, someone investigating your new identity might go there, show your photograph around, and find someone who remembers you under your real name."

I nodded.

"So you go to a different part of the country. But avoid small communities where everybody knows everybody else and can tell an investigator immediately whether someone who looks like you ever came from there. Pick a city; there's less continuity; memories are shorter. Let's say you choose Los Angeles or Seattle. Go to the public library there and read newspapers that came out a few years after you were born. You're looking for disasters—house fires, car accidents, that sort of thing—in which entire families were killed. That detail's important because you don't want anyone left alive to be able to contradict your story. Study the obituaries of the victims. You're looking for an ethnically compatible male child who, if he had lived, would be the same age you are now."

"And then?"

"Let's say the victim you choose to impersonate was named Robert Keegan. His obituary will probably tell you where he was born. You send away for a copy of his birth certificate. Not a big deal. People lose copies of their birth certificates all the time. Public-record offices are used to that kind of request."

"But . . ." I frowned. "If Robert Keegan died, won't there be a note about it on his birth certificate, some kind of cross-reference?"

"Not in the days before computers became an essential part of our society," Payne said. "The year that you were born, information wasn't exchanged efficiently. The authorities would send you the copy of Robert Keegan's birth certificate without giving it another thought. Wait a while so that a further inquiry about Robert Keegan won't attract attention. Then contact the hall of records for a copy of Robert Keegan's *death* certificate. The reason I mentioned Los Angeles and Seattle earlier is that the states of California and Washington put Social Security numbers on their death certificates. Many parents apply to get a Social Security number for their children while they're filling out birth certificate forms in the hospital, so the odds are Keegan had one, even though he died young. With his birth certificate and his Social Security number, you can get a driver's license, a passport, and any other major identification that you need. You can get a job, pay taxes, and open a bank account. In short, you can assume his identity." Payne gave me a long look. "But we're not talking about you."

"No, we're talking about my brother. If Lester Dant were dead, could Petey have assumed his identity the way you just explained?"

Payne kept studying me. "Before your brother was first arrested, photographed, fingerprinted, and booked as Lester Dant? Theoretically."

"Then I'm not crazy." I let out a long breath. "Petey and Dant *could* be the same person. Dant could be Petey's alias."

"But it didn't happen," Payne said.

"What?"

"Your brother didn't assume Lester Dant's identity."

"How can you be so damned sure?"

"Because earlier this morning, I paid a visit to Gader. We knew each other when I was with the Bureau. For old times' sake, I asked to be allowed to review Dant's file."

I felt uneasy about what Payne was leading up to.

"The file was very revealing," Payne said. "You were so insistent that your brother and Dant were the same man, Gader had Dant's background double-checked. There's no death certificate anywhere. Moreover, Dant didn't even apply for a Social Security number until he was a teenager. The signature on the application is consistent with the signatures Dant had to give at the various times he was arrested. Dant and your brother are two different people."

"*No.*"

"It's the truth," Payne said.

"That means my wife and son are dead!"

"Not necessarily. Without evidence to the contrary, there's always a reason to hope."

"Without their corpses, you mean."

Payne didn't reply for a moment. "I'm sorry, Mr. Denning."

I stared toward the fish tank. "You didn't see the look in Petey's eyes when he told me about the goldfish that he and I had buried in the backyard and how the neighbor's cat dug it up. He didn't say it as if he were remembering something he'd heard. His eyes had the clarity of someone who'd been there. *That was Petey talking to me.*"

"Perhaps. But I haven't the faintest idea how you can prove it."

"I will." I stood. "Believe me, somehow I will."

"Before you go, I've been meaning to ask you something."

I stopped at the doorway and looked back at him.

"From my years with the Bureau, my nose is sensitive to the smell of cordite. That smell is on my right hand from when we shook hands when you came in. Have you been using firearms, Mr. Denning?"

15

"Ready on the firing line!" the female instructor barked.

We straightened.

"Ready on the right!"

We checked in that direction.

"Ready on the left!"

Through safety glasses, we checked in *that* direction, making sure that nobody was doing anything careless.

"*One,*" the instructor yelled, "grip your holstered weapon! *Two,* draw and aim from the waist! *Three,* raise your weapon to your line of sight! *Four,* press the trigger!"

Eight almost-simultaneous shots filled the long, narrow indoor shooting range. They echoed off the concrete walls, my protective earphones making the reports sound oddly distant.

Although the instructor was directly behind me, she too sounded muffled. "Aim to the right of the target! To the left!"

We obeyed, not firing, but checking for other targets, which she'd warned could pop up at any time.

"Weapon to your waist! Secure it!"

As one, the eight of us completed the sequence and took our hands from our holstered firearms.

The range became silent.

"Not bad," she said. "Let's see if anybody hit anything."

Each of us stood in a slot, with a ledge in front for ammunition and spare magazines. A button to the left engaged a motorized pulley that brought in the targets.

The instructor studied the results. "Okay. Nobody hit the bull's-eye, but I don't expect you to at this point. At least none of you missed the target completely. Denning, you hit closest, but you're still a little high and to the left. Practice more dry-firing at home. Stop twisting your wrist when you press the trigger."

She went on to correct the other students. We put masking tape over the holes in our targets, touched a button that returned the targets to the end of the gallery, and straightened when she shouted, "Ready on the firing line!"

16

I went to a fitness center every day. I'd never been in top physical condition, but since Petey had taken Kate and Jason, I'd fallen apart. A junk-food diet in combination with too much alcohol and no activity had caused me to put on twenty pounds. No longer. I hired a trainer. Knowing that I had to start slowly, I was nonetheless impatient to get on with it. I progressed from thirty to sixty minutes a day on the machines. I started jogging, at first at the center's indoor track and then outside in the cold. One mile. Two. Five. I lost the weight I'd put on. Fat became muscle.

I took self-defense classes. Angle. Force. Mass. Architect's language. I no longer pretended to try to work. As far as I was concerned, I had only one job, so I disbanded my company, giving my employees a generous severance package. When I wasn't preparing myself by shooting and physical training, I spent my time searching the Internet, using other Web addresses that Payne had given me.

In my former life, I'd always been too busy to explore the Internet. Now I was amazed at how much information I could obtain, provided that, thanks to Payne, I knew where to look. I found Lester Dant's birth information, which was exactly as the FBI had indicated: He'd definitely been born in Brockton, Indiana, on April 24, a year before Petey had been born. I searched the databases for every state in the union but couldn't find corresponding *death* information about Lester Dant. Without proof that Petey had assumed Dant's identity, I grudgingly tested the FBI's theory that Dant had assumed *Petey's* identity, but no matter how far I spread my search, I couldn't find any proof that Petey had died, and, if he had, whether he'd been murdered.

Thanksgiving (the holiday's name made me bitter) had passed. Kate's parents had asked me to spend it with them. I'd refused, hardly in a social mood. But then I'd thought that they were as desolate as I was and we might as well try to console one another. The three of us drank some wine and watched football in the kitchen while we made the dinner, but I never managed a holiday spirit, constantly worrying that the Denver police or Gader and Payne had mislaid the phone number I'd given them in case Kate and Jason were found while I was away.

For Christmas, Kate's parents came to visit. But as soon as I saw Kate's father, I wished that I'd saved them the trouble and gone to them. I could barely conceal my dismay at how this once tall, robust man had been so stooped by his heart condition, aggravated by worry. As hard as we tried to be festive, we kept remembering former, better Christmases, like when I'd been dating Kate in college and I'd realized I was making progress when she'd invited me to spend Christmas with her and her parents.

Of the many difficult things about the season, choosing the tree had been especially hard for me because Kate and Jason had always joined me—a big family event. As soon as we'd gotten home with it, we'd always begun putting on the decorations, often not finishing until after dark. This time, every bulb that I'd put on the tree racked me with greater loss. Normally, there'd have been plenty of presents under the tree, but this year, Kate's parents and I had agreed not to exchange gifts. After all, there was only one thing we wanted, and it couldn't be put under a tree. As usual, Kate's mother made eggnog. It was as delicious as every other year, but I could hardly get it down. A few days later, they went back to Durango. Kate's father felt so poorly that her mother had to drive.

Phil Barrow invited me next door for a New Year's Eve party. I did my best to be sociable, but for me, the holiday was a wake. I went home an hour before the countdown at midnight. As hard as I tried, I couldn't remember what Kate and Jason sounded like.

Spring came.

May.

June.

They'd been gone a year.

17

"I'm leaving town," I told Payne.

"Yes, sometimes it's a good idea to get away from bad memories," he said.

"I was hoping that you wouldn't mind if I had my mail forwarded to you."

"Sure," Payne said. "No problem."

"I've asked the police and the FBI to leave messages with you in case they learn something new."

Payne nodded. "I'll phone you the second I hear anything. Just give me the number where you'll be and—"

"At the moment, that's a little uncertain. I'll have to phone *you*."

"You don't know where you're going?"

"Not exactly."

"But you don't just board a plane without having a reservation to someplace."

"I'm not going on a plane. I thought I'd simply get in my car and drive. See the country. Go wherever the roads take me."

Payne's eyes narrowed. "Who are you kidding?"

"I don't understand."

"Go wherever the roads take you? Give me a break. You're up to something. What is it?"

"I told you. I just need to get away."

"You worry me."

I avoided his gaze and looked at the fish tank.

"Don't tell me—you're going out there to try to find him," Payne said.

I kept looking at the fish tank.

"How the hell do you figure to do it?" Payne demanded. "It's impossible. You don't have a chance."

At last, I looked back at him. "I've done everything else I can think of."

"Without any leads? It's for damn sure you'll be going where the roads take you. All you'll do is wander."

"But I *do* have leads," I insisted.

Payne leaned his ample body forward. "Tell me."

"It's hard to explain."

"Give it a try."

"Petey wanted to take my place."

"And?" Payne looked baffled.

"Now I'm going to do it in the reverse. I'm going to take *Petey's* place."

"What?"

"I'm going to put myself in his mind. I'm going to think like him. I'm going to become him."

"Jesus," Payne whispered.

"After all, we're brothers."

"Mr. Denning . . ."

"Yes?"

"I'm as sorry for you as it's possible to be. God help you."

Part Three

Part Three

1

Put myself in Petey's mind? Think like him? It was desperation, yes, but what was the alternative? At least it would be motion. It would keep me from losing my *own* mind.

I went to the street where Petey had first approached me outside my office—or what had used to be my office. The time was shortly after 2:00 P.M., as it had been exactly a year earlier. Petey had shouted my name from behind me, which meant that he'd been waiting to the left of the building's revolving door. I walked to a large concrete flower planter, where I guessed that he'd been resting his hips. I studied the front door, trying to put myself in his place. Why hadn't he gone into my office? As I leaned against the planter, feeling invisible to the passing crowd, I understood why he'd done it the way he had. In my office, he'd have been under *my* control, whereas on the sidewalk, yelling my name from behind me, *he* was in charge.

I recalled our initial conversation, this time from *his*

perspective as he told me things that only my brother could have known, seeing my amazement, winning me over. I went to the delicatessen across the street, where our conversation had continued. I sat where *he* had sat. I imagined myself from his perspective as he continued to persuade me that my long-lost brother had finally returned. I went home and pretended to be him coming into my house, looking around, seeing all my possessions, the things that he'd never been able to have. Was it at this point that his plan had formed? *I* deserve this, not *you,* he would have thought. Picking up this and that object, he would have worked hard to conceal his anger. *You ruined my life, and this is what you got for it, you bastard.*

Kate would have been easy to look at: her long legs, her inviting waist. But what about Jason? What would Petey really have thought of him? A damned nuisance. Petey's background didn't leave room for paternal instinct. But Jason was part of what Petey would've had if I hadn't destroyed his life by sending him home from the baseball game. Jason went with the package, with the attractive wife and the big house, so Petey wanted him. Petey wanted *everything* that I had.

I recalled the dinner that Petey had eaten with us and how polite he'd been, helping to clean the dishes. Later, he'd played catch with Jason. He must have hated every second of it, just as he'd hated pretending to enjoy reminiscing about our childhood before I ruined his life. But the worst moment of all, the most hateful for him, would have been when I'd brought him the baseball glove that he'd dropped when the man and woman had grabbed him. He must have wanted to shove the damned glove down my throat.

I went to Petey's room. I lay on his bed. I stared up at
the ceiling and discovered that I'd picked up the baseball
glove and was slamming my fist into it again and again.
He would have wanted a smoke, but he wouldn't have
ruined his plan by lighting up in the house and annoying
Kate. So he'd crept downstairs, through the French doors
off the kitchen, into the moonlit backyard, where he'd sat
angrily on a lounge chair and lit a cigarette. I remembered looking from our bedroom window and seeing him
down there. I imagined him pretending not to notice
when my face appeared. I put myself in his mind. What
are you doing up there? he'd have thought. Screwing the
wife, are you, bro? Enjoy it while you can. It'll soon be
my turn.

2

The next morning, I went to the barbershop where I'd taken him. I sat in the chair, feeling the scissors against my head, imagining that he'd festered from the insult that I thought he looked like shit and I was going to make him presentable. Then I went to the Banana Republic where I'd bought him new clothes. Then the shoe store. Then the dentist, where I'd made him feel self-conscious about his chipped tooth, reinforcing his sense that I thought he looked like shit.

When I walked into the dentist's office, the receptionist glanced up in surprise. "We weren't expecting you today, Mr. Denning. We're just about to close for lunch. Is this an emergency?"

"No." Confused, I realized that I'd almost tricked myself into believing that I could truly repeat the pattern from a year ago. "I must have gotten my days mixed up. Sorry to have bothered you."

As I reached unsteadily for the doorknob, I remembered waiting in the reception area while Petey had gone in to have his teeth cleaned and the chip in his tooth smoothed away. I tried to project myself into Petey, to imagine him sitting angrily in the dentist's chair. Since he hadn't been to a dentist in years, he would have been nervous, tensing a little as the dentist came at him with . . .

"Actually, there might be a way you can help." My hand trembling, I released my grip on the doorknob and went over to the counter that separated the receptionist from the waiting area.

She looked at me expectantly.

"A year ago, I was in here with my brother." My heart pounded from the shock of the idea I'd just had.

"Yes, I remember. I'm terribly sorry about what happened to your wife and son."

"It's been a difficult time." I fought to keep my voice steady, to hold my emotions in check. "The thing is, I was wondering . . ." I held my breath. "Do you know if any X rays were taken of my brother's teeth?"

3

"There!" I told Gader. "This'll prove it!"

The somber man frowned at what I'd set on his desk. "Prove what?"

"That my brother and Lester Dant are the same man!"

"Are you still trying to—"

"My brother had dental X rays taken a couple of days before he kidnapped my wife and son. When I was a child, my parents made sure that Petey and I went to a dentist for regular checkups. Show these X rays to our family dentist back in Ohio. He can compare them to his records. He'll prove that the teeth belong to the same person."

"But a nine-year-old's teeth wouldn't be the same as those of a man in his thirties," Gader objected.

"Because he wouldn't have had all his permanent teeth by the time he disappeared? No. My dentist says that my brother would have had *a few* permanent teeth, and even if they changed over the years because of work done on them, the *roots* would have kept the same structure. What would it hurt you to look into it?"

Gader set down a thick file he'd been reading. "All right," he said impatiently. "To settle this once and for all. In Ohio, what was the name of your family dentist?"

"I . . . don't remember."

He looked more impatient.

"But Woodford wasn't a big town," I said. "There weren't many dentists. It shouldn't be hard to track down the one we went to."

"Assuming he's still in business. Assuming he kept records this long." Gader's phone rang. As he reached for it, he told me, "I'll get back to you."

"When?"

"Next week."

"But that isn't soon enough."

He didn't hear me. He was already speaking into the phone.

4

Saturday morning, I rose from Petey's bed, put camping gear in the Expedition, and packed sandwiches in a cooler. As much as possible, I did everything the same as a year earlier, and at nine, exactly when we'd set out the last time, I took Interstate 70 into the mountains. The peaks were still snowcapped, the same as they had been the previous June. Ignoring their beauty, as Petey would have, I worked to recall our conversation. I squirmed as I sensed a pattern: Almost every time Jason had said "Dad" and asked me something, Petey had answered first. He'd been practicing to take my place, getting used to being called "Dad."

When I headed north into the Arapaho National Forest, I imagined him hiding his anticipation. I reached the lake and stopped where the three of us had stopped the previous year. I looked at where Petey, Jason, and I had pitched our tent. I hiked around the lake to the stream that fed it, climbing the wooded slope to the gorge from which the stream thundered. All the while, I thought of him looking around for a spot to get rid of me and make it seem like an accident.

I climbed loose stones to the ridge above the gorge. I felt Petey's excitement when Jason went around the boulder to urinate. Now! Brad's back was exposed.

"Dad!"

No, the kid was returning too soon!

Unable to stop, I hurtled my goddamned brother into the gorge, then spun toward the kid, whose face was frozen in terror.

My mental image of Jason's fright shocked me into the present. Snapping from Petey's mind-set, I was nauseated from the darkness of pretending to be him. Despite a chill breeze, sweat soaked me. Working down the loose stones to the trail at the bottom of the ridge, I couldn't help wondering how Petey would have climbed down without falling, given that he had a frightened, struggling boy to contend with. Then I realized that there was only one way he could have done it. The answer made me sick as I imagined what it had been like to carry an unconscious boy through the trees and back to the Expedition.

Since the vehicle didn't have a trunk, Petey would have had to tie and gag Jason, putting him on the back floor, covering him with the tent. As Petey, I drove carefully home through the mountain passes, never exceeding the speed limit, lest a state trooper stop me and wonder about the squirming sounds beneath the tent in the back.

Arriving home, I drove into the garage and pressed the remote control. With a rumble, the door came down. As I got out of the car, I envisioned Kate coming into the garage from the kitchen. She'd have just gotten back from the all-day seminar she'd been conducting. The trim gray business suit she'd been wearing when we'd left that morning made her long blond hair more bright.

"How come you're back so soon?" She frowned. "Where are Brad and Jason?"

"We had an accident."

"An accident?"

He'd overpowered her, bound and gagged her, gone into the house, found her car keys, then put her and Jason in the Volvo's trunk. The car had a backseat that could be flipped down so the trunk could hold long objects, such as skis. He'd probably opened the seat partway to allow air to circulate into the trunk, using the numerous objects he'd looted from the house to keep the seat from opening completely and allowing Kate and Jason a way to escape. He'd hurriedly packed suitcases, making sure to take some of my clothes. After all, as long as he was replacing me, he might as well look like me.

Around 6:00 P.M., just as Petey had, I got in the Volvo, which the police had returned to me, and drove from the house. At 6:21, exactly when Petey had, keeping my head low from the camera as Petey had, I got money from the same ATM that he'd used. But as I headed north from Denver, following Interstate 25, I realized that, with all the objects Petey had stolen from me, the Volvo would have looked as if he were running an appliance store out of the car. Worried that a policeman might get suspicious, Petey would never have left Denver with all that stuff. He would have sold it as quickly as possible. But he was new in town. When would he have had time to find a fence? Rethinking the previous days, I suddenly remembered that, after the dentist, Petey had wanted some time alone in a park "to get my mind straight." The son of a bitch had used the afternoon to arrange to sell what he'd planned to steal from me.

I drove to a rough section of town and imitated the transaction, filling the few minutes that it would have taken. Then I returned to the interstate, and this time, I felt invisible, one of countless vehicles on the road, nothing to make me conspicuous.

5

A road sign informed me that Casper, Wyoming, was 250 miles ahead. I set the Volvo's cruise control to make sure I stayed under the speed limit. When sunset approached and I put on my headlights, I felt even more inconspicuous, blending with thousands of other lights. I passed Cheyenne, Wyoming, able to distinguish little, except that its buildings seemed low and sprawling. Then, four hours after having left Denver, I approached the glow of Casper. For most of the drive, I'd sensed only flat land in the uninhabited darkness around me. Now the shadow of a mountain hulked on my left, blocking stars.

A few miles north of town, I saw a sign for the rest area. Traffic was sparse, most of the vehicles having driven into Casper. An arrow pointed toward a barely visible exit ramp. Following it off the interstate, I approached two squat brick buildings whose floodlights silhouetted three pickup trucks and a minivan.

But Petey would have needed more seclusion, so I

took a gravel road that veered to the right from the pavement that led to the rest area. The floodlights at the buildings reached far enough to show picnic tables and stunted trees in back. Satisfying myself that no one had emerged from the rest rooms and seen what might have seemed unusual behavior, I reduced my headlights to parking lights and got just enough illumination to see a redwood-fenced area, behind which the tip of a Dumpster showed.

I parked behind the Dumpster, shut off my parking lights, and walked in front of the fence, verifying that no one, a state trooper, for example, had seen what I'd done and was coming to investigate. Confident that I was hidden, I unlocked the trunk.

What I imagined pushed me back. Kate and Jason on their sides. Squirming. Terrified. Duct tape pressed tightly across their mouths. Hands tied behind their backs. Ankles bound. Eyes so wide with fright that their whites were huge. Moans that were half apprehension, half pleas. The stench of bodily excretions, of carbon dioxide, of sweat and fear.

Petey would have taken off their gags and allowed them to catch their breath while he'd warned them not to scream. They'd have been too fear-weakened and groggy from the foul air in the trunk to manage much of an outburst. He'd have needed to lift them one at a time from the trunk, loosening their clothes so they could relieve themselves. That unpleasant intimacy would have tested his commitment to his new family. But his obligations were just beginning. For example, they'd have been terribly thirsty. Had he planned ahead and stopped at a fast-food place in Casper to get soft drinks, possibly french fries and hamburgers also? As he regagged them and put them back in the trunk, would he have said any reassuring words?

"I love you."

I shut the trunk. From the darkness behind the Dumpster, I stared toward the vehicles in front of the rest rooms. I walked in that direction, my footsteps crunching on pebbles. The floodlights at the two buildings made me feel naked the closer I came. By then, most of the vehicles had departed, leaving only a midsize sedan. I went into the men's room and found it empty. I stepped outside. Insects swarmed in the overhead light.

A woman left the other building, pulled keys from her purse, and approached the sedan. She didn't look in my direction. I imagined Petey starting to rush her, then pausing as headlights flashed past on the interstate, not a lot, but enough that there was never a gap, never a moment when somebody driving by wouldn't have seen a man attack a woman.

So Petey had waited for another opportunity, gone into the women's room, and subdued his victim there. He'd watched the interstate until there were just enough gaps between headlights that no one would see him in the few seconds that it took him to carry the unconscious woman around to the darkness. Behind the Dumpster, he'd tied and gagged her. Then he'd returned to the rest area, used the woman's key to start her car (a Caprice, the police had told me). He'd kept the headlights off and driven back to the darkness behind the fence, where he would have had to use a knife to make ventilation holes through the backseats into the Caprice's trunk before he transferred Kate and Jason into it.

But when he'd put the driver in the trunk with them,

hadn't it worried him that there might not have been enough air for three people? Why had he risked suffocating Kate and Jason by putting the woman in the trunk with them? As it was, the woman had died. Why hadn't he killed her and hidden her body in the Dumpster? No one would have found her for quite a while, if ever. Again I felt Kate and Jason's horror as the asthmatic woman fought to breathe with the duct tape pressed over her mouth, her frenzied movements, her gagging sounds, her gradual stillness, the release of her bladder, probably her bowels. As the Caprice sped along the interstate, Kate and Jason would have been seized by the out-of-control fear that, if it had happened to the woman, it could happen to *them*.

The question kept nagging at me: *Why hadn't Petey just killed her and hidden her body in the Dumpster?* The only answer that made sense to me was that, no matter how indifferent Petey had felt toward the woman, he hadn't intended for her to die. Killing me was one thing. As far as Petey was concerned, I deserved to die for ruining his life. But this woman had merely happened to be in the wrong place at the wrong time. It was the first indication of humanity that I'd detected in him. It gave me hope for Kate and Jason.

He could have left the Volvo behind the Dumpster, where it might not have been discovered for days. Instead, he'd gone to the trouble of moving the Volvo to the front of the rest rooms, where it would be in plain sight. Because he wanted it to be found soon. He wanted it to point the way north, just as abandoning the Caprice outside Billings, Montana, made it seem that he was heading toward Butte. He'd been thinking with frightening control.

6

I drove back to the interstate. A road sign indicated that Billings, Montana, was 250 miles away. My eyelids felt heavy. But I had to keep moving. I had to complete Petey's escape.

Had he slept along the way? Doing that certainly tempted me. But I was afraid that if I steered off the interstate and found a secluded spot—a camping area, for example—where I could get a few hours' sleep, I wouldn't waken until daylight. In Petey's case, the Caprice might have been reported by then. He had to get to Billings. Imitating him, I kept driving.

I played the radio loud. In the middle of the night, it was hard to find a station. The ones I did find broadcast mostly evangelists riddled with static.

A mountain range stretched from north to south on my left. Moonlight glowed off the snowy peaks. My eyelids weakened. To stay awake, I bit my lips. I dug my finger-nails into my palms. Interstate 25 became 90. I passed

Sheridan, Wyoming, and entered Montana. The signs changed character: Lodge Grass; Custer Battlefield National Monument; Crow Agency. . . . At Hardin, the interstate veered west. Meanwhile, as the miles accumulated, I imagined that Petey would have worried that his captives weren't getting enough air. He'd have stopped periodically on deserted roads to check on them. It pained me to think of Kate's and Jason's frightened eyes peering desperately up at him. They flinched when he reached in to touch their brows to calm them. As for the Caprice's driver, he barely looked at her.

When I finally read a sign for Billings, I was troubled that the distance between Casper and Billings should have taken me only four hours, but with frequent stops, pretending to check on my captives, I'd taken ninety minutes longer than I should have.

Even so, it was still dark when I came to the rest stop on the other side of Billings. A sign called it a scenic vista, but with the moon having set, I had only a vague sense of mountains to the north and south. Two vehicles were parked at the rest rooms: a pickup truck and a sedan. Here, too, a service road led behind the buildings. I parked in the darkness. Adrenaline overcame my exhaustion as I got out of the car. The air was surprisingly cold. Two men in cowboy hats came out of one of the concrete-block buildings. I waited while they got in the pickup truck and drove away. At this predawn hour, there was almost no traffic on the interstate. I walked quickly toward the rest rooms and listened for activity in either one. If I heard voices, if there was more than one person, I'd wait for a better opportunity. But if there was only one set of footsteps . . .

At that hour, few women felt safe to drive alone. I assumed that the victim would have been male. Use a tire iron to knock him unconscious in the men's room. Drag him into the darkness. Take his car to the back. Put Kate, Jason, and the driver into its trunk.

Would it have been at this point that Petey had discovered that the owner of the Caprice had choked to death from the duct tape over her mouth? He wouldn't have been overwhelmed with sorrow. He'd given her a chance. As far as he was concerned, it wasn't his fault. The penalty for kidnapping was the same as for murder, so with nothing to lose, instead of trying to hide her body, he'd left it with the Caprice. Then he'd gotten into its replacement and driven onto the interstate. But instead of continuing toward Butte, where he wanted the police to think he was going, he'd taken the next exit ramp, crossed the overpass, and reaccessed the interstate, reversing direction, heading back toward Billings.

I kept after him. By then, it was dawn. I saw mountains, ranches, and oil refineries. Crossing the Yellowstone River, I no longer had the police report to guide me. Petey had been as tired as I was. Where the hell had he gone next?

7

The interstate forked. I had to choose—take 94 northeast through Montana, way up into North Dakota, or else retrace 90 south into Wyoming. I chose the latter. I didn't fool myself that intuitively I was doing what Petey had. My decision was totally arbitrary.

But as tired as I was, if I didn't soon find a place to sleep, I knew I'd have an accident. Petey must have felt the same. Even charged with adrenaline, he couldn't have kept going much longer. For certain, he wouldn't have dared risk an accident. He didn't have a driver's license, and the car wasn't registered to him. A state trooper questioning him would eventually have gotten suspicious enough to look in the trunk. Meanwhile, as the sun got higher, warming the car's interior, I imagined how hot the trunk would have gotten. No matter how many ventilation holes Petey had made, Kate, Jason, and the car's owner would have roasted in that confined space, the sun's heat turning the trunk into an oven, the air getting thicker, smothering. If Petey was going to keep them alive in the trunk, he had to rest by day and drive by night.

Because the Denver detectives had said that duct tape had covered the dead woman's mouth, I presumed that Petey had done the same to Kate, Jason, and the man whose car he'd stolen. I took my right hand off the steering wheel and pressed it over my mouth, forcing myself to breathe only through my nose. Spring allergies had caused mucus to partially block my nostrils. My chest heaved. I couldn't seem to get enough air. I had to concentrate to control my heartbeat, to inhale and exhale slowly. I couldn't bear the thought of breathing self-consciously, of taking in a minimum of air for what felt like forever in a hot, closed space.

Definitely, no one in the trunk would have had a chance of surviving unless Petey drove only when it was cooler—at night. But where could he have stopped? A motel would have been dangerously public. But what about a camping area? Tourist season was only beginning. Petey might have been able to find a wooded area that didn't have visitors. Listening for the approach of vehicles, he could have risked letting his prisoners out of the trunk. If there was a stream where they could clean themselves, so much the better.

He'd have needed to get food again. At the next exit, I saw a McDonald's, went to the drive-through lane, and ordered an Egg McMuffin, coffee, and orange juice. While I waited behind other cars, I frowned at my beard-stubbled image in the rearview mirror. But the beard stubble wasn't what bothered me. I'd been trying to imitate Petey's thoughts, and I'd forgotten one of the most important things about him: the scar on his chin. It would have attracted attention. I pulled a pen from my shirt pocket and drew a line where Petey's scar would have been. I wanted to know what it felt like to have people staring at my chin.

When I paid for my food, the woman behind the counter pointed toward the ink mark. "Mister, you've got—"

"Yeah, I know," I said. "I can't seem to get the darned thing off."

I'd intended to ask her if there were nearby camping areas, but feeling conspicuous, I paid for my food and drove away. Squinting from the glare of the morning sun, I decided to let my beard keep growing and hide the streak on my chin.

A likely place for a campground would be along a river, so when I crossed the Bighorn, I took the first exit. There, I debated whether to follow the river north or south. A sign indicated that south would take me to the Crow Indian Reservation. That didn't sound like a place where I'd be invisible, so I headed north.

Traffic was sparse. The land was fenced. In a while, I came to a dirt road that took me to the left, toward the river. It soon curved to the right to parallel the river, although bushes and trees along the bank prevented me from seeing the water. A weed-overgrown lane went into the trees. I drove down it, parked behind the trees, walked to the road, and satisfied myself that the car was hidden.

I had no illusions that this was the spot where Petey had stopped, but logic suggested that it was similar. Petey would have ignored the car's owner while he tried to re-assure Kate and Jason, saying that he wouldn't hurt them unless they forced him to, that if they did what they were told, there wouldn't be trouble. He would have kept one of them in the trunk while he let the other bathe, making sure that a rope was tied to one and then the other's waist to prevent them from trying to run. He would have allowed them to change clothes. He would have studied them while they ate their fast-food breakfast.

"I'll take care of you."

They wouldn't have known what to make of that.

As frightened as Kate was, she'd have had all night to analyze the danger they were in. She'd have already decided that their only chance was for her to use her stress-management skills to try to keep him calm. "Thanks for the food."

"You like it?"

Despite their fear, Kate and Jason would have been so hungry that they'd have gulped their hamburgers.

"I said, *Do you like it?*"

"Yes," Kate would have answered quickly.

"It isn't much, but it's better than nothing."

Was there a threat in the way he said it, that if they gave him trouble, he could make sure that was exactly what they got: nothing? Kate would have taken another deep swallow from her soft drink, knowing that it wouldn't be enough to replenish her fluids. She'd have brushed her tangled hair from her face, aware that she had to try to look as presentable as possible. Make Petey think of you as a human being, not an object. Thank him for courtesies he showed. Behave as if the situation were normal. Make him want to go through efforts for you so he can get the gratification of being appreciated.

But what about Jason? As young as he was, lacking

Kate's training, he'd have been nearly out of his mind with terror. Gagged, Kate wouldn't have been able to talk to him in the trunk. She couldn't have coached him. She had to depend on giving him significant looks and hoping that he'd understand her motives, that he'd follow her lead.

"What are you going to do with us?" she'd have asked when the time seemed right.

"I told you, I'm going to take care of you."

"But why did—"

"We're a family."

"Family?" Don't react. Make even the outrageous seem normal.

"Brad had an accident."

"What?"

"He fell off a cliff. I'm taking his place."

Kate's stomach would have plummeted as if *she* had fallen from a cliff.

"I'm your husband. Jason, you're my son."

Fighting to keep tears from swelling into her eyes, Kate would have echoed Petey's earlier words, reinforcing their import. "Take care of us."

Petey probably wouldn't have been familiar with the term "the Stockholm principle," but he was a skillful-enough manipulator that he would have understood it. After a period of time, captives grow weary of their roller-coaster emotions. Grateful to be shown small kindnesses, they tend to accept their situation and to bond with their captors.

That would have been Petey's hope. But of course he wasn't accustomed to providing for a wife and son. The breakfast would have quickly disappeared, and then there'd have been the problem of what to do about lunch and supper. Petey wouldn't have thought that far ahead, but even if he had, how was he going to keep hamburgers and fries from spoiling, and what about a way to reheat them? He needed to buy a cooler, a camping stove, pots and pans and . . . What had started as an urge to take my place suddenly didn't have the gratification it had promised. Everything was getting too complicated. Why not admit that he'd made a mistake and chuck the whole business? Why not do what he wanted with Kate and Jason, kill them and the driver in the trunk, hide their bodies, drive into the nearest big town, abandon the car, buy a bus ticket, and adios?

The thought made me shudder. No, that's how Lester Dant would have acted, I tried to assure myself. Lester Dant would have killed Jason right away, then driven Kate to a secret spot and dumped her body down a ravine when he got tired of abusing her. He certainly wouldn't have taken the time and the risk to lay a false trail all the way to Montana. That only made sense if *Petey* had abducted them, if he was determined to take over my life and make Kate and Jason his family.

But his patience would have been sorely tested. The only way he could have felt at ease enough to go to sleep was by putting Kate and Jason back into the trunk so they wouldn't try to escape while he was dozing. The shade of the trees would have prevented the trunk from becoming lethally hot. Still, Petey would have had no idea how long he might sleep. He'd have loved eight hours. Even with numerous ventilation holes, Kate, Jason, and the man whose car he'd stolen probably wouldn't have been able to survive that long in the trunk without the lid being opened periodically to vent carbon dioxide. Two people, though, would have a chance. There'd have been one-third more air for them if . . . That's when I knew that Petey had deliberately killed the second driver, whereas the first death had been an accident.

Sleep. I could barely keep awake. But as I opened a back door, staring at my suitcase, knapsack, laptop computer, and printer, I realized that I was going to have to put them in the front seat so I could stretch out in the back. It would have annoyed Petey to move his four suitcases. Another complication. Another nuisance. In addition, I was going to have to disable the car's interior light so I could leave a back door open and stretch my legs while I slept—to prevent the car's battery from dying. One more damned thing to do.

No, this wouldn't have been at all like what Petey had wanted.

8

The sound of a passing vehicle startled me awake. I sat up sharply. Before I checked my watch, the angle of the sun told me that the time was late afternoon. Out of sight from the trees, the vehicle kept bumping along the dirt road. My mouth felt pasty as I got out of the backseat and peered through the trees, seeing that the vehicle was a pickup truck, a rancher in a hurry to get somewhere. My back was sore.

Thus Petey's nervous schedule would have resumed: checking on his captives, lifting them out so they could relieve themselves and wash their faces in the river. At some point, he would have had to take care of himself. His clothes would have felt grimy. Probably he changed them for some of the clothes that he'd stolen from me. Perhaps he'd felt angry as the rumblings in his stomach told him that he had to start thinking about getting more food for everybody. He couldn't go on like this. Either he had to find a place in which to settle or he would have to kill Kate and Jason for creating his problems.

No! The only way I could shove that mind-threatening thought away was by imagining how Kate and Jason might have reacted to Petey's growing impatience. Kate's training would have told her that she had to accommodate Petey as best she could, to make things less complicated for him, to ease the strain he felt.

"I can try to wash these dirty clothes in the river. Tie me to a tree and watch me on the bank. That way, you'll be sure I can't run away. What about these suitcases you moved to the front? Why don't I return them to where they were? There's a lot of housekeeping I can take care of."

Jason might have caught on by then. He might have understood what Kate was doing and tried his best to appear the obedient son. Reinforce Petey's fantasies. Make him believe that his risk and effort were worthwhile. That was the only way they were going to stay alive. In a way, it was the captives trying to make the *captor* fall into the Stockholm syndrome.

Petey would have been too close to where he'd abandoned the Caprice. The new vehicle he was driving would soon have been reported missing. Maybe it had license plates from several states away, suggesting that the driver had a distance to go before arriving home and wouldn't be reported missing until at least the end of the day. All the same, Petey wouldn't have been able to depend on that. He needed to get on the move. But he didn't dare show the car until darkness made him invisible. That meant waiting to get food for Kate and Jason. But it also meant that Kate and Jason had more time to talk with him, a chance to try to bond with him, to personalize themselves, so that killing them wouldn't be easy.

Petey brought out the rope and the duct tape.

"I need to ask you to do something," Kate said.

Petey tied her hands behind her back.

"Please, listen," Kate said. "I understand why you need to put the duct tape over our mouths. You're afraid we'll yell and make somebody call the police."

Petey tied her feet.

"Please," Kate said. "It's almost impossible to breathe when the trunk gets hot. When you press the duct tape across our mouths, I'm begging you to . . ."

Petey tore off a section of tape.

"*Please.* It won't threaten you if you cut a small hole where our lips are. We still won't be able to yell. But we'll be able to breathe better."

Petey stared at her.

"You promised you'd take care of us," Kate said. "What good are we to you if we're dead?"

Petey's harsh eyes were filled with suspicion. He pressed the tape over her mouth and set her in the trunk. He did the same to Jason. Kate looked beseechingly up at Petey, who reached to close the trunk, paused, then pulled out a knife and slit the duct tape over their lips.

I hoped. But when darkness finally came and I returned to the interstate, I couldn't repress my unease that I was totally wrong about my reenactment of what had happened. In Wyoming, I came to another fork in the interstate. My palms broke out in a sweat as I tried to decide what to do next. I could retrace my route on 25, eventually returning to Denver, or I could veer east on the continuation of 90, heading into the Black Hills of South Dakota. I couldn't imagine Petey returning to Denver. But the Black Hills would surely have appealed to him. Plenty of places in which to hide.

9

Footsteps paused outside the entrance to the men's room. This was at a rest area in South Dakota, shortly after three in the morning. In the harsh overhead light, I stood at a urinal. At that quiet hour, sounds were magnified. That was probably the only reason I noticed the footsteps approaching. Waiting for them to resume, I looked over my shoulder, past the toilet stalls, toward the door on my right. The place had the chill of concrete after the heat of the day had faded.

I waited for the door to swing open. The silence beyond it grew. Still peering over my shoulder, I zipped up my pants. I went over to the sink and washed my hands, fixing my gaze on the mirror before me, which gave a direct view of the door. There weren't any paper towels, only one of those power dryers that force warm air over wet hands. They sound like a jet engine. Needing to hear everything, I didn't press its button.

As my fingers tingled from the water on them, I stared

toward the door. The silence beyond it persisted. It's only a tired driver who pulled into the rest area, I thought. He didn't need to relieve himself, just to stretch his legs. He's standing out there, enjoying the stars.

And if I'm wrong?

I told myself I was overreacting. After all, I didn't have any firm reason to believe that someone was out there waiting to surprise me when I opened the door. But I'd been in the foulness of Petey's mind for so long, imitating his movements, re-creating his logic, stalking rest areas, that I couldn't subdue the suspicion. My imagination was so primed that I could *feel* the danger out there as if it were seeping through the wall.

When I'd parked outside, mine had been the only vehicle, an attraction to a predator. He was listening for voices, for more than one set of footsteps, wanting to make sure I was alone. Hearing only me, he'd soon push the door open. I thought of the pistol in the suitcase in my car and cursed myself for being a fool. What good was learning how to use it if I put it where I couldn't get it if I needed the damned thing?

My legs were feathery. I trembled. No! I thought. What if I'd tracked down Petey? What if *he* was outside that door?

I pushed the button on the hand dryer. Its harsh roar obscured my footsteps as I shifted toward the back of the door. Braced against the wall, I felt a spurt of fear in my stomach as the door swung open.

A man in his mid-twenties, wearing cowboy boots, jeans, and a cowboy hat came quickly in, holding a tire iron. The door swung shut behind him as he stopped at the sight of the empty rest room. Puzzled, he stared at the roaring hand dryer. He peered toward the toilet stalls.

Abruptly he saw my reflection in the mirror over the sink. He tried to turn. I was already rushing, slamming his back with such force that he hurtled forward, his mustached face hitting the mirror, smashing it into shards. Blood streaked the mirror as I grabbed him by the back of his collar and his thick belt, ramming him toward the hand dryer, driving his head against it so powerfully that the nozzle on the fan broke off. The dryer kept roaring as I backed him up and drove his head against it even harder. Blood sprayed from the force of the unshielded fan. The tire iron fell from his hand, clanging on the concrete floor. I slammed his head once more and dropped him. He lay like a pile of old clothes. Eyes shut, he moaned. Except for the rise and fall of his chest, he barely moved.

My stomach was on fire. The anger that had brought me close to killing him frightened me. But the emotion that primarily seized me, making me want to shout, was that I'd won.

10

"Federal Bureau of Investigation," the receptionist said.

"Special Agent Gader, please." I gripped my cell phone so tightly that my fingers ached.

It was nine in the morning. Sunlight glinted off a secluded lake surrounded by lumpy bluffs studded with pine trees. The ridges were dark gray stone, making it clear how the Black Hills had gotten their name. I'd reached this area before dawn, but when I'd noticed that the map indicated only barren open land beyond them, I'd decided that Petey would have stopped earlier than he'd planned, going to ground for the day.

The beauty of the lake looked odd to me. After what had happened at the rest area, I felt as if I'd stepped into an alternate reality.

"Agent Gader is out of town on an assignment."

I picked up a rock. Frustration made me hurl it at the lake.

"May I ask who's calling?" the woman asked.

"Brad Denning. I—"

"Agent Gader mentioned that you'd be contacting him. He said that he'd spoken to Mr. Payne about the matter you were interested in, and if you'd talk to—"

I broke the connection.

11

"I guess you haven't been back to Woodford in a while," Payne said.

Pressing the cell phone to my ear, I walked close to the lake. Its cool air drifted over me. My beard stubble scraped against my hand. I worked to calm myself. "Not since my mother and I moved away when I was a kid."

"How big was it then?"

"Not very. About ten thousand people."

"A one-factory town," Payne said.

"That's right. My dad was a foreman." I suddenly missed him so much. "How did you know?"

"Because Gader says the factory shut down and went to Mexico ten years ago. Now Woodford's a bedroom community for Columbus, and its population has doubled to twenty thousand. There are several dentists, but none of them ever heard of the Denning family."

The air at the lake became colder. "But surely they know the dentists who worked there before them."

"Nope. Gader says you don't remember the name of the dentist you went to or his address."

My head throbbed. "It was too long ago."

"Then it's a dead end. Gader says he's sorry."

"Yeah, I bet."

"He says if you're relying on dental records to prove that Lester Dant is really your brother using an alias, you're setting yourself up for a big disappointment. Anyway, how's that going to help find your family?"

"I don't know, but I can think of words that are a whole lot stronger than *disappointment*."

The cell phone's reception became staticky.

"Where are you calling from?" Payne asked.

"South Dakota."

"Nice there?"

"I didn't come for the scenery," I said.

"Well, as long as you're determined to be on the road, do you want some advice?"

"Provided it's not 'Take it easy and get some rest.' "

"No, something else. This might surprise you," Payne said. "It'll sound like encouragement."

"Then go ahead and surprise me."

"Until I put on all this weight and I got to relying on the Internet," Payne said, "I was a hands-on kind of investigator. That's why I noticed things others didn't. When there's time, nothing beats going to the places and people you want to know about."

" 'When there's time.' "

"Which you seem to have plenty of."

"You're suggesting that if I'm determined to find that dentist, I should do it myself?"

"More or less."

"You're right—it does sound like encouragement. Why the change?"

"Because I'm worried about you."

The reception became staticky again. I listened hard.

"I'm afraid, if you don't satisfy yourself one hundred percent that you've done everything you can, if you lose hope . . ."

I strained to hear, but the static became worse.

". . . you'll destroy yourself."

"I'll get back to you later in the week," I said.

"What? I can't hear you."

I broke the connection.

12

As I imagined spending days in secluded places asleep in the back of the car, using my nights to drive as far as I could, I knew that Petey wouldn't have tolerated that routine much longer. The one thing that would have kept him motivated was his discovery—from the widespread news reports on the car radio a couple of days later (the media really loved the story)—that I hadn't died in the mountains. He wouldn't have told Kate and Jason that I was alive, of course. But his secret would have given him resolve, imagining how my fear and longing for my family made me suffer. No crowing midnight phone calls to me, no gleeful postcards, nothing with an inadvertent clue that might have led the police to him. Only taunting, gloating silence.

But, damn it, where would he have taken them? I thought about the South Dakota badlands ahead. In the old days, rustlers used to hide in the maze of sun-scorched canyons, the environment so hellish that posses wouldn't go in after them. It was too desperate a choice, even for Petey. After the badlands, there were hundreds of miles of flat grassland, hardly a tree anywhere, everything exposed. But Petey wouldn't have tolerated being in the open. Hide in plain sight? I doubted it. He wouldn't have felt protected without the shelter of hills and woods.

So had he found a place in the Black Hills? A deserted cabin maybe, or a . . .

I'd come as far as intuition could take me. A dead end, just as Gader had said that the idea about the dentist was a dead end.

The dentist. "Nothing beats going to the places and people you want to know about," Payne had said.

Yes.

After sleeping in the back of the car until sundown, I set out toward where I now realized my route had already been taking me, toward where everything had started so long ago.

Toward Petey's lost youth.

Part Four

1

BROCKTON NEXT EXIT.

The sign caught me by surprise. It was two nights later. I'd gone through Iowa and Illinois and was now on Interstate 70, continuing relentlessly east through Indiana. My destination was Ohio. Just beyond Columbus. Woodford. My hometown.

But as I saw the sign for Brockton, Lester Dant's birthplace, I frowned. Although I'd long ago made myself familiar with Brockton's position on the map, this was the first time I'd realized that it, like Woodford, was close enough to 70 to merit an exit sign. Fixated on the dental records that I hoped to find in Woodford, I hadn't focused on Brockton. But at that moment, my attention rapidly shifted. I made the turn.

A two-lane road wound through shadowy farm country. After twenty miles, street lights revealed run-down houses and a bleak main street. Two-story buildings flanked it, some with FOR SALE notices on windows. A sputtering neon sign announced BROCKTON MOTEL, VA-CANCY. It too looked run-down, but with no other choice, I stopped.

A bell rang when I opened the office door. Harsh overhead lights hummed. A puffy-eyed woman in a robe shuffled from a room behind the office. "How many nights?"

I said, "Two," determined to stick around and learn as much as I could.

The elderly woman seemed puzzled that anyone would have a reason for staying in Brockton more than one night. "Cash only." She named an amount, a narrowness in her eyes suggesting that she thought the rate was a fortune, which it wasn't.

When I gave her the money, she looked relieved, handed me a key, yawned, and shuffled back to her room. "Soft-drink machine's outside next to the candy machine," she murmured over her shoulder.

"Sorry for waking you."

"Plenty of time to sleep when I'm dead."

Outside, in the humid night, a single bulb illuminated the parking area. There weren't any vehicles at any of the ten motel units. The key I'd been given was for number one. Imagining that I was Petey, I noted that all the units were behind the manager's room. In the shadows, I couldn't be seen if I took a bound and gagged woman and child from my trunk.

The room was small, the sheets thin, the mirror dusty. I stared at my thickening beard stubble. My eyes looked haunted. I was a stranger to myself.

2

"Do you know this man?"

The manager looked as tired as when I'd wakened her the previous night. Her wrinkled mouth left a trace of lipstick on her coffee cup. Behind the counter, she tilted the police photo this way and that. "Not exactly flattering. How'd he get the scar on his chin?"

"Car accident."

"Can't say I recognize him. You another FBI agent?"

"Another?"

"Last year, somebody from the FBI asked me about this guy."

My optimism sank. If Gader *had* arranged for Dant's background to be double-checked, I was wasting my time.

"He must have done something really bad for you to keep looking for him," she said.

"Yes. Something really bad. Does the name Peter Denning sound familiar?"

"Nope."

"How about Lester Dant?"

"Dant." The woman thought a moment. "That's the name the other FBI agent asked about. There used to be a couple of families named Dant around here."

I felt more discouraged.

"The hardware store's named after one of them," she said, "but the man who owns it now is Ben Porter."

Wasting my time, I repeated to myself. Tempted to drive on to Woodford, I decided not to take anything for granted. "Where's the hardware store?"

3

"I don't know him." Ben Porter was in his fifties, as was just about everybody I'd passed in the sparsely populated town. His coveralls were flecked with sawdust from boards he'd been cutting. "But that doesn't mean much."

"Why not?"

"I never met the store's original owner. I kept the name Dant on the building to maintain tradition."

In a dying town, the word *tradition* sounded brave. "You don't know *any* Dants?"

"Like I told the other FBI agent, they're before my time. I moved here only ten years ago." The expression on his face made it seem that he wished he hadn't.

"Can you think of anybody who might know about them?"

"Sure. The reverend."

"Who?"

"Reverend Benedict. The way I hear it, he's been in Brockton just about forever."

4

The white steepled church and the cottage behind it were the only two buildings in town that didn't look in need of repair. On the right, between the church and a graveyard, a path went through a rose garden. Ahead, an elderly man in a short-sleeved blue shirt with a minister's collar had his back to me. He was on his knees, his head bowed in prayer. Then his arms moved and his head bobbed, and I realized he was pruning the roses.

He had a hearing aid tucked behind his right ear. It must have been an excellent model, because he heard me walking across the grass and turned to see who I was.

"Reverend Benedict?"

His wrinkled brow developed more furrows as he came creakily to his feet. His old pants had grass stains on the knees.

"My name's Brad Denning. Ben Porter at the hardware store—"

"A fine man."

"—suggested I talk to you about a couple of families who used to live around here."

"Families?"

"The Dants."

The reverend's eyes had sparkled as if he'd welcomed the opportunity to test his memory. Now they became guarded.

"Do you remember the Dants?" I asked.

"Are you with the FBI?"

"No."

"Someone from the FBI asked me about the Dants last year," the reverend said.

"I know that. But I'm not with the Bureau. Did the agent show you this photograph?"

"Yes. That's Lester. I told the agent the same thing."

"You're sure of that? It's Lester Dant?"

"He was younger. He didn't have that scar on his chin. But there's no doubt it's Lester."

I felt sick. The theory I'd worked so hard to believe toppled. Lester Dant, *not* my brother, had taken Kate and Jason. He wouldn't have had a reason to keep them alive.

"Why do you want to know about him?"

"It doesn't matter anymore, Reverend," I managed to say. Hollow, I turned to leave.

" 'Just a routine investigation,' the FBI agent told me."

I looked back at him. "Hardly routine."

"What's wrong, Mr. Denning? You seem in terrible distress."

I hadn't intended to explain, but something about him invited it. In despair, I started to tell him. I tried to keep my voice steady, but the more I revealed, the more it shook.

The reverend stared. He seemed to hope that I was finished, but then I told him more—and more—and his shocked look turned to pity for someone who, because of a boyhood mistake, had been condemned to the torment of hell.

"*Lester* did all that?"

"Or my brother pretending to be him. That's what I needed to find out."

"God help him. God help *you*."

"If only God would."

"All prayers are eventually answered."

"Not soon enough, Reverend."

He seemed on the verge of telling me to have faith. Instead, he sighed and motioned me toward a bench. "There are several things you need to understand about him."

" 'Understand'? I hope that doesn't mean make excuses or sympathize, because what I really want to do, Reverend, is *punish* him. And please don't tell me to turn the other cheek or let God take care of vengeance."

"You just said it for me."

We studied each other.

"You're positive that the man in this photograph is Lester Dant?" I asked.

"Yes."

I felt sicker. Even so, I had to know the truth. "All right then, Reverend." Despondent, I sat on the bench. "Help me 'understand' him."

5

"And his parents," the reverend said. "You also have to understand his parents." He thought for a moment. "The Dants." His frail voice strengthened. "There were six families of them originally. They lived around here for as long as anybody can remember. That's what my predecessor told me, at any rate, when I was assigned here. But they weren't really part of the community. You couldn't even say that they were part of the United States."

"You've lost me, Reverend."

"They were separatists. Tribalists. Loners. Somewhere in their history—my predecessor had a theory that it went as far back as the Civil War—something terrible had happened to them. They came from a place that they desperately wanted to forget, and they settled around here, determined to be left to themselves."

A bee buzzed my face. I motioned it away, fixing my attention on the reverend.

"Of course, to keep their families going, they couldn't

be entirely insular. They had to interact with nearby communities, looking for young people to marry. On the surface, they had a lot to recommend them. They knew their Bible. They owned property. They didn't drink, smoke, gamble, or swear. For a while, they attracted new members, usually from families so poor that marrying a Dant was a step up. But word got around how severe they were, and the Dants had to look farther, mostly among other strict groups, trying to negotiate marriages. Their options became more limited. By the time my predecessor arrived, the families had dwindled to three."

I shook my head, puzzled. "If they were determined to stay to themselves, how come somebody named Dant owned the hardware store?"

"A lifeline. No matter how hard they tried, they couldn't be self-sufficient. Even in a good year, with bountiful crops, there were necessities that they couldn't produce for themselves. To them, Brockton was like a foreign country. The hardware store was their embassy. They exported their excess produce through it and imported lumber, tools, clothing. . . ."

"Medicines."

"No," Reverend Benedict said, "never medicines. The Dants were as fundamental religiously as they were politically. To them, sickness was a sign of God's disfavor. They felt it was a sin to use human means to interfere with God's intention."

"Because of our fallen nature?"

"For which the Dants believed God punished us," the reverend said.

"With a self-destructive attitude like that, it's a wonder the families survived."

"That's the point—they're all gone now." Reverend Benedict pointed a wizened finger toward the photograph. "Except for Lester."

"When did you meet him?"

"After the fire."

"The fire?"

"I'll get to that. First, you need to know that, because the Dants avoided doctors, the town had no idea of the birth and death rate out there. Every so often, emissaries would come to town and get supplies. Mostly men, but sometimes women and children. I suspect that their motive was to show everybody in the family how corrupt the outside world was. It could be that we looked as strange to them as *they* did to us."

"Strange?"

"The effects of inbreeding were starting to show."

"The law let them get away with it?"

"Once in a while, a state trooper went out to check on things, but what was he going to charge them with, except wanting to be by themselves?"

"Child endangerment."

"Difficult to prove if the children are well nourished and can quote their Bible."

"Isn't there a law that children have to go to school?"

"The Dants hired an attorney who argued that the children were getting an adequate education at home. It came down to religious freedom. These days, I suppose we'd call them survivalists. But they weren't hoarding weapons and they weren't plotting to overthrow the government, so the authorities decided that dragging the Dants into court was worse than leaving them alone. Live and let live became the motto. Until the weekend when Lester's mother was one of the emissaries who came to town."

I listened harder.

"Her name was Eunice. She was visibly pregnant, but evidently her husband believed that she wasn't far enough along not to travel. She came out of the hardware store. The next thing, she collapsed on the sidewalk, writhing in pain. Her husband, Orval, tried to make light of it, tried to pick her up and put her in the car. But when he saw the blood on her dress and the pool of it around her, he froze in confusion, just long enough for a doctor and a police-man—we had several of both back then—to notice what was happening and rush her to the clinic that served as our hospital. Orval tried to stop them, but suddenly, it was obvious that Eunice wasn't having a miscarriage. She was about to give birth to a premature baby."

"The creep was willing to risk her life?"

"He didn't do it easily. Orval told the doctor and the po-liceman that the baby meant more to him than anything else in the world; that he and Eunice had already lost three children to stillbirths; that they'd tried persistently to have another child and finally God had blessed them with this pregnancy. But to rely on a doctor was the same as telling God that they didn't have faith, Orval said. If they inter-fered with God's plan, the baby would be damned. Orval felt so strongly about this that he actually tried to pick up Eunice and carry her from the clinic. But the doctor warned him that the wife and the baby would die if they didn't stay and receive medical attention. The policeman was more blunt. He threatened to arrest Orval for at-tempted murder if Orval tried to remove his wife. By then, the baby was on its way, and even Orval realized he was going to have to allow medical help, whether he wanted it or not. Eunice nearly died from loss of blood. The baby nearly died from being so small."

"The baby was Lester?"

"Yes. Orval and Eunice didn't believe in giving their children names that had religious connotations. They compared it to idolatry. No Matthew, Mark, Luke, or John for them. Once you take away the Bible as a source for a name, there aren't many choices. The name Lester was neutral, a default."

"And then?"

"My predecessor retired. I came here to take his place. Before he left, he explained about the community and told me what I've just told *you*. He said that, despite the doctor's expectations, the baby lived. In fact, a week before I arrived, Orval had brought the child to town to show how healthy the boy was, to prove to the doctor that God's will was the only thing that mattered."

"But . . ." I felt more puzzled. "What's this got to do with . . . You said you met Lester after a fire."

"Years later."

I leaned forward.

"The smoke woke just about everybody in town. I remember it was a Labor Day weekend. A heat wave had just broken, so most people had their air conditioners off and the windows open, taking advantage of a breeze. My wife and I stepped outside, coughing, wondering whose house was on fire. Then I realized that the fire wasn't in Brockton. Even with the smoke in the streets, I could see a glow on the horizon, to the south, in the direction of where Orval and Eunice had their farm. I knew that it couldn't be any other Dant's place, because by then Orval, Eunice, and Lester were the only Dants left.

"Somebody rang the alarm at the fire station, the signal for volunteers. But when I got there, people had realized that the fire wasn't in town. There was a lot of confusion about whether we should go out to help them or whether we should let Orval and Eunice pay for insisting that they didn't need us. In the end, the town made me proud. The fire brigade had a truck filled with water. They drove it out there, and a whole lot of people went in cars. But even before we got close, it was obvious from the extent of the glow on the horizon that even a *dozen* trucks filled with water wouldn't make a difference.

"It hadn't rained in a month. The wind got stronger. On the left, flames streaked across pastures. Sections of timber were ablaze. Far off, a house and a barn were on fire. We did what we could to stop the flames from spreading across the road. Other than that, we were helpless. By then, it was dawn, and somebody shouted toward a burning field. I looked that way and saw a young man stumble ahead of the flames. He swatted at his smoking clothes, reached a fence, and toppled over it. I got to him first. He was sobbing. I'd never seen eyes so big with fear, but it was obvious that they weren't registering anything. He was blind from hysteria. I tried to stop him, but he lurched to his feet and staggered along the road. It took three of us to get him to the ground and smother the smoke coming off him."

"That was Lester?"

The reverend nodded. "He wasn't able to tell us what happened until three days later. After we got him to the ground, something seemed to shut off in him. He became catatonic. We took him to the clinic. He didn't have any serious burns or other obvious injuries, so the doctor treated him for shock. When it was safe to move him, my wife and I brought him here." Reverend Benedict indicated the cottage behind the church.

His eyes saddened. "When Lester was alert enough, he told us about the fire, how the smoke and the dogs barking had wakened him. He'd shouted to warn his parents. He'd tried to run down the hall to their room, but the flames were outside his door, and he had to climb out his window. In the yard, he kept shouting to warn his parents. Past the flames in their bedroom, he heard them screaming, but when he tried to get in through the window and pull them out, the heat was like a wall that wouldn't let him through. The breeze had spread the fire beyond the house. The barn and the outbuildings, the fields and the woods—everything was on fire. The only way he escaped was by throwing himself into a cattle trough, soaking himself, and running across a pasture while the fire chased him. In the week that he stayed with us, sometimes he woke screaming from nightmares of hearing his parents' screams."

Imagining their agony, I shook my head from side to side. "Did anybody ever learn what caused the fire?"

"Lester said that a light switch had stopped working in the kitchen. His father had planned to fix it the next day."

"I know about buildings. It sounds like an electrical short," I said. "Fire can spread along faulty wires and accumulate behind the walls. When it breaks through, the flames are everywhere at once."

"According to Lester, it was terrifyingly fast."

"And *then* what happened? You said that he stayed with you for a week."

"We wanted him to stay longer, but one morning, my wife looked in on him, and he was gone."

"Gone?"

"We'd bought some clothes for him. They were missing. A pillowcase was missing also. He must have used it as a duffel bag. Bread, cookies, and cold cuts were taken from the kitchen."

"He left in the middle of the night? *Why?*"

"I think it had something to do with my being a minister and the cottage being next to a church."

"I don't understand. Lester was raised in a religious family. The church shouldn't have bothered him."

"Their beliefs were drastically different from mine."

"I still don't . . ."

"The Dants believed that God turns His back on us because of our sinful nature. What *I* preach is that God loves us because we're His children. I've always suspected that the night before Lester ran away, he overheard me practicing my Sunday sermon. He probably thought he was hearing the words of the Devil."

"And you never saw him again?"

"Not until last year when the FBI agent showed me that photograph."

In despair, I peered down at it—at Lester Dant, not my brother. The hope upon which I'd based my search no longer kept me going.

Reverend Benedict looked even sadder. "My wife and I wanted children, but we weren't able to have any. While Lester recuperated, she and I had talked about becoming his guardians. When he ran away, we felt as if we'd lost a child of our own." He turned his gaze toward the cemetery beyond the rose garden. "She died last summer."

"I'm sorry."

"Lord, how I miss her." He looked down at his wrinkled hands. "The last I heard about Lester . . ." Emotion made him pause. "A month after he ran away, he was in Loganville. That's a town about a hundred miles east of here. A fellow minister happened to mention a helpless young man who showed up one day and whom members of the congregation were taking care of. I went there to find out if it was Lester and to try to persuade him to come back home, but he was gone by the time I got there. If I'd somehow convinced him to stay with us"—the reverend drew a breath—"perhaps none of the tragedies he caused would have happened."

"You did everything possible. *Lester's* the one to blame."

"Only God can determine that."

The effort of explaining had obviously tired him. I stood from the bench and shook his hand. "Thank you, Reverend. This was painful for you. I appreciate the effort."

"My prayers go with you."

"I need them. You said that Orval and Eunice lived south of town?"

"About eight miles."

"Everything's different now, I suppose."

"An agribusiness wound up farming the land. But not much has changed. If you head that way, you can just make out the burned farmhouse from the road."

6

I don't remember driving south of town. I was so dazed by what I'd learned that it's a wonder I didn't drift off the narrow road and hit something. I really had no idea why I was going out to where the fire had happened. But the alternative was to drive pointlessly back to Denver, and I refused to do that. Payne's words kept coming back to me: "Nothing beats going to the places and people you want to know about." The ruined Dant farm became one of those places.

A sign at the side of the road was weathered, partially overgrown with brush. But something in my subconscious noticed it, bringing me to attention. A large piece of plywood. What I assumed had once been black letters had faded to gray.

REPENT.

That was all, but it was enough to make me realize that I'd entered Dant country. On the right, beyond a pasture, I saw a farmhouse. It was distant, but even from the road,

I could tell that it was listing, about to collapse, and that its windows had been broken. The roof on a barn next to it had already caved in.

But the reverend had said that Orval Dant's property had been on the left, so I focused my attention over there and soon noticed scorched stumps bordering fields of knee-high crops. I came to a section of trees, where tall burned timber stood among comparatively shorter, lush new trees. Then the land opened out again, and I saw the weed-covered furrows of a dirt lane stretching back what seemed a quarter of a mile to a wide mound of something near another section of new trees.

A metal gate blocked my way. It had a lock on a chain. I got out and tested the lock, finding it secure. A strengthening breeze carried a hint of moisture. Earlier, the sky had been stark blue, but now it was hazy, darkening on the horizon. The rain wouldn't reach me for a couple of hours. Even so, I reached into the car and got my knapsack, which had trail food, water, and a rain jacket, among other things. The jacket was what most concerned me, but the truth was, I'd learned the hard way that even an apparently harmless walk in the woods might not work out as planned. I'd also learned from what had happened at the rest area four nights earlier. My pistol was in the knapsack.

I felt the pack's satisfying weight against my back as I climbed the fence. Dust puffed around my sneakers when I came down on the opposite side. I started at a walk, but as I looked at the bushes around me, I was reminded of something that Kate, Jason, and I had done the summer before they'd been kidnapped. An architect friend had bought an old cabin up in the mountains. Trees and un-

dergrowth had almost smothered the log building, so one
Sunday he'd invited his friends up to help clear the place
in exchange for barbecued steaks and all the beer we
could drink. Our families were welcome also. Jason had
thought it would be fun working next to me, helping to
drag the cut bushes away, and I'd felt my chest swell with
pride that the little guy had tried so hard. He made Kate
laugh when he objected to her wiping the dirt and sweat
from his face and making him look like a sissy.

Now, frustrated that I was no closer to finding them, I
increased speed along the lane, anger pushing me. I
stretched my legs as far and fast as I could, the sun hot on
my face, sweat beading my skin, my jeans and shirt sticking to me.

A quarter of a mile was too short. I felt so infuriated
that I could have run for miles, as I used to before I'd left
Denver. But back in Denver, I'd been hopeful, whereas
my frantic speed along that lane was a measure of how
strongly I felt defeated.

I reached the end and slowed. The wide mound that I'd
seen from the road revealed itself to be the blackened
walls of a collapsed wooden structure. Its boards had
been reduced to long slabs of charcoal that had toppled
into a chaotic pile. Dead leaves were wedged in the gaps.
Thorny bushes and vines whose three-leafed pattern
warned of poison ivy sprouted from the debris. Beyond,
a larger structure (presumably the barn) had similarly
burned and collapsed.

Despite the sweat I'd worked up, I felt cold. I told myself that I was only imposing my mood on what I was
seeing. All the same, I couldn't ignore what had happened there. Lester Dant's parents had burned to death

thirty feet from where I stood. Blackness overwhelmed me.

What the hell am I doing? I thought. I was about to go back to the car, when something beyond the gutted house caught my attention: an area of about thirty by thirty feet enclosed by a low stone wall. The stones had been darkened by the fire. Some had fallen. I passed the ruins, trying to avoid the poison ivy as I approached the walled-in area. It had an opening where a gate had once been, and when I came closer, I saw that the enclosed area, too, was filled with poison ivy, dead leaves, and thorny bushes. But, amid the chaos, I noticed regularly spaced clumps. Stepping closer, I realized that they were small piles of rocks arranged in rows. The pattern was too familiar not to be recognized as a graveyard. Instead of mounds, there were depressions, the earth having settled onto decaying wooden coffins and the moldering bodies within them. The depressions were common to most old graveyards. The only reason they didn't appear in modern cemeteries was that coffins were now made from metal and graves had sleeves of concrete onto which a concrete lid was placed after the coffin was lowered and the mourners had departed.

In that dismal enclosure, generations of Dants had been buried. I imagined the pain and the loneliness with which their loved ones had laid them to rest. What struck me most was how many of the graves were short, indicating the deaths of children.

I don't know how long I stared at the graves, meditating about the independent community that the Dants had hoped to establish and how severely their dreams had failed. At last, I stepped away, going around the back of the ruins.

A small animal skittered through trees behind me. A squirrel perhaps. But because I'd detected no signs of life around the place, the sound startled me. There weren't even any birds.

Sweating from the stark sun, I noticed that the storm clouds were a little closer. Wary of more poison ivy, I continued around the back of the burned house. Abruptly my legs felt unsteady. For an instant, I feared that something was wrong with my brain, that I was having a stroke and my balance was gone. My footing became even more unsteady. My lungs fought for air when I realized in panic that it wasn't my brain or my legs. The ground beneath me parted. I plunged.

With a gasp, I stopped, caught at my hips. My legs dangled in an unseen open area. Heart racing, I pressed my hands against the ground and strained to push myself up through the hole that trapped me.

Immediately my hands felt as unsteady as my legs had. The more I pushed them against the earth, the more they sank into it. I dropped again, but not before I flung out my arms, blocking my fall an instant before the widening hole would have sucked me all the way down.

My legs dangled helplessly, my body swaying in the emptiness beneath me. Only my head and shoulders were above ground, my weight supported by my outstretched arms. Hearing muffled rattles below me, I couldn't make my lungs work fast enough to take in all the air I needed. The ground sagged again. As the rattles got louder, I shouted and plummeted all the way into the hole.

7

With a shock, my feet hit bottom. The impact bent my knees and threw me backward into darkness, jolting me against something. My knapsack jammed against my back, the flashlight, water bottle, and pistol in it walloping against my shoulder blades. I cracked my head and almost passed out. A moldy earthen smell widened my nostrils. The furious whir of rattles made me press harder against what I'd struck.

It felt like a wall. It was made from wood that had turned spongy. Simultaneously, I realized that what I'd fallen onto was the rotted remains of a wooden floor. Concrete showed through. It was pooled with water and had soaked my pants. But none of that mattered. All I cared about were the rattles in the darkness across from me and the rippling movement in the sunlight that came down through the hole in the ground.

Snakes. I scrambled to my feet, pressing into a corner. The flashlight, get the damned flashlight, I thought. Frantic, I tugged the knapsack off my back, yanked at its zipper, and reached in, fumbling for the light. In a rush, I turned it on and aimed its powerful beam at the darkness across from me.

The floor over there was alive with coiled snakes, their angry rattles echoing. A moan caught in my throat. I switched the flashlight's aim toward the scummy water at my feet, fearing that snakes would be coiled there. But the green-tinted water was free of them. It was about two inches deep, and I prayed that something in its scum was noxious to them. The floor tilted down toward the corner I was in, which explained why the water had collected there, but to my right and left and in the corner across from me, the raised part of the floor was dry, which was why the snakes had gathered on that side.

How far can a rattlesnake spring? I thought. Twice its length? Three times? If so, the snakes could fling themselves across the water at me. But my fall had startled them, making them dart back before they coiled. Their writhing mass was on the other side of the enclosure, a sufficient distance to keep me safe for the moment.

The enclosure. What the hell had I fallen into? It was about the size of a double-car garage. To the left of the opposite corner, a portion of the wall had collapsed. Behind its wooden exterior, insulation and concrete had toppled inward, exposing dank earth. A downward channel in the earth showed that whoever had poured the concrete for this chamber had failed to put in adequate drainage behind it. Rain had filtered down, accumulating behind the concrete until its weight had overwhelmed that section of the wall.

The gap explained how water had gotten into the

chamber. So did the roof—not concrete, but made of timbers with plywood slabs on top (the hole in the roof showed the layers) and a waterproof rubber sheet above that, with six inches of earth over everything. Nothing prevented mice and other small animals from burrowing through the earth, reaching the rubber sheet and chewing through it. Once rain soaked down to the support beams, the process of rot would have begun, ultimately making the roof incapable of bearing weight.

But the chamber had obviously been built years earlier. During that much time, more than just a few inches of water would have accumulated where I was standing. There had to be a crack in the floor that allowed the water to seep away. That would have caused further erosion, explaining why the floor tilted toward the corner I was in.

I stared toward the fallen section of the wall. In the exposed earth, a channel angled toward the surface—the snakes used it to come and go. I wondered desperately if I could dig up through it, piling the earth in the chamber behind me as I went.

But how was I going to get past the snakes? As the rattles intensified, I braced the flashlight under my right arm and fumbled in my knapsack, gripping the pistol. Immediately I realized the flaw in what I intended. Even with fifteen rounds in the magazine and one in the chamber, not to mention a further fifteen-round magazine in the knapsack, I couldn't hope to kill every snake. Oh, I could hit most of them. There were so many that it would be difficult for me to miss. But *all* of them? Killing them, not merely wounding? No way. Besides, I had to consider the effect of the gunshots. The reports would send the surviving snakes into a frenzy, making them strike insanely at anything that moved, even if it meant flinging themselves across the water to get at me. And what about ricocheting bullets slamming back at me?

I pressed harder into the corner. Stay quiet, I warned myself, trying to control my hoarse breathing. Once the snakes realize you're not a threat, they'll calm down.

I hoped. But I hadn't brought spare flashlight batteries. In a couple of hours, the flashlight would stop working. A few more hours after that, the sun would go down. The hole in the roof would darken. I'd be trapped in blackness, not knowing if the snakes would disregard the water (which possibly wasn't noxious to them at all) and slither close to me, attracted by my body heat.

The meager illumination through the hole in the roof would have to be sufficient. Hoping that my eyes would adjust to the shadows, I shut off the flashlight, conserving the batteries. Despite the cold water I stood in, sweat trickled down my face. Fear made me tremble. Stop moving! I warned myself. Don't attract attention! I squeezed my muscles, straining to control their reflexive tremors.

At first I wondered if it was my imagination. Long seconds after I shut off the light and willed myself not to move, the buzz from the rattles lessened. Slowly, the frenzy subsided. My shadow-adapted eyes showed me the snakes eventually uncoiling, their unblinking gaze no longer fixed on me. Their movements became less threatening. A few went up the channel toward the surface.

But snakes preferred heat. Why had they gathered in the cool chamber rather than remaining outside and basking in the sun? What had driven them down? The question made my skin feel prickly, especially when the few snakes that had gone up returned. God help me, what didn't they like up there?

The rattling had almost completely stopped, just a few snakes continuing to coil. Then, except for the hammering of my heart, the chamber became quiet. Above, I heard sounds past the hole I'd fallen through. The breeze became a wind, whistling through bushes. I heard a rumble that I hoped was an approaching car but that I suddenly understood was thunder. The light through the hole dimmed.

Lightning cracked. The wind shrieked harder. But none of that was why fear squeezed my chest tighter. No, what terrified me was the *pat pat pat* I heard on the floor, the rain falling through the hole.

8

It came faster. The snakes that were positioned under the hole jerked when the drops hit them. Some slithered toward their companions on the far side of the enclosure. They accumulated on something slightly higher than the floor, a long, flat object that the shadows kept me from identifying, its soft contours having dissolved after years of periodic flooding. But other snakes veered in my direction, the floor seeming to waver as they approached the scummy water.

Some slithered onto it. Rank fumes from the water assaulted my nostrils. I aimed my pistol, trembling, holding fire when I saw that the snakes on the water reversed direction and headed back toward the dry floor. Others had paused at the water and angled away. I'd been right. Something in the water repelled them.

But the rain fell rapidly through the hole, splashing the floor, widening its circle of moisture. A small pool formed, trickling toward my corner. Soon the entire area would be covered. When there wasn't a dry space, the snakes wouldn't have a reason to avoid my corner.

Feeling smothered, I turned on the flashlight and searched for something that I could use to hit the snakes if they came at me. Sections of wood and concrete that had fallen from the opposite wall were too far to reach without putting myself within striking distance of the snakes. As the water spread across the floor, the snakes crowded into a narrower area across from me. It wouldn't be long before they set out in all directions, looking for a place that was dry. I thought about attempting to rip a board from the wall. It might make a club. I had to try it.

Lightning flashed beyond the hole in the roof. The water spread to the snakes across from me, forcing them to pile on top of one another. Some dispersed. They'd soon be everywhere. I shoved the pistol under my belt and aimed the flashlight to my right, looking for a crack in the wall that would give my hands sufficient purchase to yank off a board.

What had been shadows in my peripheral vision were, I saw now, support beams that had fallen from the roof, leaning against the wall. Maybe I could use the beams to build a ramp. Maybe I could climb up and pull down other beams, claw through the earth and reach the surface. I didn't dare worry that the entire roof might collapse and crush me. No matter what, I had to get away from the snakes.

So much rain had fallen through the hole in the roof that the floor was now totally wet. Across from me, more snakes dispersed, rippling over the water. I moved to the right and pressed a shoe against one of the beams that leaned against the wall, to test it. Dismayed, I found that the wood was so rotten that it crumbled under my weight. The sudden lack of resistance threw me off balance. Struggling not to land in the water, I lurched forward and struck the wall behind the beams.

The impact jolted my shoulder. I almost dropped the flashlight. Worse, the noise disturbed the snakes, sending several of them into another frenzy of rattling. I was certain that I'd go crazy, start shooting, and be killed by a dozen bites. My terror so preoccupied me that it took me a moment to register that the wall I'd hit sounded hollow.

More snakes crossed the water toward me. I shoved the other beam to the side and uncovered a door. The nearest snake was three feet away when I gripped the rusty doorknob. I turned it, but the rust had frozen the mechanism. I turned harder, felt it budge, and thrust against the door with all my strength.

It creaked. Another desperate shove, and it suddenly swung inward with a crash, taking me with it. I sprawled on wet concrete, banging my chin but ignoring the pain, concentrating to protect the flashlight. Dazed, I whirled toward the doorway. A snake had coiled, about to strike. I kicked at the door, but its old hinges didn't respond soon enough. The snake leapt. The door banged shut halfway along its body, pinning it, the snake's front half whipping this way and that. The light from the hole in the roof was no longer visible. Only my flashlight, trembling in my hand, showed how the snake was caught. Its agonized movements tore its front half from the door. Its jagged midsection spewed blood as it flopped into the water and thrashed toward me.

I lurched backward. My head banged against something, and as the snake struck the bottom of one of my sneakers, I stood frantically, using my other sneaker to stomp the snake's head, its bones cracking beneath my sole.

The snake's severed body thrashed under my heel, its spastic movements slowing, becoming less violent. When it was finally still, I raised my shoe and aimed the flashlight at the flattened, bloody head. Reminding myself that a prick from its fangs could be poisonous even after it was dead, I kicked the torso toward the door.

When it splashed down, I raised my light to make sure that the door was closed and that no other snakes could get past it. I swung around to find out where I was and if this place, too, was inhabited by snakes. Nothing slithered. No rattling unnerved me. But even though I'd escaped from the first enclosure, I remained trapped.

I was in a tunnel roughly five feet wide and twenty feet long, with a ceiling I could touch if I raised my hand. The end opposite the door was choked with the objects I'd banged against: blackened timbers and other debris from the fire. Unlike in the first chamber, the concrete of the walls and the floor hadn't been covered with wood. The ceiling, though, had the same poor design: timbers with presumably plywood slabs, a rubber sheet, and earth on top. The timbers had not yet fallen, but water seeped between them, and eventually the timbers would rot to the stage of collapse.

As I noticed two rusted metal ducts that went along the ceiling and into the chamber, the rain streamed from the ceiling in greater volume. Rivulets poured down through the wreckage at the end of the tunnel. The water on the floor rose to my ankles. The crack at the door's bottom was too narrow to allow the water to drain. I was trapped in what amounted to a cistern.

How much rain could a strong June storm unload? An inch? Two? That didn't seem a threat unless you considered the expanse of the ground above the tunnel and the square footage of the burned house, both of which collected the water and funneled it into the five-by-eight-by-twenty-foot space that held me. The water probably wouldn't rise all the way to the ceiling, but there was a strong chance it would get high enough that I'd have to dog-paddle to keep my head above the surface. But how long could I do that as the water chilled me and hypothermia set in? Once I started shivering, I'd be dead in three hours.

In fact, I'd *already* started shivering. My flashlight showed wisps of my breath as I splashed toward the debris that blocked the tunnel. I braced the light between scorched boards, its slanted glare making it difficult for me to see as I grabbed a burned timber and strained to tug it loose. The effort made me breathe faster. Inhaling deeply, I coughed from the smoky odor coming off the wet wood.

I pulled harder and freed the timber. With a minor sense of triumph, I was about to shove it behind me, when the debris shifted and caused the flashlight to tumble. I grabbed for it, but my fingers only grazed it. As it flipped from my grasp, I lunged, using my hands like scoops to catch it the instant before it would have fallen into the water. I pulled it to my chest, treasuring it. Almost certainly, it would have stopped working if it had gotten soaked. The panic of nearly having lost my light made me shiver more severely.

The chill water rose to my shins. I tried holding the flashlight with one hand while I used the other to pull at the boards that blocked my way, but I couldn't get a decent grip. Reluctantly, I again tried bracing the flashlight among the debris, but it almost fell the moment I pulled out another board.

My pistol dug into the skin under my belt. It gave me the idea of cramming the flashlight under the opposite side of the belt, but there wasn't room. Think! I told myself. There has to be a way! I took off my knapsack, opened a side pocket, and shoved the flashlight into it. When I resecured the knapsack to my back, the light glared toward the ceiling, but when I leaned forward to grab at debris, the light did what I wanted, tilting in that direction.

My frenzied movements echoed so loudly that my ears rang. Breathing stridently, I pulled out more boards, thrusting them behind me. Water poured down through the debris and rose to my knees. No matter how hot I felt from my exertions, I couldn't stop shivering. I freed another board and stared at a soot-smeared concrete step that led upward. With greater determination, I pulled two more boards loose, found *another* step, and felt a growing surge of hope. If I could uncover enough steps so I could climb above the water, the danger of hypothermia would lessen. I had food in my knapsack. I'd be able to eat and rest, conserving the flashlight's batteries, using them only while clearing the stairwell.

Desperate, I grabbed a timber and dragged it free, about to shove it behind me, when I heard a crack and gaped up at a huge plug of debris snapping loose. I tried to scramble back, but a jumble of scorched timbers and boards crashed down on me. The force took my breath away, knocking me toward the water. I didn't dare let the flashlight get soaked! Deafened by the reverberating rumble, I fought to raise myself, to keep the knapsack from filling with water. I pushed at the timbers weighing against me. I thrust the boards away. I grabbed something that didn't feel like wood. It was round and soft.

I screamed when I realized that I was holding the snake, its severed body drooping in my hands, the fangs of its crushed head close to my arm. As I hurled it away, a floating timber knocked against me. I fell. The foul water went over my head. It rushed into my ears, crammed my nostrils, and filled my mouth. Gasping, I bolted to the surface, coughing, spitting out soot-tasting water, struggling to breathe. I wiped at my eyes, frantically realizing that my lack of vision had nothing to do with water in them.

The flashlight had gone out.

9

In absolute darkness, my other senses strained to fill the void: the echo of waves splashing and wood thudding against the walls; the feel of my wet clothes clinging to me; the taste of soot and dirt; the stench of the water making me gag. My most extreme sense, though, was terror. Afraid to move lest I touch the fangs of the dead snake floating around me, I stood rigidly, trying to keep balanced in the darkness while I listened to the lapping of the waves slowly subsiding. Soon, all I heard was water streaming from the roof and through the debris in the stairwell.

My wet knapsack was heavy on my back. Blind, I took it off, looped its straps over a shoulder, and carefully took out the flashlight. I shook it. I pressed its on/off button. Nothing. I unscrewed its cap, removed the batteries, dumped the water from the cylinder, and blew on the poles of the batteries to attempt to dry them. After reinserting the batteries, I pressed the button. The darkness remained total. No, I was wrong. My eyes, straining to adapt to the blackness, became sensitive to a slight glow on my left wrist—the luminous coating on the hour marks of my watch. The speckled circle floated, disembodied.

I poured water from the knapsack, put the flashlight in it (and my pistol, which had dug deeper into the skin under my belt). Then I made sure that the pack's zippers were tightly closed and strapped it to my back. Meanwhile, the cold water rose above my knees.

Move! Wading, I groped ahead. I flinched from a chill, clammy, pitted surface, belatedly identifying it as a concrete wall. When I'd lost my balance and fallen, I must have gotten turned around. Now I had to make a choice: right or left. One direction led to the door, the other to the choked stairwell.

I eased to the left, pawing through the darkness. Something pricked my hand. Oh Jesus, I'd touched the snake's fangs. Jerking my hand back, grabbing where I'd been stung, I felt an object stuck in my palm. No. A splinter. Only a splinter. I'd scraped against a board.

I'd found the stairwell. As my watch's luminous dial zigzagged ghostlike in the darkness, I tugged at boards. I yanked at timbers. I pulled and heaved, shoving debris behind me. My hands were in pain, cut and gouged, but I didn't care. I had to clear more space before the water rose fatally higher. My shoulders ached, and my back throbbed. My mouth became dry. I had trouble getting air down my throat and finally had to pause to take my canteen from the knapsack and gulp water, making my mouth and throat feel less swollen, able to get more air.

But the brief rest didn't give me energy. I felt light-headed and realized that carbon dioxide was accumulating in the tunnel, becoming denser as the water rose. I didn't need to worry about hypothermia. I was going to die from suffocation.

With a greater frenzy, I grabbed sightlessly for debris and hurled it behind me. I freed one step after another, working higher, but the water followed, tugging at my hips. I felt unsteady. My mind whirled. Even though I couldn't see, spots wavered in front of my eyes.

The air thickened. My movements slowed. Debris floated against me. When a timber broke in my hands, I jerked backward, almost falling into the water. Then I pulled a chunk of wreckage, releasing not only it but a pool that had gathered in the ruins above me. With the force of a broken dam, it rushed onto me, so strong that it swept me off the steps, knocking me against floating timbers. I was dazed, barely able to keep my head above the surface. I flopped one arm and then the other against the water, trying to swim but remaining in place.

I was so weak, struggling not to sink, that it took me a moment to notice that the air had a hint of sweetness. I stared toward the stairwell and feared that my mind was tricking me, because the darkness was shaded. I saw vague contours of the wreckage. Gray filtered down. Bolstered by the fresh air seeping in, I found the strength to swim to the stairwell. I wavered up the steps and pulled at timbers, the gray beckoning, urging me upward.

When I finally squirmed up through an ooze of soot, squeezing past the jumbled skeleton of the collapsed house, the sky was thick with clouds. The air turned grayer, making me think that the hidden sun was setting and that in my delirium it had taken me all day to burrow up from the stairwell.

The cold rain persisted. It pelted me, but the grime that covered me was like grease and wouldn't come off. I clawed up through wreckage. I strained and dragged myself higher. Several times, boards snapped in my hands, threatening to hurtle me back into the pit. My blood-smeared fingers hooked onto the top of a foundation wall. I pulled myself over, flopping onto mushy ground. It took me several minutes before I could stand. As I plodded through mud, I wondered if I'd have the strength to reach my car.

10

Steam rose around me, but I couldn't get the bathwater hot enough. The cold penetrated to my bones. To my soul.

What use had the chamber served? I kept asking myself. Why had Orval, who'd possessed construction skills, not built the roof with concrete? What had been the purpose of the two ducts that had gone along the roof of the tunnel and into the chamber? If the chamber had been a storage area, there wouldn't have been a need to panel the walls, cover the floor, and use insulation. I couldn't make sense of it. Unless . . .

"Where they kept me a prisoner was an underground room," the man who'd claimed to be my brother had said. Not Petey, God help me, but Lester Dant. Why would Orval and Eunice Dant have kept their only child in an underground room? The horror of it made my mind swirl.

The puzzle of the roof's poor construction now became clear. By working after dark, using no more than the lights from the house, Orval could have dug the space for the tunnel and the underground chamber without anyone who drove by noticing and wondering. Working at night, he could have mixed concrete in small amounts and used a wheelbarrow to transport it for the floor and walls of the tunnel and the chamber.

But the ceiling would have been a problem. To construct it properly, he would have needed to make concrete slabs. Once the slabs were ready, however, he would have needed a small crane to hoist them into place: precision work that would have required more than just standard illumination from the house. Outsiders would have noticed and been curious about so much light in back of his house after dark. Better to be cautious by using wooden beams for the roof, easily and quickly installed. Or maybe there'd been a deadline. Maybe Orval had been forced to compromise with the roof's construction because a timetable was hurrying him.

Sickened, I added more hot water to the tub, but I still couldn't chase the cold from my soul. Making me even colder was my uneasy conviction that I hadn't learned everything I could have out there. I was sure there was something darker. God help me, I didn't want to, but I knew I had to go back.

11

I walked along the lane to the ruin. The time was a little after ten the next morning. My night had been fitful, sleep coming only toward dawn. My nervousness grew as I stepped closer. I removed my pistol from a fanny pack that I'd bought. Clutching the weapon helped to keep my scraped hands from shaking. The thought of the snakes made bile rise into my mouth.

I paused where I had the previous day. From the lane, I couldn't see the spot where I'd fallen into the chamber. It was as if the earth had sealed itself. But I had a general idea of where the tunnel and the chamber were, and I plotted a direction that avoided them.

I studied the long grass for quite a while, on guard against the slightest ripple. Finally I aimed the pistol and took one cautious step after another. Weeds scraped against my pants. The poison ivy seemed harder to avoid.

I took a wide arc around the back of the house, approaching a group of trees behind the house. The previous night, I'd imagined the design problems that Orval had needed to solve. Insulate the prison chamber. Get heating ducts leading into it. But what about ventilation? One of the ducts would have taken air *from* the furnace in the house. The other duct would have returned air *to* the furnace. A closed system.

That would have been adequate if the chamber had been merely a storage room. But if I was right and the chamber had been a cell, the system would have needed to be modified so that carbon dioxide and other poisonous gases didn't accumulate and kill the prisoner. To prevent that from happening, there would have had to be another duct into the chamber, powered with a fan, to bring in fresh air. The logical place for that duct would have been just below the ceiling, but the snakes had prevented me from noticing the duct if it was there.

The outlet would have had to project above the ground. Otherwise, it would have gotten clogged with dirt. But how had Orval disguised it? The area behind the house was flat. After the fire, the townspeople would have swarmed around the wreckage, hoping to find survivors. They hadn't stumbled over the vent. If they had, they'd have wondered about its purpose and eventually have discovered the underground chamber. So where in hell had Orval hidden the outlet so that nobody had found it back then?

The trees were the obvious answer. Between fallen logs, or inside a stump. Ready with the pistol, I continued through the weeds and long grass. The sun was hot on my head, but that wasn't the reason I sweated. Each time a breeze moved blades of grass, I tightened my finger on the trigger.

I reached the trees, where the grass was welcomely shorter as I crisscrossed the area. Whenever I nudged a log, my muscles cramped in anticipation of finding a coiled snake. I picked up a stick (making sure that it was in fact a stick), then poked through leaves that had collected in hollow stumps. I found nothing unusual.

But the outlet had to be in the area. I turned in a slow circle, surveying the trees. Damn it, where would Orval have hidden the outlet? Ventilation ducts became inefficient the longer they extended. The outlet had to be somewhere among the charred logs and stumps. Everything else in the area was flat.

No, I realized with a chill. Not everything. The graveyard. On my left, about fifty feet from the chamber, it looked so bleak that it discouraged me from going near it. A perfect place to . . .

I stepped from the trees, entering the long grass, and the first rattle took my breath away. I stumbled back, saw the snake under a bush, and blew its head off. The reflex and the accuracy with which I shot surprised me. Hours and hours of practice no doubt explained my reaction. But for over a year, hate and anger had been swelling in me. More than anything, I wanted to kill something. No sooner had I shot the first snake than a second one buzzed. I blew *its* head apart. A third coiled. A fourth. A fifth. I shot each of them, furious that the snakes seemed to be trying to stop me. My shots rang in my ears. The sharp stench of cordite floated around me. Relentlessly, I shifted through the grass. A sixth. A seventh. An eighth. Pieces of snakes flew. Blood sprayed through the grass. Yet more kept rattling, and it seemed that it wasn't my pistol but my raging thoughts that shot them, so directly and instantly did their heads explode the moment I fixed my gaze on them.

The last empty cartridge flipped to the ground. The slide on the pistol stayed back. As I'd done hundreds of times in class, I pushed the button that dropped the empty magazine. I drew a full one from my fanny pack, slammed it into the pistol's grip, pushed the lever that freed the slide, and aimed this way and that, eager for more targets.

None presented itself. Either I'd frightened the rest away or they were hiding, waiting. *Let them try,* I thought in a fury as I picked up the empty magazine and proceeded more relentlessly through the grass. Reaching the graveyard's low stone wall, I climbed over. Brambles and poison ivy awaited me. The place was too foul even for snakes.

The piles of stones in front of each grave made my nerves tighten as I stepped forward. Glancing behind me, I thought I detected a slight furrow in the ground, where earth seemed to have settled. It was so minor that I never would have paid attention to it if I hadn't been looking for it. Faint, it ran from where I'd fallen into the chamber. It went under the graveyard's wall. Even less noticeable, it led to the grave nearest the underground chamber.

A short grave. A child's grave. Angry, I knelt. I pulled away the pile of stones at the head of the grave. For a moment, I couldn't move. The stones had concealed an eight-inch-wide duct sticking up. The duct had a baffle on it so that rain would pour off and not get into the ventilation system.

I was right: The chamber had been a cell. I remembered the long, flat object that the snakes had piled onto to avoid the rising water. Over the years, the object had so deteriorated that, in the shadows, I hadn't been able to identify it. But now I knew what it was. The remains of a mattress. It had been the only object in the room. There hadn't even been a toilet. Had Lester been forced to relieve himself in a pot, contending with the stench until his captors took it away? Their *son*? The horror of it mounted as I stared at the child's grave that they'd desecrated to hide their sin.

12

Reverend Benedict was where I had met him the previous day, kneeling, trimming roses in the church's garden. His white hair glinted in the sunlight.

"Mr. Denning." He stood with effort, shook my hand, and frowned at the scratches on it. "You've injured yourself."

"I took a fall."

He pointed toward my chin, where my beard stubble couldn't hide a bruise. "Evidently a bad one."

"Not as bad as it could have been."

"At the Dant place?"

I nodded.

"Did you find anything to help you locate your family?"

"I'm still trying to make sense of it." I told him what I'd discovered.

The wrinkles in his forehead deepened. "Orval and Eunice held their only son prisoner? *Why?*"

"Maybe they thought the Devil was in him. I have a feeling a lot of things happened out there that we'll never understand, Reverend." My head pounded. "How did Lester escape from the underground room? When the fire broke out, did Orval and Eunice risk their lives to go down to the basement and free him? Did the parents somehow get trapped? In spite of how they'd treated him, did Lester try but fail to save them, as he claimed?"

"It fits what we know."

"But it doesn't explain why he didn't tell everybody what he'd suffered. When something outrageous happens to us, don't we want to tell others? Don't we want sympathy?"

"Unless the memory's so dark that we can't handle it."

"Especially if a different kind of outrage happened out there."

Reverend Benedict kept frowning. "What are you getting at?"

"Suppose Lester somehow got out of that room on his own. Or suppose the parents released him every so often as a reward for good behavior. Did *Lester* start the fire?"

"Start the . . . Lord have mercy."

"One way or another, whether they tried to rescue him or whether he got out on his own, did he trap his parents? Did he stand outside the burning house and listen with delight to their screams? Is that something he'd have wanted to describe to anyone? But that's not all that bothers me."

"Good God, you don't mean there's more."

"I'm from Colorado," I said.

The apparent non sequitur made Reverend Benedict shake his wizened head in confusion.

"Every once in a while, there's a story about somebody who went into the mountains and came across a rattlesnake," I said. "Not often. Maybe it's because the snakes have plenty of hiding places in the mountains, and they're not aggressive by nature—they prefer to stay away from us. But Indiana's a different matter. Lots of people. Dwindling farmland. Have you ever seen a rattlesnake around here?"

"No."

"Have you ever heard of anybody who *has* come across one?" I asked.

"Not that I can think of," the reverend said. "A farmer perhaps. Rarely."

"Because the spreading population has driven them out."

"Presumably."

"Then how come there are *dozens* of rattlesnakes on the Dant property? In southern states, in Mississippi or Louisiana, for example, so many snakes might not seem unusual, but not around here. What are they doing on Orval's farm? How did they get there?"

"I can't imagine."

"Well, *I* can. Do you suppose that the Dants could have been practicing snake handling out there?"

The reverend paled. "As a religious exercise? Holding them in each hand? Letting them coil around their neck to prove their faith in God?"

"Exactly. If the snakes didn't bite, it meant that God intervened. It meant that God favored the Dants more than He did the people in town. If you've got a bunker mentality, if you've got a desperate 'us against them' attitude, maybe you want undeniable proof that you're right."

"It's the worst kind of presumption."

"And I suspect it destroyed them."

"I don't understand."

"You said that there were three Dant families when Lester was born. By the time of the fire, only *one* family—Orval, Eunice, and Lester—remained. You wondered if the other families might have moved away or had gotten deathly ill. But *I'm* wondering if the snakes didn't send the Dants a different message than they expected."

"You mean the snakes killed them?" the reverend murmured.

"The Dants would never have gone to a doctor for help."

"Dear Jesus."

"Snake handling would explain how so many got to be out there. The Dants brought them," I said. "What it *doesn't* explain is why the snakes remained. Why didn't they spread?"

"Perhaps they stayed where they belonged."

At first, I didn't understand. Then I nodded. "Maybe. That's a foul, rotten place out there, Reverend. I think you're right. If I were in your line of work, I'd say that the snakes are exactly where they feel at home."

Several bees buzzed my face. I motioned them away.

"Just one more question, and then I'll leave you alone," I said.

"Anything I can do to help."

"You mentioned that after Lester ran from your home,

he showed up in a town a hundred miles east of here, across the border in Ohio."

"That's right."

"What did you say it was called?"

Part Five

Part Five

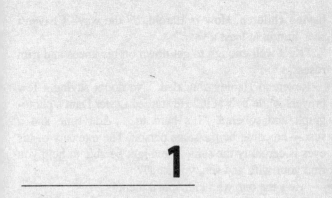

1

Loganville was better than I expected: a picture-postcard town with a prosperous-looking main street and a welcoming park in front of its courthouse. I asked directions to the Unitarian church, whose minister I'd phoned to make an appointment. The portly, gray-haired man was stacking hymnals in the vestibule.

"Reverend Hanley?" I'd explained on the phone why I needed to talk with him. I showed him Lester Dant's photograph and asked about the teenager's arrival at the church nineteen years earlier. "I realize that's a long time ago, but Reverend Benedict seemed to think that you'd remember what happened back then."

"I certainly do. It's difficult to forget what happened that summer. That boy meant a great deal to Harold and Gladys. They wanted so much to become his guardians."

"Harold?"

"Reverend Benedict. Their greatest regret was not

having children. How *is* Harold, by the way? I haven't seen him in at least a year."

"He's well enough to get down on his knees and trim roses."

Reverend Hanley chuckled. "No doubt saying a few prayers while he's at it." He studied Lester Dant's photograph and sobered. "It's hard to ... Add time and a scar—he could be the same person. The intensity of his eyes is certainly the same. He might be able to help you find your wife and son, you said?"

"He's the one who kidnapped them."

The minister took a moment to recover from what I'd said. "I wish I could help you. But I didn't get to know him well. The person you need to talk to is Agnes Garner. She's the member of the congregation who took the most interest in him. And she's the one he most betrayed."

2

Climbing the porch steps at the address I'd been given, I found a woman in a wheelchair. From her pain-tightened face, I might have guessed that she was almost seventy, if Reverend Hanley hadn't already told me that she'd been thirty-eight when Lester Dant had come into her life nineteen years earlier. "Ms. Garner?"

"*Mrs.*"

"Sorry. Reverend Hanley didn't tell me you were married."

"Widowed."

"He didn't tell me that, either."

"No reason he should have."

Her abrupt manner made me uncomfortable. "Thanks for agreeing to see me."

Her hair was gray. Her dress had a blue flower pattern. She had a cordless telephone on her lap. "You want to know about Lester Dant?"

"I'd appreciate any information you can give me."

"Reverend Hanley called and explained about your wife and son. Do you have a photograph of them?"

"Always." With longing, I pulled out my wallet.

She stared at the picture. Kate's father had taken it when we were visiting Kate's parents in Durango. The magnificent cliff ruins of Mesa Verde aren't far from there. We'd made a day trip of it. The photo showed Kate, Jason, and me standing in front of one of the half-collapsed dwellings. We wore jeans and T-shirts and were smiling toward the camera. In the photo's background, next to an old stone wall, a stooped shadow looked like a human being, but there wasn't anything to account for the shadow. Jason had insisted it was the ghost of a Native American who'd lived there hundreds of years earlier.

Ghosts. I didn't want to think I was looking at ghosts.

"A wonderful family."

"Thank you" was all I could say.

"There's so much sorrow in the world."

"Yes." Emotion tightened my throat. "Mrs. Garner, do you recognize this man?" I showed her the photo.

It pained her to look at him. She nodded and turned away. "It's Lester. I haven't thought about him in years. I try my hardest not to."

She's going to send me away, I thought.

"Do you honestly believe that what I tell you can help?" she asked.

"I don't know any other way."

"Hurt him."

"Excuse me?"

"We're supposed to forgive those who trespass against us, but I want you to hurt him."

"If I get the chance, Mrs. Garner, believe me, I will."

She gripped the sides of her wheelchair. "There was a time when I could walk. I was always the earliest to arrive for Sunday services."

The change in topic confused me.

"I made a point of getting to the church before everyone. Now I wonder if I wasn't too proud and that's why God punished me."

"Whatever happened, Mrs. Garner, it wasn't God's fault. It was Lester Dant's."

3

He'd sat at the top of the church steps with his back against the door.

"A teenager," Mrs. Garner said. "His head was drooped, but even without seeing his face, I could tell that I didn't know him. His clothes were torn, so the first thing I thought was that he'd been in some kind of accident. The next thing I thought was, the way his head hung down, he might be on drugs. But before I could make a decision whether to hurry to help him or run away, he raised his head and looked at me. His eyes were so direct, there was no way he could have been on drugs. They were filled with torment. I asked him if he was hurt. 'No, ma'am,' he said, 'but I'm awful tired and hungry.'

"By then, other members of the congregation had arrived. The reverend came. But neither he nor anybody else recognized the boy. We asked him his name, but he said that he couldn't remember. We asked where he came from, but he couldn't remember that, either. From the rips in his clothes and the freshly healed burn marks on his arms, we figured that he must have had something terrible happen to him, that he was in shock.

"The reverend offered to take him home and get him something to eat, but the boy said, 'No. These people are waiting for the service to begin.' That sounds too good to be true, I know. But you weren't there. Everybody who came to church that morning felt so concerned about the boy and so touched by his unselfish attitude that we had a sense of God's hand among us. We took him inside. I sat next to him and handed him a Bible, but he didn't open it. I wondered if he was too dazed to be able to read. Imagine my surprise when the congregation read out loud from the Scriptures and the boy recited every passage from memory. I remember that the reverend said something in his sermon about keeping compassion in our hearts and helping the unfortunate. He paused to look directly at the boy. Afterward, everybody said that it was one of the most moving services that we'd had in a long time. The reverend took the boy home. He asked me and a couple of other church members to help. We made a big meal. We got the boy fresh clothes. He did everything slowly, as if in a daze.

"Who *was* he? we wondered. What had happened to him? Where had he come from? A doctor examined him but couldn't get him to remember anything. The chief of police got the same results and asked the state police if they knew about anybody who matched the boy's description and had been reported missing. The state police didn't learn anything, either."

That made sense, I thought. Loganville was in Ohio, but the fire had happened in Indiana. The Ohio police had probably decided that the boy's arrival in Loganville wasn't important enough for out-of-state inquiries. Even if they *had* gone out of state, inquiries to the Indiana state police might have been pointless, the fire having been basically a local matter that the state police wouldn't have monitored.

"Various members of the congregation offered to take the boy in," Mrs. Garner said. "But the reverend decided that since I'd found him, I had the right to take care of him if I wanted. My husband was the most generous soul imaginable. Five years earlier, we'd lost a son to cancer." She paused, caught in her memories. "Our only child. If Joshua had lived, he'd have been the same age as the teenager I'd found on the church steps seemed to be. I couldn't help thinking that God had sent him into our lives for a reason. As a . . ."

Mrs. Garner had trouble saying the next word.

"Substitute?" I asked.

She nodded, her pain lines deepening. "That's another reason I believe I was punished. For vain thoughts like that. For presuming that God would single me out and give me favorable treatment. But back then, I couldn't resist the idea that something miraculous was happening, that I was being given a second son. I told my husband what I hoped for, and he didn't take a moment to agree. If I wanted the boy to live with us while his problems got sorted out, it was fine. My husband loved me so much and . . ."

Her voice dropped. She turned her wheelchair slightly so that she looked even straighter at me. "The boy came to live with us while the authorities tried to figure out who he was. He was awfully skinny. It took me days of solid home cooking, of fried chicken and apple pies, to put some weight on him. His burns had healed, but the scratches on his arms and legs, where his clothes had been torn, got infected and needed their dressings and bandages changed a lot. I didn't mind. It reminded me of taking care of the son we'd lost. I was pleased to do it. But I couldn't help wondering what on earth had happened to him.

"I left books and magazines on his bedside table so he'd have something to amuse him while he was resting. After a while, I realized that none of them had been opened. When I asked him if they didn't suit him, if he'd like to read something else, he avoided the question, and it suddenly occurred to me that the boy couldn't read."

I'd taken a seat on a porch swing. Now I frowned. "But you said that he could recite passages from the Bible."

"Any passage I asked him."

"Then I don't understand."

"I asked him to read the back of a cereal box. I asked him to read the headline of a newspaper. He couldn't do it. I put a pencil and paper in front of him. He couldn't write the simplest words. He was illiterate. As for the Bible passages, there was only one explanation. Someone had taught him the Bible orally, had made him memorize passages that were read to him. It chilled me when I realized that. What on earth had happened to him?"

"That's one of the few questions I have an answer for."

Her gaze was intense. "You know?"

Wishing that I hadn't interrupted, I nodded. "His parents held him prisoner in an underground room."

"*What?*"

"As much as I've been able to figure out, they believed that the Devil was in him, that the only way to drive Satan out was by filling his head with the Bible."

Mrs. Garner looked horrified. "But why wouldn't they have let him learn how to read and write?"

"I'm still trying to piece it together. Maybe they believed that reading and writing were the Devil's tools. The wrong kind of books would lead to the wrong kind of ideas, and the next thing, sin would be all over the place. The Bible was the only safe book, and the surest way to guarantee that the Bible was the *only* book Lester knew was to teach it to him orally."

Mrs. Garner's eyes wavered as if she'd become dizzy. She lowered her head and massaged her temples.

"Are you all right?" I asked.

"The things people do to one another."

"I've told you what Lester did to my family. What did he do to *you*?"

Seconds passed. Gradually, she looked up at me, the pain in her eyes worse. "He was the politest boy I ever met. He was always asking to help around the house. At the same time, I'd never met anyone so troubled. Some afternoons, he'd lie in bed for hours, staring at the ceiling, reliving God knew what. In the nights, he couldn't go to sleep unless his closet light was on. He often woke screaming from nightmares. They seemed to have something to do with the fire that had burned his arms. I'd go into his room and try to calm him. I'd sit holding him, stroking his head, whispering that he was safe, that nothing could hurt him where he was, that he didn't have to worry anymore."

She paused, rubbing her temples again.

"Are you sure you're okay?" I asked.

"So long ago. Why does the memory still hurt so much?"

"I don't mean to upset you. If you need to rest for a while, I can come back when—"

"I never spoke about this to anyone. Ever. Maybe I should have. Maybe it wouldn't keep torturing me if I'd told someone, if I'd tried to explain."

"Do you want to explain it to *me*?"

She looked at me in anguish for the longest while, searching my eyes. "To a stranger. Yes. Someone whose judgments I'll never have to face again."

"I don't make judgments, Mrs. Garner. All I want is to get my wife and son back. Do you know anything that can help me do that?"

She struggled with her thoughts. "One night, he kissed me on the cheek. Another night, after one of his nightmares, after I held him and calmed him, he pecked my cheek again. Or tried to. He grazed my lips, as if he'd aimed for my cheek and missed. It was an awkward moment. I stood as soon as I got him settled in bed. I felt uncomfortable, but I kept telling myself that I was imagining things, that the boy hadn't meant anything."

"Mrs. Garner, you don't need to—"

"I have to. Somehow I have to get it out of me. I wanted to take care of the boy so much that I was in denial. Each intimacy seemed innocent. Like when I tried to teach him to read and write. That's what I used to be: a teacher at the high school. This happened at the end of summer. School hadn't started yet. I had time to try to teach him. I used the Bible, since he already knew the words. We sat together at the kitchen table. Our chairs were close. There was nothing wrong. We were just a teacher and a student sitting at a table working on a school problem, and yet, in retrospect, I realize that he sat closer than he needed to. When he helped me make dinner, our hands would touch briefly. I didn't think anything of it. One of the reasons I haven't told anybody about this is that I'm afraid it'll seem as if I took some kind of"—she had trouble saying the word—"enjoyment. . . . That's the furthest thing from the truth. I know that there are a lot of twisted people in this world, Mr. Denning. But I'm a churchgoing, God-fearing woman, and I assure you that I am not capable of enjoying the touch of a teenager whom I considered to be like a son."

An uncomfortable silence gathered. I made myself nod, encouraging her to continue.

"But it's because I wanted so desperately to take care of him that everything happened. One night, after another of his nightmares, when I held him, he grazed my . . ." Self-conscious, she looked down at the front of her dress. "It seemed accidental, yet I finally admitted that too many accidental gestures like that had happened, and I told him that certain kinds of touching weren't appropriate. I told him that I wanted the two of us to be close but that there were different kinds of closeness. He said that he didn't know what I meant but that if I wanted him to keep a distance, he would."

"The next night . . ." She couldn't get the words out. Her eyes glistened, close to weeping. "May I see the photograph of your wife and son again, please?"

Puzzled, I took out my wallet.

She studied it even longer than the first time. "Such a wonderful-looking family. What are their names?"

"Kate and Jason."

"Are you happily married?"

"Very." Now *I* was the one who had trouble speaking.

"Is your son a good boy?"

"The best." My voice became hoarse.

"How will this help you find them?" Moisture filled her eyes.

If Kate and Jason are still alive, I thought. What I'd learned from Reverend Benedict filled me with despair.

"I'm betting that he has habits." I struggled to hide my discouragement. "If I can understand him, I might be able to follow his trail."

"A trail that started nineteen years ago?"

"I don't know where else to go."

"He raped me."

The porch became deathly silent, except for her sobs as tears trickled down her cheeks.

I felt paralyzed, trying to get over my shock. "I'm sorry. I shouldn't have asked you to talk about it."

"Don't talk about it?" Her tears made scald marks on her cheeks. "God help me, I've been holding it inside all these years. *That's* the torture. My husband was the principal of the school where I taught. Around dark, the janitor called about a water pipe that had burst. My husband hurried down to learn how serious the damage was. I got ready for bed. The boy . . . The rotten son of a bitch bastard—"

The torrent of what for Mrs. Garner were the crudest of obscenities shocked me.

"He came into my bedroom while I was undressing, threw me on the floor, and . . . I couldn't believe how strong he was. He was so frail-looking, and yet he overpowered me as if he had the force of the Devil. He kept calling me Eunice, but he knew very well that my first name is Agnes. I tried to fight him off. I scratched. I kicked. Then I saw his fist coming at me. Twice. Three times. I almost choked on my blood, lying there half-unconscious while he . . ."

Her voice faltered. She pulled a handkerchief from her dress, raising it to her cheeks.

"Afterward . . ." Some of her tears dripped from her chin. "After I vomited . . . After I found the strength to stand, I saw drawers open and realized that he'd stolen anything of value that he could stuff into his pockets. But that was the last thing on my mind. I staggered to the phone to call the police and get an ambulance, and all at once, I realized that I couldn't do that. I thought of the congregation and the town and the high school where my husband and I worked, and I imagined everybody staring at me. Oh, sure, they'd be sympathetic. But that wouldn't stop them from telling everybody they knew about what had happened to Agnes Garner. Being sympathetic wouldn't stop them from staring, and it wouldn't stop word from getting around to the students, who would stare even more than their parents. Rape. Rape.

"I wavered in front of the phone. I remember telling myself that I had to call for help, that I was close to passing out. Instead, I forced myself into the bathroom. I used all my strength to get in the tub and wash myself where he'd . . ." She wiped more tears from her face. "*Then* I got dressed. *Then* I called the police. And no doctor ever had a chance to examine any part of me except my smashed lips and my bruised cheeks. I told everybody that I'd come into the bedroom and found him stealing money and jewelry. Not that I had much jewelry. I'm not that kind of a woman. All told, he took about three hundred dollars, which could be replaced, but a simple necklace that my grandmother had given me could *never* be replaced.

"My husband got home just after the police car arrived. The police searched for the boy but never found him. Maybe he slept in the woods. Maybe he hitchhiked and got a ride out of the area. The next day, Reverend Benedict arrived from Brockton. I learned that the boy's name was Lester Dant. I learned about the fire that had killed his parents. But I never told Reverend Benedict or Reverend Hanley what had really happened in my bedroom. I never told my husband. I never told *anyone*. When word got around, people stared, yes, but it was a kind of staring that I could tolerate. We'd taken a boy into our home. He'd repaid us by beating me and stealing from us. I was the kind of victim that the town could deal with."

"I can't tell you how sorry I am," I said.

"Eunice." She sounded anguished. "*Why on earth did he call me Eunice?*"

I didn't answer.

"You know about the underground room where his parents kept him prisoner. What *else* do you know? Have you any idea why he called me Eunice?"

Her tone was so beseeching that I found myself saying, "Yes."

"Tell me."

"Are you sure you want the answer?"

"The same as *you* need answers."

I hesitated. "Eunice was his mother's name."

Mrs. Garner moaned.

"It sounds as if he was punishing . . ."

"His mother. Punishing his *mother*. God help me." Her voice cracked with despair. "Hurt him. Remember your promise. When you find him, hurt him."

"You have my word."

4

All the way to my car, I tried not to let Mrs. Garner see my discouragement. "When you find him," she'd said. But I no longer believed that I would. With no information about where Lester Dant had gone that night, I hadn't the faintest idea what to do next. Worse, I didn't see the point of trying. Lester was far more disturbed than the FBI's information about him had revealed. I couldn't imagine him keeping Kate and Jason alive.

Grieving for them, I slumped behind the steering wheel. Hate fought with grief. "Hurt him," Mrs. Garner had pleaded. Yes, hurt him, I thought. Furious, I drove past well-maintained lawns and neatly trimmed hedges. I reached a four-way stop and turned to the right. At the next four-way stop, I turned to the left. No reason. No direction.

I went on that way, at random, for quite a while, driving through the prosperous farm town until I realized that I was passing certain homes and stores for what might have been the fifth or sixth time. Fatigue finally caught up to me, making me stop at a motel called the Traveler's Oasis on the edge of town.

It was almost five, but for me it felt like midnight as I carried my suitcase and backpack into a room that faced the parking lot. Too exhausted to survey the Spartan accommodations, I returned to the car for my printer and laptop computer. I wondered why I'd bothered to bring them. They took up space. I hadn't used them.

Maybe it's time to go home, I thought.

In Denver, it was two hours earlier. I picked up the phone.

"Payne Detective Agency," a man's familiar voice said.

"Answering the phone yourself?"

Payne didn't reply for a moment. "Ann had a doctor's appointment." Ann, his receptionist, was also his wife. "How are you, Brad?"

"Is my voice that recognizable?" I imagined the portly man next to his goldfish tank.

"You've been on my mind. When you called the last time, you were in South Dakota. You said you'd get back to me, but you didn't. I've been worried. What are you doing in . . ." I heard Payne's fingers tapping on a computer keyboard. "The Traveler's Oasis in Loganville, Ohio."

"Sounds like you've got a new computer program."

"It keeps me distracted. What are you doing there?"

"Giving up."

"I'm sorry to hear that. I figured that as long as you were in motion, you wouldn't do anything foolish to yourself. You didn't learn anything, I gather."

I sat wearily on the bed. "The opposite. I learned too much. But it hasn't taken me anywhere."

"Except to the Traveler's Oasis in Loganville, Ohio."

Payne tried to make it sound like a joke, but it didn't work. "I was hoping to find a pattern," I said into the phone.

"Sometimes a pattern's there. We just don't recognize it."

"Yeah, well, *my* pattern's been aimless." Something Payne had said caught up to me—the somber way he'd said it. "Ann had a doctor's appointment? Is everything okay?"

"We'll see."

". . . Oh."

He hesitated. "A lump on her breast, but it might just be a cyst. The doctor's doing a biopsy."

I took a tired breath. "I'll say a prayer."

"Thanks."

"Before all this began, that isn't something I'd have said."

"That you'd pray for somebody?" he asked.

"The last few days, I spoke to a couple of ministers and a very religious, very decent lady. I guess some of their attitudes wore off on me. The trouble is, I also learned about a man whose parents turned him into a monster. Lester Dant."

"You believe in him now."

"Oh, I believe in him all right. God help me."

"Another prayer," Payne said.

"I'll be starting home tomorrow. I'll phone as soon as I get back. Maybe you'll have the results of the biopsy by then."

"Maybe." Payne's voice sank. "Have a safe trip."

I murmured, "Thanks," and hung up.

Please, God, keep his wife healthy, I thought.

I lay on the bed and closed my eyes. The draperies shut out the late-afternoon light. I wanted to sleep forever.

Please, God, I hope you didn't let Kate and Jason suffer.

I couldn't help thinking about the good and bad things that religion could do to people. I couldn't help thinking about Lester Dant running from one church and showing up at another and . . .

5

The shock of the idea made me sit up. I found myself standing excitedly, thinking about what Lester Dant, posing as my brother, had told me more than a year earlier.

"As I wandered from town to town, I learned that an easy way to get a free meal was to show up at church socials after Sunday-morning services."

Jesus, I thought, he would have continued doing what worked. He'd have gone to another church in another small town. Payne had been right. The pattern was there. I just hadn't recognized it.

In a rush, I arranged my computer and printer on a table next to the bed. I unplugged the room's phone from the wall and attached my own phone line, connecting it to my computer. Then I turned on the computer and made adjustments to my Internet-access program so I could shift from AOL's Denver phone number to one that it used in the Loganville area.

The next thing, I logged on to an Internet geography

site and printed a map for Ohio, along with ones for the surrounding states of Michigan, Indiana, Kentucky, West Virginia, and Pennsylvania. What I wanted was a list of towns. Dant would have avoided cities. I was sure of it. After the smothering closeness of having been imprisoned underground, I imagined him recoiling from the congestion of cities.

The maps gave me hundreds of names. Too many to be of use, but a start. I made the list more practical by eliminating the names of towns that were on the extreme reaches of the other states. I further reduced the list by eliminating Indiana, convinced that Dant would have avoided going back to where he'd been imprisoned. That left Ohio, Michigan to the north of it, Kentucky and West Virginia to the south, and Pennsylvania to the east.

But the towns in them weren't what I cared about. What I wanted were the names of *churches* in those towns. I typed "Churches in Ohio" into the Internet's "Search For" box. A list appeared, complete with their locations and their Web site addresses. I matched them with the towns on my list. I did the same with churches in Kentucky, West Virginia, Pennsylvania, and Michigan. I eliminated any church with a saint's name in it, certain that Dant would have avoided Catholic, Anglican, and Greek Orthodox churches. Their theology and ritual would have been alien to him. I need to identify Protestant congregations, I thought, and then I can—

A loud knock on the door distracted me.

I jerked my head in that direction.

Sunlight had long since faded from behind the draperies. I looked at my watch. Almost seven hours had passed. The hands were close to midnight.

The loud knock was repeated. "Mr. Denning?" a man's voice asked.

When I stood, my legs ached from having sat so long. I went to the door, squinted through the tiny lens, and saw an elderly man in a jacket and tie. I kept the security chain on the door when I opened it and peered through the five-inch gap. "What is it?" The stark floodlights in the parking lot made me blink.

"I just wanted to make sure that everything was all right. Our computer shows that you've been on the phone since around five o'clock, but when I tried to access the line to make sure you hadn't fallen asleep and left the phone off the hook, all I got was static."

"I've been catching up on office work."

The man looked puzzled.

"On the Internet," I said, pointing toward my computer on the corner table, which I later realized he couldn't see.

The man looked more puzzled.

"You have my credit-card number," I said. "I'll gladly pay all the phone charges."

"As long as everything's okay."

"Couldn't be better."

"Have a nice night."

He left, and I became aware of throbbing in my head, of cramps in my stomach. Through the crack in the door, I saw a harsh red-and-blue neon sign across the street. The words it flashed were STEAKS 'N' SUDS. Two eighteen-wheeler trucks were at the edge of the crowded parking lot. Begrudging the time I'd be wasting but telling myself that I couldn't be any use to Kate and Jason if I didn't maintain my strength, I disconnected from the Internet, locked the room behind me, and walked toward country music—a jukebox playing something about a one-man woman and a two-timing man—coming from the restaurant's open windows.

6

Forty minutes later, the steak sandwich I'd eaten felt heavy in my stomach. I recalled the strict healthy diet that I'd put myself on in preparation for my search. Tomorrow, I'll rededicate myself, I vowed. Tomorrow.

"Here's your coffee to go," the waitress said.

"Thanks."

As I left the restaurant, about to cross the parking lot, a noise made me pause. The jukebox had stopped, but the conversations of the crowd inside were loud enough that I had to strain to listen harder. On my right. Around the side of the restaurant. I heard it again. A groan.

A *woman's* groan.

"Think you can leave me?" A man's muffled voice came from around the corner. "You're dumber than I always said you were."

I heard a metallic thump, as if someone had fallen against a car. Another groan.

Inside, the jukebox started playing again: something

about lonely rooms and empty hearts. The careful Brad I'd once been would have gone back into the restaurant and told the manager to call the police. But how long would it take the police to arrive, and what would happen in the meantime?

Imagining Kate being punched, I unzipped the fanny pack I always wore. Knowing that I could draw the pistol if I needed it, I walked to the restaurant's corner. There were only a few windows on that side. Away from the glare of the neon lights, my eyes needed a moment to adjust before I saw moving shadows between two parked cars: a man striking a woman.

"Stop," I said.

The man spun toward my voice. The minimal light showed a beefy face. A chain on his belt was attached to a big wallet in his back pocket. "This is a private conversation. Stay out of it." He shoved the woman to the asphalt. "You don't want to live with me anymore? Well, either you live with me or you don't live at all."

"I told you to stop."

"Get lost, pal, or when I finish my family business, I'll start on *you*."

"Get lost? You just said the two words I hate the most."

"You heard me, buddy." The man jerked the woman to her feet and pushed her into a car. When she tried to struggle out, he struck her again.

"But you're not hearing *me*." Conscious of the pistol in my fanny pack, I stepped closer.

"All right, I gave you a chance to butt out!" The man spun toward me again. "Now it's *your* turn."

"Must be my lucky night."

He lunged.

The take-out coffee was in my left hand, the liquid so hot that it stung my fingers through the Styrofoam cup. I yanked the lid from the cup and threw the steaming contents at the man's face, aiming for his eyes.

The man shrieked and jerked his hands toward his scalded face.

I drove stiff fingers into his stomach, just below the V of the rib cage, the way I'd been taught.

Sounding as if he might vomit, the man doubled over.

I kicked sideways toward a nerve that ran down the outside of his left thigh.

Paralyzed, his leg gave out, toppling him to the pavement, where he shrieked harder from the pain in his leg.

I yanked his hands from his face and drove the heel of my right palm against his nose, once, twice, three times. Cartilage cracked. I stepped back as blood spurted.

He dropped to the pavement and lay motionless. Ready to hit him again, I shoved him onto his side so the blood would drain from his nose. I felt for a pulse, found one, smelled his sour alcohol-saturated breath, and turned to the woman slumped in the car. "Are you all right?"

She moaned. I was appalled by the bruises on her face.

"Are you strong enough to drive?" I asked.

"I don't . . ." The woman was off-balance when I helped her from the car. Her lips were swollen. "Yes." She took a deep breath. "I think I can drive. But . . ."

"Do it."

Behind me, the man groaned.

"Hurry," I said. "Before he wakes up."

Through blackened eyes, the woman looked around in confusion. Bruises that deep couldn't develop in just a few minutes, I knew. They were the consequence of numerous other beatings.

"*Drive?*" she asked plaintively. "*How?* I ran here. I hoped I could borrow money from a girlfriend who works in this place. It turns out she called in sick. *He* was waiting instead."

Stooping beside the man on the pavement, I satisfied myself that he was still too dazed to realize what was going on. I pulled his car keys from his pants. Then I took his big wallet from his back pocket and removed all the money he had—what looked like a hundred dollars.

"Here," I told the woman. I pulled out my own wallet and gave her most of the cash I had—around two hundred.

"I can't accept this," she said.

"My wife would have wanted me to give it to you."

"What are you talking about?"

"Take this. Please. Because of my wife."

The woman looked at me strangely, as if trying to decipher a riddle. "I have a sister in Baltimore," she said as I gave her the man's car keys.

"No, it's the first place he'll look," I said. "If you'd robbed a bank, would you hide at your sister's? Too obvious. You have to pretend that you're running from the police."

"But I haven't done anything wrong!"

"Keep telling yourself that. You haven't done anything wrong. But that son of a bitch over there certainly has. You have to keep reminding yourself that your only goal in life is to stay away from him." In Denver, when life had been normal, I'd been proud of the volunteer work Kate had done as a stress counselor at a shelter for battered women.

I knew the drill. "Pick a city where you've never been. Pittsburgh." I chose it at random. "Have you ever been to—"

"No."

"Then go to Pittsburgh. It's only a couple of hundred miles from here. Leave the car at a bus station, and go to Pittsburgh. Look in the phone book under 'Community Services.' Look for the number of the women's shelter."

7

I trembled in my motel room, amazed by the rage that had overtaken me. For a moment, as the bastard had come at me, I'd almost shot him. The only thing that had stopped me was the realization that the shot would have sent people scurrying from the restaurant. Someone might have seen me. The police would have come after me. How could I have looked for Kate and Jason if I were in jail?

8

For reasons important to my family and me, my E-mail said, *I'm looking for information about a young man who might have come to your church in the late summer or in the fall nineteen years ago. I realize that it's hard to remember that far back, but I think that the circumstances would have been unusual enough that someone in your congregation would recall him. The boy would have been in his midteens. He would have collapsed against the front door of your church early before Sunday services, so that the first person to arrive would have found him there. He would have been wearing torn clothes and would have had scrapes and scratches, suggesting that he'd been in an accident of some sort. He wouldn't have been able to recall his name or what had happened to him or how he had come to be at your church. Members of the congregation would have taken care of him—in particular, women—because something about his eyes invites mothering. He would have been able to quote the Bible from memory but otherwise would have been unable to read or write. Someone, probably a woman, would have tried to teach him. Ultimately, he would have stolen from the people who helped him, perhaps have beaten them also, and have fled town. It may be that near the end he "remembered" that his name was Lester Dant. If you have any knowledge of someone like this, please send me an E-mail at the above address. I very much need to learn everything I can about this person. A year ago, he kidnapped my wife and son.*

9

The next morning, after a torturous sleep, I sent that message to the E-mail address of every church on my list. Staring at my computer screen, I silently asked God to help me. All I could do now was wait.

The need to urinate finally made me move. But once in motion, I remembered Payne's remark that as long as I stayed in motion, I was less likely to do something foolish to myself. I went for a five-mile run. I returned and checked to see if I had any E-mail. Nothing. I did an hour of exercises, then checked my E-mail again. Still nothing.

What did I expect? That someone at each church would faithfully read the church's E-mail every morning, that word of my message would spread instantly throughout each congregation, that people who remembered something like the events I'd described would immediately send an E-mail back to me? I have to be patient, I warned myself. Even in small towns, news doesn't get around as fast as I want it to. If there's a reply to be had, I probably won't receive it until evening.

So I showered, dressed, and tried to read. I went out and got a sandwich. I took a walk. I watched CNN. But mostly I kept checking to see if any E-mail had arrived. None did. By midnight, I gave up, shut off the lights, and tried to sleep.

But unconsciousness wouldn't come, and finally, betraying my resolve of the previous night, I went down the road to a bar and grill, where I wasn't likely to be recognized. If the man I'd beaten was looking for me, the logical place he'd do it was the restaurant across from the motel. This time, it took four beers and a shot of bourbon before I felt stupefied enough to go back to my room and try to sleep. I'm going to hell, I told myself.

I *am* in hell.

Around dawn, I woke, but there still wasn't any message. I faced another day of waiting. Time dragged on, until I admitted that I'd been a fool to have hoped. I hadn't been brave enough to identify with Lester Dant as closely as I'd needed to. I'd been wrong in my prediction of where he'd gone nineteen years previously and of what he'd done when he'd arrived there. Vowing that I couldn't persist in leading my life the way I was, wondering if I wanted to lead my life at all, I checked my E-mail and tensed at the discovery of four messages.

10

I was certain that they didn't exist, that I'd tricked myself into seeing things. With a sense of unreality, I stared at them. Unsteady, I printed them out. Each was from a different state: Kentucky, West Virginia, Pennsylvania, and Ohio. Initially, their sequence was alphabetic, based on the sender's name, but after I reread them several times, I arranged them so that they formed a geographical and chronological narrative.

Mr. Denning, the first began. *Your message so disturbed me that it took me a long time to face up to answering it. My husband told me not to pain myself, but I can't bear the thought that other people have suffered.* The writer identified herself as Mrs. Donald Cavendish, and the details of her message paralleled what Mrs. Garner had told me. If a rape had occurred, Mrs. Cavendish didn't mention it, but I had a disturbing sense of a deeper hurt than even the strong facts of her message accounted for. He hadn't called himself Lester, though. He hadn't used any name at all. The night that he'd disappeared, he'd burned down their house.

This had happened in November, a month after he'd brutalized Mrs. Garner. What had occurred in the interval? I checked my maps and found that the town in Kentucky was two hundred miles from Loganville, Ohio. After Lester spent the money that he'd stolen from Mrs. Garner, had he wandered, subsisting on the proceeds from house break-ins and liquor-store robberies until his aimless path took him to Kentucky?

The next message (as I arranged them) was from the neighboring state of West Virginia and described events *one year later,* when Lester (he used only his first name) had been welcomed by a churchgoing family whose teenage daughter he eventually victimized. It was the daughter who sent me the E-mail, revealing what she'd hidden from her parents until she was an adult. Lester had warned her that if she told anyone what he'd done, he'd come back one night and kill her. To prove his point, he'd strangled her cat in front of her. The next night, he'd robbed the house, stolen the family car, and disappeared. The police had found the fire-gutted car two hundred miles away, but although Lester was gone, it had taken the daughter a long time before she'd stopped having nightmares about him.

The third message (from Pennsylvania) described events a surprising *eight years* later. He'd shortened his first name to Les. His methods had changed. In his mid-twenties now, he no longer had the air of vulnerability that had made it so easy to portray himself a victim and win the compassion of a small-town congregation. Instead, he'd showed up at the church and offered to do odd jobs in exchange for meals. His amazing ability to quote any Bible passage from memory had endeared him to the congregation. This time, it was the church that he'd burned.

But it was the fourth message that disturbed me most. It was from a man who described events *thirteen years* after the fire in which Lester Dant's parents had been killed. It came from a town in central Ohio. This time when Lester had disappeared, he'd taken the man's wife. She'd never been found. But Lester hadn't used his first name or its abbreviation, Les. He'd used an entirely different first name. It turned me cold.

Peter.

Shivering to the core of my soul, I stared at the maps and the placement of the towns. From Brockton southeast to Loganville in Ohio, then farther southeast to the town in Kentucky, then east to West Virginia, then northeast to Pennsylvania, then northwest to the town in Ohio, a hundred miles from where I was raised in the middle of that state. One month. One year. Eight years. Thirteen years.

He'd been to far-off places in the country during the intervals (his FBI crime report made that clear), but something kept making him return to this general area, and I couldn't help feeling that the placement of towns on the maps wasn't random, that it had a center, that he'd been skirting his ultimate destination, each time getting closer, drawn relentlessly back to where everything had begun.

Part Six

1

It had been more than a quarter of a century since my mother and I had been forced to leave Woodford to live with her parents in Columbus. Payne had told me that the town was now a flourishing bedroom community for the encroaching city. But I hadn't fully realized what that meant. After I steered from the interstate, following a newly paved road into town, I tested my memory. I'd been barely fourteen when Mom and I had left. Even so, from all the times that she and Dad had taken Petey and me to visit her parents, I remembered that there'd been a lot of farmland on the way to the interstate. Much of that was gone now, replaced by subdivisions of large houses on small lots. The panoramic outdoor view that owners had initially been attracted to had been obliterated by further development. Expensive landscaping compensated.

On what had once been the edge of town, I passed the furniture factory where my dad had been a foreman. It was now a restaurant/movie theater/shopping mall com-

plex. The industrial exterior had been retained, giving it a
sense of local history. Downtown—a grid of six blocks
of stores—looked better than it had in my youth. Its ad-
joining two-story brick structures had been freshly sand-
blasted, everything appearing new, even though the
buildings came from the early 1900s. One street had been
blocked off and converted into a pedestrian mall, trees
and planters interspersed among outdoor cafés, a foun-
tain, and a small bandstand.

The area was busy enough that it took me a while to
find a parking spot. My emotions pushed and pulled me.
When I'd been a kid, downtown had seemed so big. Now
the effect was the same, but for different reasons—helplessness made me feel small. Despite the passage of
years, I managed to orient myself as I passed a comic-
book store and an ice-cream shop, neither of which had
been in those places when I was a kid. I came to the corner of Lincoln and Washington (the names returned to
me) and stared at a shadowy doorway across the street. It
was between a bank and a drugstore, businesses that *had*
been in those places when I was a kid. I remembered because of all the times my mother had walked Petey and
me to that doorway and had taken us up the narrow echoing stairway to our least favorite place in the world: the
dentist's office.

That stairway had seemed towering and ominous
when I'd climbed it in my youth. Now, trying to calm
myself, I counted each of its thirty steps as I went up. At
the top, I stood under a skylight (another change) and
faced the same frosted-glass door that had led into the
dentist, except that the name on the door was now COS-
GROVE INSURANCE AGENCY.

A young woman with her hair pulled back looked up from stapling documents together. "Yes, sir?"

"I . . . When I was a kid, this used to be a dentist's office." I couldn't help looking past the receptionist toward the corridor that had led to the chamber of horrors.

She looked puzzled. "Yes?"

"He has some dental records I need, but I don't know how to get in touch with him because I've forgotten his name."

"I'm afraid I'm not the person to ask. I started working for Mr. Cosgrove only six months ago, and I never heard anything about a dentist's office."

"Perhaps Mr. Cosgrove would know."

She went down the hallway to the office that I'd dreaded and came back in less than a minute. "He says he's been here eight years. Before then, this was a Realtor's office."

"Oh."

"Sorry."

"Sure." Something sank in me. "I guess it was too much to hope for." Discouraged, I turned toward the door, then stopped with a sudden thought. "A Realtor?"

"Excuse me?"

"You said a Realtor used to be in this office?"

"Yes." She was looking at me now as if I'd become a nuisance.

"Does he or she manage properties, do you suppose?"

"What?"

"Assuming that Mr. Cosgrove doesn't own this building, who's his landlord?"

2

"You mean the Dwyer Building." The bantamweight man in a bow tie stubbed out a cigarette. His desk was flanked on three sides by tall filing cabinets. "I've been managing it for Mr. Dwyer's heirs the past twenty years."

"The office Mr. Cosgrove is in."

"Unit-Two-C."

"Can you tell me who rented it back then? I'm looking for the name of a dentist who used to be there."

"Why on earth would you want—"

"Some dental records. If it's a nuisance for you to look it up, I'll gladly pay you a service fee."

"Nuisance? Hell, it's the easiest thing in the world. The secret to managing property is being organized." He pivoted in his swivel chair and pushed its rollers toward a filing cabinet on his right that was marked D.

"Dwyer Building." He searched through files. "Here." He sorted through papers in it. "Sure. I remember now. Dr. Raymond Faraday. He had a heart attack. Eighteen years ago. Died in the middle of giving somebody a root canal."

After what I'd been through, the grotesqueness of his death somehow didn't seem unusual. "Did he have any relatives here? Are they still in town?"

"Haven't the faintest idea, but check this phone book."

3

"... a long time ago. Dr. Raymond Faraday. I'm trying to find a relative of his." Back at my car, I was using my cell phone. There'd been only two Faradays in the book. This was my second try.

"My husband's his son," a suspicious-sounding woman said. "Frank's at work now. What's this got to do with his father?"

I straightened. "When my brother and I were kids, Dr. Faraday was our dentist. It's very important that I get my brother's dental X rays. To identify him."

"Your brother's dead?"

"Yes."

"I'm so sorry."

"It would be very helpful if you could tell me what happened to the records."

"His patients took their records with them when they chose a new dentist."

"But what about patients who hadn't been his clients

for a while? My brother and I had stopped going to Dr. Faraday several years earlier."

"Didn't your parents transfer the records to your new dentist?"

"No." I remembered bitterly that after my father had died in the car accident and it turned out that his life-insurance policy had lapsed, my mother hadn't been able to afford things like taking me to a dentist.

The woman exhaled, as if annoyed about something. "I have no idea what my husband did with the old records. You'll have to ask him when he gets home from the office."

4

The baseball field hadn't changed. As the lowering sun cast my shadow, I stood at the bicycle rack where my friends and I had chained and locked our bikes so long ago. Behind me, the bleachers along the third-base line were crowded with parents yelling encouragement to kids playing what looked like a Little League game. I heard the crack of a ball off a bat. Cheers. Howls of disappointment. Other cheers. I assumed that a fly ball, seemingly a home run, had been caught.

But I kept my gaze on the bicycles, remembering how Petey had used a clothespin to attach a playing card to the front fender of his bike and how it had created a *clackclackclackclack* sound against the spokes when the wheel turned. It pained me that I couldn't remember the names of the two friends I'd been with and for whom I'd destroyed Petey's life. But I certainly remembered the gist of what we'd said.

"For crissake, Brad, your little brother's getting on my nerves. Tell him to beat it, would ya?"

"Yeah, he tags along everywhere. I'm tired of the little squirt. The friggin' noise his bike makes drives me nuts."

"He's just hanging around. He doesn't mean anything."

"Bull. How do you think my mom found out I was smoking if *he* didn't tell *your* mom?"

"We don't know for sure he told my mom."

"Then who *did* tell her, the goddamn tooth fairy?"

"All right, all right."

Petey had nearly bumped into me when I'd turned. I'd thought about that moment so often and so painfully that it was seared into my memory. He'd been short even for nine, and he'd looked even shorter because of his droopy jeans. His baseball glove had been too big for his hand.

"Sorry, Petey, you have to go home."

"But . . ."

"You're just too little. You'd hold up the game."

His eyes had glistened with the threat of tears.

To my later shame, I'd worried about what my friends would think if my kid brother started crying around them. "I mean it, Petey. Bug off. Go home. Watch cartoons or something."

His chin had quivered.

"Petey, I'm telling you, go. Scram. Get lost."

My friends had run toward where the other kids were choosing sides for the game. As I'd rushed to join them, I'd heard the *clackclackclack* of Petey's bike. I'd looked back toward where the little guy was pedaling away. His head was down.

Standing now by the bicycle rack, remembering how things had been, wishing with all my heart that I could return to that moment and tell my friends that they were jerks, that Petey was going to stay with me, I wept.

5

Unlike the baseball field, the house had changed a great deal. In fact, the whole street had. The trees were taller (to be expected), and there were more of them, as well as more shrubs and hedges. But those changes weren't what struck me. In my youth, the neighborhood had been all single-story ranch houses, modest homes for people who worked at the factory where my dad had been a foreman. But now second stories had been added to several of the houses, or rooms had been added to the back, taking away most of the rear yards. Both changes had occurred to the house I'd lived in. The front porch had been enclosed to add space to the living room. The freestanding single-car garage at the end of the driveway had been rebuilt into a double-car garage with stairs leading up to a room.

Parking across the street, seeing the red of the setting sun reflected off the house's windows, I was so startled by the change that I wondered if I'd made a mistake.

Maybe I wasn't on the right street (but the sign had clearly said Locust) or maybe this wasn't the right house (but the number 108 was fixed vertically next to the front door, just as it had been in my youth). I felt absolutely no identification with the place. In my memory, I saw a different, simpler house, the one from which my dad and I had hurried that evening, scrambling into his car, rushing toward the baseball diamond in hopes of finding Petey loitering along the way.

A wary man from the property next door came out and frowned at me, as if to say, What are you staring at?

I put the car in gear. As I drove away, I noticed half a dozen FOR SALE signs, remembering that in the old days everyone on the street had been so dependent on the furniture factory that no one had ever moved.

6

Mr. Faraday had thin lips and pinched cheeks. "My wife says your brother died or something?"

"Yes."

"That's why you need the dental records? To identify him?"

"He disappeared a long time ago. Now we might have found him."

"His body?"

"Yes."

"Well, if it wasn't something important like that, I wouldn't go to the trouble." Faraday motioned me into the house. I heard a television from the living room as he opened a door halfway along the corridor to the kitchen. The quick impression I got was of excessive neatness, everything in its place, plastic covers on chair arms in the living room, pots on hooks in the kitchen, lids above them, everything arranged by size.

Cool air rose from the open basement door. Faraday

flicked a light switch and gestured for me to follow. Our descending footsteps thumped on sturdy wooden stairs.

I'd never seen a basement so carefully organized. It was filled with boxes stacked in rows that formed minicorridors, but there wasn't the slightest sense of clutter and chaos.

Two fans whirred: from dehumidifiers at each end of the basement.

"I can't get rid of the dampness down here," Faraday said. He took me along one of the minicorridors, turned left, and came to a corner, where he lifted boxes off a footlocker.

"What can I do to help?" I asked.

"Nothing. I don't want to get things mixed up."

He raised the lid on the locker, revealing bundles of documents. "My wife complains about all the stuff I save, but how do I know what I might need later on?" Faraday pointed toward a stack of boxes farther along. "All my tax returns." He pointed toward another stack of boxes. "The bills I've paid. And *this* stuff . . ." He indicated the documents in the locker. "My father's business records. The ones I could find, anyway." He sorted through the bundles and came up with a stack of file folders. "What was your brother's name?"

"Peter Denning."

"Denning. Let's see. Denning. Denning. Ann. Brad. Nicholas. *Peter*. Here." His voice was filled with satisfaction as he held out the file.

I tried to keep my hand steady when I took it.

"What about these others? Do you want yours? Who are Ann and Nicholas?"

"My parents." I felt heavy in my chest. "Yes, if it's okay with you, I'll take them all."

"My wife'll be thrilled to see me getting rid of some of this stuff."

7

By the time I got back to the car, dusk had set in. I had to switch on the interior lights so I could see to search through Petey's file. No longer able to keep my hand from trembling, I pulled out a set of X rays. I'd never touched anything so valuable.

Back in Denver, when I'd gone to the dentist to get a copy of the X rays he'd taken of the man who claimed to be my brother, I'd made sure to get a duplicate set in case the FBI lost the ones I gave them or in case I needed copies in my search. Now I could barely wait to get to a motel. Driving to the outskirts of town, I picked the first one I saw that had a vacancy. After checking in, I rushed to my room, too hurried to bring everything from my car except my suitcase, which I yanked open, pulling out the X rays from Denver.

A child's teeth and an adult's have major differences, which made it difficult to tell if these X rays came from the same person. For one thing, when Petey had been kidnapped, some of his permanent teeth would not yet have grown in. But *some* of them would have, my dentist had said. Look at the roots, he'd said. On a particular tooth, are there three roots or four? Four are less common. Do the roots grow in any unusual directions?

With the adult's X rays in my left hand and the child's in my right, I held them up to my bedside lamp. But its shade blocked much of the illumination. I almost took off the shade before I thought of the bathroom and the bright lights that motels often have there. Hurrying past the bed, I found that this particular motel had a large mirror in front of a makeup area. When I jabbed the light switch, I blinked from the sudden glare above the mirror. After raising both sets of X rays to the fluorescent lights, I shifted my gaze quickly back and forth between them, desperate to find differences or similarities, frantic to learn the truth. The child's teeth looked so pathetically tiny. I imagined Petey's frightened helplessness as he was grabbed. The adult's. Whose *were* they? Slowly, I understood what I was looking at. As the implications swept over me, as the various pieces of information that I'd found began fitting into place, I lowered the X rays. I drooped my head. God help Kate and Jason, I prayed. God help us all.

8

An organ blared as I opened the church's front door: a solemn hymn I didn't recognize. To the right of the vestibule, stairs led up to the choir loft. They creaked as I climbed them. It was shortly after noon. I'd been to eleven Protestant churches before this one. With only six more to go, I was losing hope.

The choir loft was shadowy except for a light above the organ. As the minister finished the hymn, in the gathering silence my echoing footsteps made him turn.

"Sorry to bother you, Reverend." I walked nearer, holding out the photograph. "The secretary at your office said that you were almost done getting ready for choir practice. I'm trying to find this man. I wonder if you recognize him."

Puzzled, the minister took the photograph, pushed his glasses back on his nose, and studied it.

A long moment later, he nodded. "Possibly."

I tried not to show a reaction. Even so, my heart hammered so loudly that I was sure the minister could hear it.

"The intensity of the eyes is the same." The minister put the photograph under the organ's light. "But the man I'm thinking of has a beard." He pointed toward my own.

Beard? I'd been right. He'd grown a beard to hide his scar. "Perhaps if you put your hand over the lower part of his face." I tried to sound calm, despite the tension that squeezed my throat.

The minister did so. "Yes. I know this man." He looked suspicious. "Why do you want to find him?"

"I'm his brother." I managed to keep my hand steady as I shook hands with the minister. "Brad Denning."

"No. You're mistaken."

"Excuse me."

"Denning isn't Pete's last name. It's Benedict."

I didn't know what struck me more, that Petey was using his own first name or that he'd taken the last name of the minister who'd wanted to adopt him after the fire. My stomach soured. "So he still won't use the family name."

The minister frowned. "What do you mean?"

My heart pounded harder. "We used to live around here. But a long time ago, Pete and I had a falling-out. One of those family arguments that cause such bad feelings, it splits the family apart."

The minister nodded, evidently familiar with what that kind of argument had done to some families in his congregation.

"We haven't spoken to each other in years. But recently, I heard that he'd come back to town. This was the church we used to go to. So I thought someone here might have seen him."

"You want to be reconciled with him?"

"With everything that's in me, Reverend. But I don't know where he is."

"I haven't seen him since . . ." The minister thought about it. "Last July, when Mrs. Warren died. Of course, he was at the funeral. And before that, the last time I saw him was . . . Oh, probably two years. I'm not even sure he's in town any longer."

"Mrs. Warren?"

"She was one of the most faithful in the congregation. Only missed one service that I can remember. When Pete showed up two years ago and volunteered to do handiwork for the church for free, Mrs. Warren took a liking to him. She was amazed by how completely he could quote Scripture. Tried to trick him several times, but he always won."

"That was my dad's doing, teaching Pete the Good Book."

"Well, your father certainly did an excellent job. Mrs. Warren finally offered him a handyman's job on her property. Our loss, her gain. When she missed that service I mentioned, I was convinced she must be sick, so I telephoned her, and I was right—she had a touch of the flu. The next time she came to church, Pete wasn't with her. She told me that he'd decided to move on."

"Yeah, Pete was always like that. But you say he was here for her funeral?"

"Evidently, he'd come back and was working as her handyman again. In fact, the way I hear it, she left her place to him."

"Her place?"

"Well, she was elderly. Her husband was dead. So were her two children. I suppose she thought of Pete as the closest thing she had to family."

"Sounds like a kind old lady."

"Generous to a fault. And over the years, as she sold off portions of the farm her husband had worked—it was the only way for her to survive after her husband died—she made sure to let eighty acres around her house go wild for a game preserve. Believe me, the way this town's expanding, we could use more people like Mrs. Warren to preserve the countryside."

"Reverend, I'd appreciate two favors."

"Yes?" He looked curious from behind his glasses.

"The first is, if you see Pete before I do, for heaven's sake don't tell him that we've spoken. If he knows I'm trying to see him, I'm afraid he'll get so upset that he might leave town."

"Your argument was that serious?"

"Worse than you can imagine. I have to approach him in the right way and at the right time."

"What's the second favor you want?"

"How do I find Mrs. Warren's place?"

9

Two miles along a country road south of town, I reached a T intersection. I steered to the left, and as the minister had described, the paved road became gravel. My tires threw up dust that floated in my rearview mirror. Tense, I stared ahead, hoping that I wouldn't see a car or a truck coming toward me. The countryside was slightly hilly, and at the top of each rise, I was afraid that I'd suddenly come upon an approaching vehicle and that *he'd* be driving it. Maybe he wouldn't pay attention, a quick glimpse of another driver, but maybe he paid attention to everything. Or maybe he wouldn't recognize me with my beard, but if he did, or if he recognized Kate's Volvo (Jesus, why hadn't I thought to bring another car?), I'd lose my chance of surprising him. I'd have even less chance of finding Kate and Jason.

Sweating, my shirt sticking to my chest, I saw the expanse of thick timber and undergrowth that the minister had said would be on my left. I passed a mailbox, a

closed gate, and a lane that disappeared into the forest.
Mrs. Warren's house was back there, the minister had
said, where she could watch the deer, the squirrels, the
raccoons, and the rest of what she'd called "God's children" roaming around the property. Relieved that I hadn't
seen anybody and hence that no one had seen me, I kept
driving, more dust rising behind me. At the same time, I
couldn't help worrying that the reason I hadn't seen any
activity was that Petey wasn't there, that he'd moved on.

Petey.

Yes.

Each X ray had shown a particular tooth with four
roots that grew in distinctive directions. The child's had
been smaller and less pronounced than the man's.
Nonetheless, it hadn't been difficult to see that one had
evolved into the other. Not that I'd relied on my opinion.
Before going to the various churches, I'd made sure to be
at a dentist's office when it opened. With cash I'd gotten
from a local bank, I'd paid the dentist a hundred dollars
to examine the X rays before he attended to his scheduled
patients. He'd agreed with me: Man and boy — the X rays
had belonged to the same person.

So there it was. The man who'd claimed to be my
brother had told the truth. The FBI had been wrong.
Lester Dant hadn't assumed Petey's identity. *Petey* had
assumed *Lester's*. But that disturbing discovery settled
nothing. The reverse. It prompted far more unnerving
questions to threaten my sanity.

This was clear. After Petey had tricked the police into
thinking that he was heading west through Montana, he'd
taken Kate and Jason in the reverse direction — back to
Woodford. Because he no longer had to lay a false trail by

abandoning vehicles that he'd carjacked, it wouldn't have been hard to avoid capture. All he had to do was carjack a vehicle that had a license for a distant state. The driver wouldn't have been expected for several days. By the time he or she was reported missing, Petey would have reached Mrs. Warren's property and hidden the car. Meanwhile, he'd have switched license plates several times and hidden the car owner's body somewhere along the interstate.

Mrs. Warren. Petey had been confident that he could intimidate her, because that's what he'd done a year earlier. At the church where I'd learned about Petey and Mrs. Warren, the minister had mentioned that Petey was Mrs. Warren's handyman, that she never missed Sunday service except for an uncharacteristic absence one Sunday two years earlier, *one* year before Petey took Kate and Jason from me. Petey must have done something so dismaying to Mrs. Warren that she found it impossible to go to church that Sunday. When the minister phoned her, certain that only something dire would have kept her away, she'd claimed that she had the flu. The next Sunday, she'd been in church again. Meanwhile, she'd said, Petey had left the area.

The minister's phone call had probably saved Mrs. Warren's life. His concern for her must have made Petey think that the minister was suspicious, must have driven Petey away. But when Mrs. Warren felt safe, why hadn't she confessed the horrors that had happened out there? The answer wasn't hard to figure. Like Mrs. Garner in Loganville, she'd been ashamed to let the other church members know what Petey had done to her. What's more,

Petey had no doubt terrified her with a threat to return and punish her if she caused trouble for him.

Maybe she started feeling secure again, but then, to her fright, Petey came back a year later. He might have found a way to hide Kate and Jason from her. No matter—her torment resumed. He intimidated her severely enough to make her put him in her will. "He feels like a son to me," she'd have been forced to tell her lawyer, coached to sound convincing. Petey would have stood next to her in the lawyer's office when she signed the document, a reminder of his warning that if she turned against him, he'd make sure that she spent her remaining years in agony. Then he'd have kept her a prisoner at the house while he dropped a word here and there among the congregation that she hadn't been feeling well lately. That way, people would have been prepared when she died. After all, as the minister had said, Mrs. Warren was elderly. Maybe one night she passed away in her sleep— with help from a pillow pressed over her face.

As I sped back to town, I used my cell phone to call Special Agent Gader, but his receptionist told me that he wouldn't be in the office for a couple of days. I phoned Payne's office but got a recording that said he wouldn't be in the office for the rest of the week. I had a hollow feeling in the pit of my stomach that told me his wife's biopsy hadn't been good.

That left getting in touch with the local police, but when I parked outside the station (the same brick building from years ago), I had a disturbing image of policemen piling into squad cars and rushing out to Mrs. Warren's. I feared that their arrival would be so obvious that if Petey *was* in that house, he'd notice them coming and escape out the back. I might never learn what he'd done with Kate and Jason. Even if the police *did* manage to capture him, suppose he refused to answer questions? Suppose he denied knowing anything about where Kate and Jason were hidden? If they were still alive, they might starve or suffocate while he remained silent. Think it through, I warned myself. I needed more information. I couldn't trust the police to go after him until I knew exactly how they should do it.

10

The pilot said something that I couldn't quite hear amid the drone of the single-engine plane.

I turned to her. "Excuse me?"

"I said, Woodford's over there."

I glanced to the right, toward where she pointed. The sprawl of low buildings, old and new, stretched toward the interstate.

She put so much meaning into the statement that I shook my head from side to side. "I don't understand."

"You told me you wanted to see how the old hometown looked from the air."

"More or less."

"Seems like less. You've barely looked in that direction. What you're interested in are those farms up ahead."

We flew closer to the eighty-acre section of woods and underbrush. Although the day was sunny, there was a touch of wind. Once in a while, the plane dipped slightly.

"You're a developer, aren't you?"

"What?"

"We've had our share of development the last five years. Seems like every time I look, there's a new subdivision."

It was an easier explanation than the truth. "Yeah, too much change can be overwhelming."

I stared down at the large dense section of trees. I saw the lane leading into it from the gravel road. I saw a clearing about a hundred yards into it where a brick house was surrounded by grass and gardens.

I'd bought one of those pocket cameras that had a zoom lens. Now I pulled it out and started taking photographs.

11

Back in my motel room, I spread out the eight-by-tens on a table. I'd paid a photographer to stay open after hours and process them. Now it was after dark. My eyes ached. To help keep me alert, I turned on the television — CNN — and as an announcer droned in the background, I picked up a magnifying glass and leaned down over the photographs. They were slightly blurred from the plane's vibration. Nonetheless, they showed me what I needed.

One thing was immediately obvious. No one would have noticed it at ground level, where the front, sides, and back of the house couldn't be viewed simultaneously. But when seen from above, the grass and gardens in back of the house looked different from those at the sides and the front. They seemed to have had work done on them recently. The area seemed slightly lower than the others.

Sunken? I wondered. As when ground settles after it's been dug up and then refilled?

In the background, the CNN announcer explained that

a distraught man with a gun was holding his ex-wife and his daughter prisoner in a house in Los Angeles. A police SWAT team surrounded it. With greater intensity, I stared through the magnifying glass at the photos, confirming that a section of grass and garden in back of the house did appear slightly lower than what was around it.

I noticed a blue pickup truck parked next to the house. I studied a stream that wound through the middle of the woods in back. But what I kept returning to was that area behind the house. The grass seemed greener there, the bushes fuller, as if they were getting more attention than those at the front and the sides.

I set down the magnifying glass and tried to calm myself. There was nothing sinister about relandscaping, the police would say. A blighted lawn and old bushes had been replaced with healthy ones. But what if the lawn and bushes had been replaced because something had been built under them?

On the television behind me, the announcer reported that the hostage situation had ended badly. As the police tightened their circle around the building, the man had shot his daughter and his ex-wife, then pulled the trigger on himself.

I stared at the television.

12

When I'd driven past Mrs. Warren's property, I'd made the mistake of using Kate's Volvo. Petey might have recognized it. This time, I drove only to the outskirts of town, where I left the car among others at a shopping mall. I put on my knapsack and hiked into the countryside.

As in most midwestern farm communities, the road system was laid out in a grid that contained squares or rectangles of land. Avoiding the road that fronted Mrs. Warren's property, I took an indirect route that added several miles, coming at the wooded eighty acres from the road behind. Under a bright, hot sun, I hiked past fields, past cattle grazing, past farmers tending their crops. I adjusted my baseball cap and moved my fanny pack to a more comfortable spot on my waist, trying to look as if I didn't have a care in the world, that I was merely out for a pleasant day of walking. In truth, I wanted desperately to run. The adrenaline burning through me needed exertion to keep it controlled. If I didn't do something to vent the pressure swelling inside me, I feared I'd go crazy. To my right, across a field, the woods got larger. Nearer. Kate and Jason. They're alive, I told myself. They have to be.

Worried about being noticed crossing the field toward the woods, I waited until a car went by and there wasn't any other traffic. The stream that I'd seen in the photographs crossed the field and went under the road. I climbed down to it. Its banks were high enough that I was out of view as I walked next to the water. In contrast with the stark sun, the air was cool down there.

After five minutes, the stream entered the trees. I ducked under a fence, climbed the slippery bank, and found myself among maples, oaks, and elms. The noise I made in the undergrowth troubled me, but who would hear me? Petey wasn't going to be patrolling his fences, guarding his property against intruders. The logical place for him to be was at the house. Or maybe he'd be off somewhere, committing God knew what crimes.

The forest cast a shadow. A spongy layer of dead leaves smelled damp and moldy. I wiped my sweat-gritted face, took off my knapsack, and pulled out a holster that I'd bought that morning. It was attached to the right side of a sturdy belt. My spare fifteen-round magazine was in a pouch to the left, along with two other newly purchased magazines. A hunting knife went next to it and a five-inch long, thumb-width flashlight called Surefire, which the clerk in the gun shop had shown me was surprisingly powerful for its size. I took the pistol from my fanny pack and shoved it into the holster. The weight of the equipment dug into my waist.

Thirsty from nervousness, I sipped water from one of

three canteens in the knapsack. I ate a stick of beef jerky and several handfuls of mixed peanuts and raisins. Uneasiness made me urinate. Then I put on the knapsack and pulled a compass from my shirt pocket. Unlike a year ago, I'd taken the time to learn how to use it. Remembering the photographs, estimating the angle that I needed to follow in order to reach the house, I took a southeast direction, making my way through the trees.

All the while, I listened for suspicious noises in the forest. The scrape of a branch might have been Petey creeping toward me, but it turned out to be a squirrel racing up a tree. The snap of a twig startled me, until I realized that it was a rabbit bounding away. Birds fluttered. Wary, I scanned the undergrowth, studied my compass again, and moved cautiously forward.

The next time I stopped to get a drink, I checked my watch, surprised to find that what had seemed like thirty minutes had actually been two hours. The air felt thicker. Sweat stuck my shirt and jeans to me. I took another step and immediately dropped to a crouch, seeing where the trees thinned.

On my stomach, I squirmed through the undergrowth, the moldy smell of the earth widening my nostrils. I crawled slowly, trying not to move bushes and reveal my position. From having designed homes for wealthy clients, I was familiar with intrusion detectors. I watched for anything ahead of me, motion sensors on posts or a wire that might be attached to a vibration detector. Nothing struck me as unusual. In fact, now that I thought about it, an intrusion detector would be useless in the woods. The animals roaming about would trigger it.

Animals? I suddenly realized that for a while I hadn't

noticed *any* animals. Nor **a** single bird. The sense of barrenness reminded me of what I'd felt at the Dant farm.

Snakes? I studied the ground ahead of me. Nothing rippled. Taking a deep breath, I squirmed forward. The trees became more sparse, the bushes less thick. Peering through low branches, I saw a clearing. A lawn. A flower garden.

In the middle was the redbrick house. I'd come at it from its right side. The two-and-a-half-story wall had ivy. White wooden lawn furniture and a brightly colored miniature windmill decorated the lawn.

I took binoculars from my knapsack and made sure that the sun wasn't at an angle that would cause a reflection off the lenses. Then I focused them and studied the downstairs and upstairs windows. All had lace curtains. Nothing moved beyond them. In the photographs I'd taken, the pickup truck had been parked on the opposite side of the house, so to find out if it was still there, I'd have to crawl around to that side.

I stayed as flat as possible while I shifted through the undergrowth. When I came within view of the back of the house, I still didn't see movement in any of the windows. I stared at the open area behind the house, which from ground level seemed to have a natural slope, its slightly sunken outline no longer apparent. An unsuspecting visitor would have noticed nothing unusual about it, except that the lawn and gardens were attractive. If there was indeed a room beneath it, I assumed that Petey watered and fertilized that area frequently to compensate for the shallow roots that the underground structure would cause. If so, today wasn't his day to work in the garden. He wasn't in sight. The place seemed abandoned.

I dared to hope that I'd gotten lucky, that he wasn't home. But as I crept through the bushes toward the other side of the house, my stomach soured when I saw the pickup truck where it had been the previous afternoon. Angry, I continued through the undergrowth on that side of the house, coming to a view of the front, where a roofed porch had a rocking chair and a hammock, homey and inviting.

But no one was visible there, either, and I retreated to a sheltered spot that gave me a view of the side, part of the back, part of the front, and all of the truck. Bushes enclosed me. I eased out of my knapsack, sipped from one of the canteens, ate more beef jerky, peanuts, and raisins.

And waited.

13

Hours later, I was still waiting. The sun eased below the trees. Seeing a light come on in a downstairs window, I felt my muscles compact. Then a light came on in an adjacent room, and another farther over. I strained to see movement through the curtains, but the house continued to seem deserted. For all I knew, the lights were controlled by timers. When an upstairs light came on and a shadow moved past a window, I held my breath for a moment.

A *man's* shadow. I was certain of it. I'd caught only a glimpse, but the broad shoulders and forceful stride obviously didn't belong to a female. Several seconds later, the shadow appeared downstairs, going from one room to another. Raising my binoculars, I strained to see through the windows and suddenly focused on a man with a beard. His face was toward me for only a few seconds before he went through an archway into the kitchen.

But a few seconds were all I needed. Regardless of the

beard, I couldn't fail to recognize him. Even through binoculars, the solid shoulders and the intense eyes were unmistakable.

The man was Petey.

"Go home," I'd told him. After a lifetime of being lost, he'd done exactly that. He'd come back to Woodford. Did he ever drive by the house where we used to live? Did he ever go to the baseball field and remember that afternoon, brooding about how different his life would have been if I hadn't preferred my friends over him and sent him away from that baseball game?

Stop thinking like that! I warned myself. Get control! Guilt and regret weren't going to change the past. They were a weakness. They could get me killed. They could get *Kate and Jason* killed.

Petey wasn't my brother any longer.

He was my enemy.

My impulse was to crawl from my hiding place, reach the window, wait for him to step into view again, and shoot. But what if I missed? My hand was shaking enough to throw off my aim. Or what if Petey noticed me outside the window before I could pull the trigger? Suppose he ducked out of sight and used Kate and Jason as hostages? Or what if I did manage to shoot him, but Kate and Jason weren't where I suspected they were?

Shoot to wound him? How did I know the wound wouldn't be more serious than I intended? Petey might die before I could question him. I'd have lost the chance to find Kate and Jason.

Stay put. Think it through, I warned myself. If I make a wrong move, it'll be the same thing I was afraid the police would do.

I had to keep watching the house. I needed to get a sense of his patterns. When I phoned the police, it had to be at the right time.

When the situation was in my favor.

Sure. And when the hell will *that* be? I wondered.

In the darkness, the air was damp and chill, making me pull a woolen shirt from the knapsack and put it on. It didn't warm me. As Petey's indistinct shape prepared food in the kitchen, I told myself that I should eat also, but I didn't have any appetite. Acid burned my stomach.

Eat! I told myself. I forced a chunk of beef jerky into my mouth and reluctantly chewed. The side dish was another handful of nuts and raisins, the dessert dehydrated apples. I had thought about bringing sandwiches, but I'd been worried that they would spoil and make me ill. After all, I had no idea how long I'd have to stay in the woods and watch the house. That was why I'd brought three canteens of water. Determined to conserve it, I took only a few sips to help me swallow the dehydrated apples.

How long would the police have been willing to hide like this? I wondered. They'd have swatted at the mosquitoes buzzing around them. They'd have felt the cold seeping through their clothes, the dampness sticking their pants to their legs. They'd have thought about hot coffee and a warm bed, someone to share it with. They'd soon have lost their patience and stormed the house.

I buttoned the woolen shirt all the way to my neck but still felt a chill. Raising the binoculars again, I stared through a window, through an archway toward the kitchen, which was on the far side of the house. There, Petey continued to prepare food. Eventually, his silhouette disappeared.

My muscles cramped from not having moved in quite a while. My arms and neck ached from keeping the binoculars raised. Minutes passed. I checked the luminous dial on my watch. A quarter of an hour became half an hour. When a full hour had passed, I couldn't ignore the pressure in my bladder. I crawled back from where I was hiding, stopped among trees, and urinated close to the ground, doing my best to make as little noise as possible.

The moment I returned through the bushes, the light went out in the kitchen. I tensed, watching Petey's shadow move from room to room downstairs, turning off the lights. A minute later, one of the upstairs lights went off also. I spent an hour gazing at the remaining upstairs light. Then it, too, went out.

The sky was overcast, hiding the stars. The house remained dark. I hugged myself, trying to keep warm. My eyelids grew heavy. I fought to keep them open, turning from the house toward the murky lawn and garden in back, under which, I was certain, Kate and Jason were imprisoned. So close. Have to get to them. Have to . . . My eyelids fluttered shut. I sank to the ground and drifted into sleep.

14

A door banged, jolting me from a nightmare of being whipped. My eyes snapped open. I jerked my head up enough to be able to see through low bushes toward the house. The clouds had passed. The sun was behind me, glinting off windows across from me. The reflection stabbed my eyes, aggravating a headache. A breeze from the day before had strengthened, ruffling bushes. The movement of the leaves around me must have been the source of my nightmare about being whipped.

I stared toward the back of the house, where I'd heard the door bang. Petey came into view. He wore a light green shirt, which contrasted with his dark beard. I recognized the shirt. It was one that he'd stolen from me a year earlier. The wind tousled his thick dark hair. He peered around, assessing the woods, then pulled a hose from a hook on the wall and went over to the area behind the house. Watering several bushes, he confirmed my suspicion that something beneath the ground caused shallow roots in need of frequent care. The wind sometimes sprayed the water back at him, eventually annoying him enough that he dropped the hose, went to the back wall to shut off the water, and returned to the house.

The sun's reflection off windows prevented me from seeing what he was doing inside. After a half hour, the wind had parched my lips so much that I reached for a canteen, only to stop when I heard another door bang, this one at the front. Petey came onto the porch. He'd changed his spray-soaked green shirt for a gray one. It, too, had belonged to me. He raised his head, almost as if he was sniffing the breeze. That's what my brother had become: an animal assessing if there was danger. Because of me.

Stop thinking that way! I again warned myself.

He came down the porch steps and rounded the house, making my pulse quicken when he got into the truck and fastened his seat belt. The truck was faced in my direction but away from the sun's glare, so that I saw his beard and his stark eyes through the windshield before he made a U-turn. Dust blew as he drove down the lane, the blue of the truck soon vanishing among the windswept trees.

For a moment, I was sure that my mind had played a trick on me. Had I actually seen what I most wanted to see? Was the sound of the truck actually diminishing in the distance? For several long minutes, I didn't move. Perhaps Petey had only gone to check the mailbox at the road and would soon be coming back. Or perhaps he had somehow suspected that someone was watching the house and had driven away in order to lure an intruder into the open. As soon as I started toward the house, would he shoot me from where he'd sneaked back and was watching from the trees?

The sun rose higher. The wind grew stronger, buffeting the bushes I hid among. But it didn't cool me. Instead, the morning seemed unduly warm. Sweat dried immediately on my dust-caked cheeks. Nervous, I checked my watch and saw that fifteen minutes had passed. If Petey had merely gone to the mailbox, he'd have been back by now, I told myself. I scanned the woods where the driveway disappeared into them. But the wind kept shifting the leaves and prevented me from noticing any movement where he might be hiding, watching for an intruder.

I stared toward the bushes behind the house. The police. Use the cell phone, I thought. But as I reached for it, I worried that if Petey was watching from another part of the forest, he'd hear me. Instead of muffling what I said, the wind might carry my voice directly to him.

Or what if Petey wasn't alone? What if someone else was in the house and would hear my voice as I used the phone? To prevent that from happening, I'd have to retreat several hundred yards into the forest before I felt safe using the phone, but that would mean losing sight of the farmhouse, and there was no telling what might happen while I was away.

The sun rose higher, no longer reflecting off the windows. Nothing moved beyond them. Last night, I'd seen no other silhouette, only Petey's. Was it safe to assume that he was alone? The police wouldn't be able to get here in time before he got back. Damn it, this might be my only chance. I crawled through the undergrowth toward the back of the house. If Petey was watching from the trees in front, he wouldn't be able to see me approach from the rear.

Squirming through low branches, I came to the edge of the clearing. I checked again for any movement behind the lace curtains. Then I drew my pistol and hurried into the open. The wind tried to push me back. I reached a lilac bush, used it for cover, then darted toward a grape arbor, which screened me while I studied the house a final time. I sprinted to the back wall and pressed against its sun-warmed bricks.

Steps rose to the back door. At the top, I raised my head warily to peer through a window. Beyond gauzy curtains, I had an indistinct view of a kitchen, cupboards, a sink, and a stove on the right, an archway and a refrigerator on the left. A small table was in the middle. A single chair suggested that Petey lived by himself.

What I started worrying about now was that Petey might have a dog, a pit bull, for example, trained not to show itself until an intruder entered the house, at which time the dog would tear the intruder apart. It would make sense for Petey to have one, but the more I thought about it, the more I doubted that he did. I'd been watching the house for over twelve hours, and Petey hadn't let a dog out to relieve itself. True, Petey might have done so while I was asleep. But wouldn't the dog have picked up my scent and attacked me? And unless Petey was super-scrupulous about cleaning up after his dog, wouldn't I have seen dog droppings on the lawn? Besides, a dog locked in the house would limit Petey's ability to stay away for periods of time. He could leave food for Kate and Jason in their prison. But it would be harder to leave enough for a big dog to survive for any length of time, and that didn't take into consideration the mess that the dog would make in the house.

No, I was increasingly convinced that Petey didn't have a dog. But on the off-chance that he did, I prepared to shoot it.

I tried the back door. No surprise—it was locked. I was going to have to smash the window, reach through, and open the lock from the other side. I changed my position so that I could look down through the window and see the area above the doorknob. The handle of a lock came into view. After I smashed the window, all I needed to do was reach through, twist the lock's handle, and . . .

Maybe only an architect or somebody in construction would have been bothered. The lock was a deadbolt, a type that I recommended. On the outside, the only way to get in was to use a key. But on the *inside*, there could be two ways to open the lock, depending on how it was installed. If there wasn't a window through which an intruder could reach, a handle on the lock was both convenient and safe. But in the case of a window, the secure way to install the lock was to use another key arrangement rather than a lock with a handle. That way, even if an intruder broke the window and reached through, he couldn't free the lock unless he had a key.

So, did it make sense for Petey to have a superior lock and an inferior installation? Granted, Mrs. Warren might have been the one who'd had the lock put in. But would Petey, with every reason to be cautious, have ignored the security lapse? I doubted it.

As I brooded about the problem, something else troubled me. The door had been installed so that it opened toward the cupboards on the right rather than toward an open space on the left, an inconvenient arrangement that prevented the door from being opened to its full range and that risked damaging the cupboards if the door was opened forcefully.

Nervous, I used the butt of my pistol to smash the window. With the barrel of the pistol, I carefully pulled the curtains toward me. Once they were outside the window, I yanked them loose, gaining a clear view of the kitchen, at least of the parts that I could see. I went back down the steps. Exposing myself to the wind, I found a dead branch on a shrub, broke it free, and snapped off the twigs. I wanted a dead branch rather than a live one because I needed the branch to be stiff. I climbed the steps again and peered down through the gap in the window. Careful not to show my head or hands, I put the branch through the broken window and pressed down on one side of the lock's handle, which was horizontal rather than round and thus could be manipulated with the stick. Moving, the lock made a scraping sound. Ready with my pistol, I turned the doorknob, stayed where I was, and pushed inward.

The shocking blast made me flinch as a ten-inch jagged hole appeared in the opened door. My ears hurt as if they'd been slapped. The stench of gunpowder widened my nostrils.

Taking a deep breath to steady myself, I inched my head forward and peered cautiously through the doorway. To the left, I saw a pantry area, where hinges on a doorjamb showed that a door had been taken off. In the pantry, a shotgun had been mounted to a worktable. A strong cord had been attached to its trigger. The cord went around a pulley behind the shotgun, then up to another

pulley, and finally overhead to a metal hook at the top of
the door on the inside. The tension on the cord had been
adjusted so that the shotgun would go off only when the
door was opened a certain distance, allowing for the intruder to show himself before the shotgun detonated.

The massive hole in the door made me wonder what
the blast would have done to my midsection. Sickened, I
warned myself not to get distracted. I still couldn't be
sure that Petey didn't have a dog.

Uneasy, I aimed toward the only other entrance to the
kitchen: the archway on the left. The ringing in my ears
prevented me from hearing anything else. I saw no
movement.

I stepped into the house.

15

The wind strengthened. When I shut the door, the gusts came through the broken window and the jagged hole beneath it. As urgent as I felt, I moved slowly. When I passed the kitchen table, my architect's training again warned me about something. The archway on the left was the only other entrance to the kitchen. That didn't make sense. There should have also been a door straight ahead that would give easy access to what I assumed were stairs in front leading up to the second story. The way the rooms on the ground floor were laid out, someone coming down from the second story had to take an indirect route from the front hall, through the rooms on the other side of the house, and finally into the kitchen. Mrs. Warren, who was elderly, wouldn't have tolerated the inconvenience. The wall straight ahead wasn't being used for anything. It would have been easy and logical to install a door there. Why hadn't it been done?

Maybe there *had* been a door in that wall at one time,

I thought. I stepped closer, noticing a slight difference between the top molding on the wall in front of me as opposed to the molding on the wall to my left. The white paint on the wall ahead of me looked slightly brighter than the white paint to my left. The plaster felt smoother. Someone had put a new wall over the doorway, preventing access to the front hall.

Had Petey done it? Why? Even for a young man, the indirect route into the kitchen would be a nuisance. Why had he deliberately wanted it?

The only answer I could think of was that Petey had blocked the other door because he wanted to force an intruder to go the long way through the house. He'd set other traps.

Of course. The kitchen didn't have a door that led down to the basement. The entrance to it must be in the front hall. But to reach it, an intruder would have to go through the other rooms.

As the wind howled, I stared through the archway toward the room on my left. I noticed a broom next to the refrigerator and waved it through the archway, moving it up and down and from side to side, checking that there weren't any other triggering devices (electronic beams, for example) linked to weapons.

Nothing happened.

I pressed the hard end of the broom onto a carpet that led through the archway.

The floor was solid. I entered the dining room, scanned its long table, chairs, and sideboard, saw no obvious further traps, and stepped toward another archway. Through it, I could see old padded chairs and a sofa in what Mrs. Warren would probably have called the parlor.

I tested another section of carpet and stepped toward the front room.

Crack! The floor gave way. My stomach surged toward my heart. Plummeting, I lurched forward, slamming my chest against the edge of the trapdoor. As the pistol and the broom flew from my hands, I clawed at the wooden floor. My hands slid. I hooked my fingers over the edge and dangled. Frantic, I peered down at a section of the basement that had been enclosed. Through a wooden platform below me, knives protruded, four inches apart in every direction, so that it wasn't possible to land among them and not be injured. One end of the carpet was attached to the floor, dangling rather than falling onto the points below and preventing them from impaling me. I'd have bled to death if I hadn't died instantly.

My arms ached as I strained to pull myself up. But I tested the floor! I thought. How the hell did I get fooled? The trapdoor must have been rigged to spring open only if a certain amount of weight was applied to it. Petey must have stepped over it when he passed through the archway. I strained harder to pull myself up and managed to prop my elbows on the trapdoor's edge. Slowly, I squirmed into the parlor. On my back on the floor, I breathed deeply. Trying to steady myself, I listened to the wind.

Petey might come back any minute, I thought.

I reached for the pistol and the broom, which had flown from my hands when I'd fallen. But caution instantly controlled me. Trying to subdue my too-fast breathing, I scanned the faded furniture, the ceiling, the corners. Nothing seemed to threaten me. Through the front windows, I studied the lane leading into the windblown forest. Petey's truck didn't speed into view. Keep moving! I told myself. Staying to the edge of the room, I pushed a chair ahead of me, wary of other traps.

To the right of the front windows, an archway led to a corridor. Stairs went up. On a landing beyond the front door, another shotgun had been rigged. As before, a cord was attached to the trigger. The cord looped back through two pulleys and connected to a hook on top of the door. When the door was opened and someone stepped through, the shotgun would blow the intruder in half. It wouldn't have been difficult for Petey to attach the cord to the hook as he pulled the door shut or for him to un-hook the cord when he returned and opened the door just enough for him to reach his hand up. For anyone who didn't suspect, though, death would have been instanta-neous.

Had I found all the traps? Straining my eyes, I studied the corridor. I fixed my gaze on a door beneath the stair-way. I was sure that it would take me down to the base-ment. Kate and Jason were only a couple of hundred feet away.

The floor had no carpet. It looked solid. Nonetheless, I stayed to the edge of the hallway and inched along. When I came to the door beneath the stairs, I tested the knob. It turned freely in my hand. But another trap might be behind it. So I pulled the flashlight from my belt, gently opened the door an inch, and scanned the light up and down, looking for a cord.

The area beyond was totally dark. Warily opening the door a few inches farther, I smelled something bitter, like camphor.

Mothballs.

I opened the door farther, aimed the flashlight, and saw coats and dresses on a rod. A closet. No! Furious, I used the blunt end of the broom to prod among the clothes. I tapped the floor. The walls. Nothing sounded hollow. Where the hell was the entrance to the basement?

Hurry! I thought.

I remembered the previous night when I'd watched Petey's silhouette through the window. He'd been cooking. Then his silhouette had disappeared. I'd assumed that he'd been eating in an area of the kitchen that was out of my view.

But what if he'd taken the food to Kate and Jason?

In the kitchen? *How?* There wasn't a door to the basement.

A shock of understanding hit me. Trying not to let my eagerness make me careless, I returned the way I'd come. I paused only once: to look through the front windows, past the windswept shrubs, and check if Petey's truck was returning. Then I stepped over the open trapdoor between the parlor and the dining room, rushing into the kitchen.

The pantry. I tapped the walls behind the canned goods on the shelves. They sounded solid. I glanced down at the floor, realized what Petey had done, and grabbed the workbench upon which the shotgun had been secured. Tugging it away, I saw the outline of another trapdoor. This one had a ring. I pulled upward and stared down at wooden steps descending into darkness.

16

"Kate! Jason!"

The names echoed back to me.

No one shouted in return.

I tilted the trapdoor back so that it rested against the shelves behind it. I positioned the workbench so that if the trapdoor accidentally fell, it would be stopped before it slammed down and possibly locked. Then I aimed my flashlight into the darkness, saw a switch on a post about five steps down, and tested the first step as I eased down to turn on the basement lights.

No, I warned myself. Petey wouldn't booby-trap the ground floor and not do something to the basement, as well. I'd gotten this far because I'd put myself in his place. I thought like him. What would Petey have done to protect the basement?

The broomstick remained in my hand. I tilted it downward, flicked the switch. . . .

And stumbled back from an arc of electricity that shot

from the switch, blackening the stick. The flash was blinding, the force so great that it knocked the stick from my hand. I felt a tingle in my palm where the current had started to reach me.

Smoke rose from the fake switch. Smelling burned wires, I aimed the flashlight again and went cautiously down a few more steps. I eased my weight onto each of them, always gripping one behind me for support in case a step broke away. The lower I got, the less I heard the wind. I scanned the flashlight across the basement, seeing boxes, a handyman's bench, tools on the wall above it, shelves of preserves, a washing machine, a dryer, an oil furnace, a laundry tub, and a water heater. A window above the laundry tub had been boarded over. The walls and floor were old concrete. The ceiling had pipes, wires, and joists exposed. Everything smelled of mold.

I eased lower and saw a switch on another post, this one at the bottom. Reaching it, I picked up the broomstick where it had fallen. Once more, I flicked with the stick, and this time, the switch was real. Lights glowed in the basement's ceiling: dim lights—sixty-watt bulbs—but nonetheless they made me squint.

"Kate! Jason!"

Again, my shouts echoed.

Again, no muffled voices answered me.

I oriented myself. The wall that faced the area behind the house was on my left. There wasn't a door, only a tall object like a bookshelf on which there were jars of preserved peaches and pears. I studied it from various angles, looking for another trap. I stepped protectively to the left and pushed with the broomstick.

The shelves slid away.

I inched my head around the corner, peering into the opening. The tunnel was about fifteen feet long. Its concrete was smooth and new-looking. Petey had imitated the arrangement that Orval Dant had used, with the difference that instead of a wooden ceiling, Petey had chosen concrete.

At the end was a metal-covered door. It had a deadbolt lock, but *this* one didn't have a knob that needed to be turned. Instead, it had a slot for a key, and I didn't have a doubt in the world that the door was locked.

I wanted to rush to it, but I hesitated. Why had Petey gone to the extra effort of building the tunnel instead of putting the cell directly next to the house? The latter setup would have been quicker and easier. Had Petey merely been imitating the arrangement that Orval had used? Or did the tunnel contain an additional trap?

I studied the bare floor, the walls, and the ceiling, unable to see a threat. About to yell to Kate and Jason again, I abruptly understood the purpose for the tunnel. If a stranger came down to the basement, Kate and Jason would be too far away to hear or be heard.

But how was I going to open the door? Noticing that its hinges were on the tunnel side, I turned to the right, toward the workbench. I grabbed a hammer and a chisel. . . .

And stopped, a sound paralyzing me.

Something dripped. In the stillness of the basement, the slight noise seemed magnified. I focused on the laundry tub, but its taps were secure. No water leaked from them.

Drip. I turned, trying to identify the direction from which the sound came. *Drip. Drip.* Steady. Relentless.

My attention focused beneath the stairs. On a pipe projecting from the wall. *Drip. Drip.* Then I smelled it. *Drip.* Gasoline. Trickle. Gasoline was coming from the pipe, spreading across the concrete floor. The flow must have been activated when I'd pressed the fake switch on the stairs. Petey's final trap. If all else failed, when enough fuel emptied onto the floor, a detonator would ignite it. The house and the intruder, the evidence against Petey—everything would be obliterated.

Clutching the hammer and the chisel, I raced into the tunnel. My frenzied movements echoed as I tried the doorknob and confirmed that it was locked. I held the chisel beneath the head of a hinge pin and hammered upward, freeing it. The pin clanged onto the floor. I did the same to the two other pins and pulled at the hinges, straining to free the door.

"Kate, I'm here!" I pounded on the door. "Jason, it's Dad! I'll get you out!"

But they didn't pound on the other side of the door. I didn't hear any muffled shouts answering me.

The door wouldn't budge. I stared at the key mechanism, hoping that I could unscrew its plate and disassemble the lock, but Petey had drilled the heads off the screws.

I used the chisel and the hammer to pound at the concrete next to the lock. Chunks flew. My arms ached as I pounded harder. Larger chunks fell away. I worried about causing sparks that might detonate the fumes, but I didn't have a choice. I had to do something, *anything,* before the house exploded. I hoped to expose the lock's bolt, but what I came to was a stout metal sleeve into which the bolt had been seated. For all I knew, the metal sleeve went several feet into the side of the wall. It would take me all day to pound away that much concrete.

I ran back to the workbench and scanned the tools above it, looking for a crowbar. There wasn't one. I swung toward a shovel and a hoe next to the bench, looking for an ax with which I could try to chop through the metal-covered door.

There wasn't one.

The smell of the gasoline was stronger. I saw a three-foot section of pipe on the floor, probably left over from a trap. I ignored it, stared again at the tools above the workbench, looked back at the pipe, and grabbed it. Gagging on fumes, I raced along the tunnel. I used the chisel and the hammer to pound at the concrete next to the middle hinge. Again, chunks flew. My arms cramped. Ignoring the pain, I hammered more fiercely against the chisel. My aim missed. I struck my fist, screamed, ignored the blood oozing from my knuckles, and pounded the chisel with greater force. When a hole opened, I dropped the hammer and chisel, rammed the pipe into the hole, and levered with all my weight. Sweating, I pushed relentlessly against the pipe. Suddenly the door budged. I strained. The gap widened. I stumbled, nearly falling as the door popped loose, leaving me sufficient space to squeeze through.

17

Please, God, let them be alive, I prayed.

I lurched into a room the size of a garage. A woman and a boy cowered, straining to get away from me. Each had a five-foot-long chain that led from a shackle on a wrist to a metal ring secured to the wall.

"Kate! Jason!"

They looked dazed. The pupils of their eyes were unnaturally large, black squeezing out the white around them. I could think of only one thing that would do that. Gader had told me that one of Lester Dant's numerous crimes had been drug dealing. I looked down at something I'd knocked over when I broke in. A waste can. Empty vials and used syringes had tumbled from it.

You son of a bitch, you drugged them! I inwardly screamed.

Kate and Jason kept cowering. They wore the kind of clothes that I associated with going to church. Kate had dark pumps, a knee-long modest blue dress, and a matching ribbon in her hair. Jason had black Oxfords, black trousers, and a white shirt topped with a bow tie. Their hair was meticulously combed, with the not-quite-natural look when someone else does the job. Their faces were pale, with hollows under their eyes. Kate wore lipstick, which was smeared.

The only furniture was a bed they'd been slumped on until the noises I'd made crashing into the room had terrified them.

"Kate, it's me! It's Brad!"

They cringed, desperate to keep a distance from me.

"Jason, it's Dad!"

Moaning, the boy squirmed back to the limit of his chain.

They'd never seen me with a beard. The drugs had so fogged their minds that they didn't recognize me. All they knew was that the violence of my entrance made me a threat.

"Listen to me! You're safe!"

I returned to the tunnel for the hammer and chisel. When I rushed toward Kate and Jason, they thrust their arms over their heads to protect themselves.

"You don't have to be afraid anymore!"

Their whimpers were obscured by the clang of the hammer against the chisel as I struck next to one of the metal rings embedded in the wall. Concrete flew. The fumes from the gasoline hadn't yet reached the chamber. For the moment, the danger of sparks didn't worry me as I slammed harder at the ring and the concrete around it. No longer whimpering, Kate and Jason were speechless with terror. Suddenly the ring to which Jason was anchored thumped onto the mattress.

I redirected the chisel toward the ring that held Kate. As I struck concrete above her head, she trembled. She reminded me of a dog that had been intimidated so often that it cowered at the sight of its owner.

My God, that's what she thinks, I realized. I imagined the drugged haze through which she and Jason must have been seeing me. My beard was the most pronounced thing about my appearance. *Petey's* beard was the feature they'd have most noticed in the swirl of their half-consciousness. Sweet Jesus, they thought I was Petey.

In outrage, I realized what had happened. Petey had tried to condition them, to make Kate call him Brad and Jason call him Dad—more important, to make them believe it. He'd drugged them until they didn't know who they were. Day after day, he'd persisted in the same routine, determined to take away their will and resistance, to mold them into the obedient, worshipful wife and son of his fantasies. He didn't want a wife and son who had minds of their own. What he needed were puppets who acted out his delusions.

"It's me! It's really me!" I pounded the chisel against the wall. "It's Brad!"

Their eyes widened with greater terror.

"Jason, I'm not who you think I am! I really am your father!"

I didn't have time to explain. I had to get them outside before the fumes spread farther and the house exploded. With one last frantic blow, I knocked away the ring that held Kate to the wall.

She and Jason were too frightened to move.

I grabbed their chains and dragged them toward the gap in the doorway. I squeezed into the tunnel and used their chains to pull them through one at a time. Immediately, I felt light-headed, realizing that the fumes were starting to suffocate me. Tugging Kate and Jason along the tunnel, I was again reminded of dogs that refused to go with their master. I reached the basement, seeing smoke billow from the fake light switch that had almost electrocuted me. The detonator. When it burst into flame, the house would blow up.

Daylight gleamed through the open trapdoor.

"You're almost free, Kate! Jason, you'll soon be out of here!"

But as we started up the stairs, Jason gaped and jerked back. He screamed. Above us, a shadow loomed into view, blocking part of the light. Then the light was blocked totally as Petey slammed the trapdoor shut.

18

Smoke billowed thicker from the fake light switch. I coughed but couldn't clear my lungs. A rumble above the trapdoor warned me that Petey was sliding the heavy workbench onto it. I drew my pistol and shot toward the noise. As four bullet holes appeared in the trapdoor, I realized in dismay that the muzzle flashes from my pistol might detonate the fumes.

My ears rang from the shots. Gasoline now covered most of the floor. Frantic, I looked around for a way to get out. Above the laundry sink, the boarded-over window caught my attention. I ran back for the hammer, raced toward the laundry sink, and pried the boards from the window.

It was the type that had to be pulled up on an angle and held in place by a hook in the ceiling. When I opened it, I heard the wind, which had become even stronger since I'd entered the house. Feeling a gust hit my face, I lifted Jason. He struggled as I pushed him through the opening.

I lifted Kate, shocked by how little she weighed. The sight of the outdoors, of freedom, gave her some life. With greater energy, she squirmed through the window's opening, desperate to get away from me.

Any moment, I feared, a searing blast would rip me apart. I climbed onto the sink, and just as I shoved my chest through the opening, the sink pulled away from the wall, crashing under my weight. I grabbed a branch on a shrub and dangled. The branch bent. I sank.

I clawed at the earth, kept slipping back into the basement, braced my elbows against each side of the window, and stopped. Below me, the concrete wall tore my jeans as I kneed against it, struggling to squirm upward. Even with the wind at my face and the smoke coming past me through the window, I smelled the gasoline.

I grabbed another branch and pulled myself hand over hand through the opening. But the buckle on my gun belt wedged against the sill. I tried to raise my hips, working to ease the buckle over the sill. I heard it scrape on the concrete. I sucked in my stomach, raised my hips as high as I could, felt the buckle slip free, and tugged forward harder, inching through the opening. My hips came through. My thighs. As soon as I was on my hands and knees, I surged up.

Adrenaline burned my muscles as I raced from the bushes at the side of the house. I saw Petey's truck, which the boards over the window had prevented me from hearing when he'd returned to the house. I didn't see Kate and Jason, but I was certain that, even dazed, they'd have known enough to run in the opposite direction from the truck. I whirled to charge after them toward the back of the house, to cross the clearing and reach the cover of the forest. . . .

And found myself ten feet from Petey, who aimed a shotgun at my chest.

He trembled with rage.

I couldn't draw my pistol and shoot before he pulled the trigger. Even if I hit him, my 9-mm bullet might not kill him, but with a shotgun at ten feet, he was sure to blow my chest apart.

"Stop, Petey!" With my beard, I couldn't be sure he recognized me. "It's me! It's Brad!"

Even before I shouted, his eyes had narrowed. He looked startled. Straining to see past my beard, he realized who I was.

The wind buffeted us so hard, I could barely hear him murmur, "Brad."

"Listen to me! *Did they tell you who Lester was?*" I shouted, doing the only thing I could think of to distract him from shooting. "*Do you know why they took you?*"

"Lester," he murmured.

"*Did they tell you Lester was Orval and Eunice's only child?*"

Smoke poured from the basement window.

Moving away from it, I had to keep distracting him. "*Did they tell you he died, that they went crazy with grief?*"

The house would soon explode.

"They'd already lost three children to stillbirths!" I kept my voice raised, inching toward the trees. "The rest of the Dants were dead! Eunice couldn't conceive any longer. Lester was their only chance of continuing the family line."

Petey sighted along the shotgun's barrel. "Lester."

As smoke billowed, I moved closer to the trees. "They were desperate to replace him. But they couldn't do it in Brockton. That was too close to home. They might have been recognized."

Petey kept pace with me, the shotgun aimed at my chest.

"So they set out on the interstate, driving from one town to another. They waited for God to direct them, to put a boy of the same age before them. They tried one town after another. They crossed from Indiana into Ohio. They passed Columbus. They came to Woodford." I spoke faster, more intensely. "We'll never know what made them leave the interstate and pick our town. Something must have seemed a sign from God. As they drove this way and that, they turned a corner, and there you were, all by yourself, pedaling down a street that seemed deserted."

" 'Can you tell us how to get to the interstate?' " Petey said it with such bitterness. " 'Do you believe in God? Do you believe in the end of the world?' "

The smoke worsened. I tasted it as I neared the trees.

He moved with me, his finger looking tighter on the shotgun.

"They took you, and they put you in that underground room, and they told you your name was Lester, and they punished you if you didn't act like their son."

"Lester."

I thought I saw flames beyond the smoke at the basement window.

" '*This my son was dead, and is alive again; he was*

lost, and is found.' Luke, fifteen, twenty-four," Petey said.

"When you told me you'd been molested, I thought you meant sexually."

I took another step.

So did Petey.

The wind gusted harder.

"But you didn't mean sexually. You meant molested in your *mind*. In your *soul*. They wanted you to be Lester so much that they beat you and starved you; they treated you like an animal, until you didn't know who you were. It was so awful that in the end you were ready to be anybody they wanted you to be as long as they didn't hurt you, as long as they took away your bodily wastes and gave you something to eat."

"They taught me the good book," Petey said. " *'The truth shall make you free.'* John, eight, thirty-two."

"The truth is, you *can* be free. I'll get help for you, Petey! It's not too late! Once the police understand why you did what you did, *they'll* want you to get help, too. I promise you, life can be better. Don't let Orval and Eunice destroy you again. Stop being what they made you into, Petey."

"Don't call me Petey!"

My voice broke. "I can't tell you how sorry I am. I know that your life changed because of me, that everything would have been different if I hadn't sent you home from that baseball game! But, damn it, we were just kids. How was I to know that the Dants were going to grab you? *Nobody* could have known about them. You were just my little brother tagging along. I didn't mean for it to happen, Petey." Tears streamed down my face. "There wasn't a night since you disappeared that I didn't beg God to bring you back safe, that I didn't plead for a second chance. Let me make it up to you, Petey. Please, let me try to give you the life that Orval and Eunice took from you."

"Stop calling me Petey!"

"You're right. When you came to my house, you asked me to call you Peter, but I didn't. We're not kids anymore. You're Peter."

"No! Don't call me that, either!"

Staring at the shotgun's trigger, I made a placating gesture. "Okay. Whatever you want, Lester."

"I'm *not* Lester!"

"Then I don't understand. Who *are* you?"

"*Brad.*"

The dark intensity in his eyes made clear how serious he was. I'd ruined *his* life. Now *he'd* stolen *mine*. Taking my wife and son, he'd convinced himself that he was also taking my identity. In his mind, he *was* me. As the depths of his insanity became obvious, my legs felt unsteady. "I'm so sorry. God help you," I murmured.

"No." His tone left no doubt that he was going to pull the trigger. "God help *you*."

19

The blast hurtled me into the bushes. Not from the shot-gun. The blast from the house. As the building exploded, the shock wave lifted me off my feet and threw me into the undergrowth. Wreckage flew, chopping tree branches, shredding leaves.

Dimly, I became aware enough to smell smoke and hear the crackle of flames. In pain, I slowly sat up. I felt dizzy, sick to my stomach. The ringing in my ears was unbearable.

I'd been thrown into a hollow. That was the only rea-son I'd survived the shrapnel from the blast. Chunks of smoking, burning wreckage lay around me. Bushes were on fire. The wind thrust the flames from tree to tree.

Coughing from the smoke, I staggered to my feet. I stared around, searching for Petey. I faced the burning crater of the house. He wasn't on the ground where we'd last stood. He must have been thrown into the un-dergrowth the same as I had been.

Flames crowded me. Kate and Jason. I had to find them. As I stumbled deeper into the forest, I prayed that they'd kept running, that they were far enough away that the fire wouldn't reach them.

And that Petey wouldn't. He'd do everything in his power to get them back.

Unless he was dead. Unless the blast had killed him.

Then where was his body? After the explosion, there was so little cover that I should have been able to see his corpse. Where *was* he?

The wind hurled smoke at me, making me cough harder as I lurched through the forest. While I'd been unconscious, the fire had spread rapidly, leaping from tree to tree. Bushes burst into flames. I zigzagged, trying to avoid flames on my right, only to discover that a new section of the forest was suddenly afire on my left.

I wanted to shout, "Kate! Jason!" But they'd been so afraid of me in the house that I doubted they'd answer me. If anything, I'd throw them into a greater panic. On the off chance that they did answer my shouts, Petey would hear them, would go to them.

Plus, if I shouted to Kate and Jason, Petey would hear *me,* would know where *I* was.

The fire roared around me. The smoke whirled past, driven by the wind. Fighting for breath, I stumbled into a clearing. Again, the fire leapt into the trees ahead of me.

How far had Kate and Jason managed to go? I remembered the stream that I'd followed into the forest. If I could reach it, if Kate and Jason could reach it, we had a chance.

Reach it? *How?* I'd been so distracted by my need to

avoid the fire that I'd lost my bearings. The same with Kate and Jason. They might be fleeing in a circle.

I fumbled for the compass in my shirt pocket. Squinting in the smoke, I aligned myself in a northwest direction, the opposite of the southeast line that I'd used to approach the house. I put the compass back in my shirt, dodged a flaming branch falling toward me, and ran toward untouched trees northwest of me.

The noise from the fire was filled with pops and cracks as wood ignited. Dry stumps exploded from the heat. A huge chunk of bark and wood blew away from a tree on my right, and I dove to the ground, realizing that one of the blasts was from Petey's shotgun.

I drew my pistol, dismayed by how violently my hand shook. In Denver, my instructor had warned that no matter how good a shooter was at target practice, nothing prepared one for controlling a gun in a kill-or-be-killed situation. When fear took charge, skill collapsed.

The fire swept closer. I couldn't stay where I was. But as soon as I moved, Petey would shoot again. I thought of everything that Kate and Jason had suffered, of everything that I'd been through to find them. I thought of Petey leaving me to die in the mountains. Fury compacted my muscles. My hand stopped shaking.

I raced toward another tree. A shotgun blast tore a chunk from it. Immediately I did what Petey would have least expected, charging back toward the flames, toward the tree where I'd hidden. I had a sense of where he'd shot from, a clump of bushes that I now put three bullets into. Smoke enveloped me. I held my breath and used the smoke for cover, rushing toward those bushes, angrily putting three more bullets into them. But when I crashed through, what I found wasn't a body, only an empty shot-gun shell.

I crouched, breathing hoarsely, scanning the under-growth for movement. But everything was in motion as the heat from the flames added to the force of the wind. The empty shotgun shell. How many times had Petey shot at me? Two that I knew of. How many shells did a shotgun hold? In the gun store where I'd taken lessons, I recalled hearing that most held four in the magazine and one in the chamber. Petey's shirt pockets hadn't bulged from spare shotgun shells. As far as I knew, he had only three shots left.

My back felt so scorched that I had to rush toward farther cover. Staying low, I reached more bushes, took advantage of the smoke around me, and raced toward another tree stump. *Blam!* The top of the stump disinte-grated. The shocking pain in my left shoulder felt as if hornets had stung me at enormous speed. I lurched back, shooting as I fell. I hit the ground, hoping that what had struck me were chunks of wood from the stump. But the blood on my shoulder warned me that I'd been struck by metal pellets. The only reason that my arm hadn't been separated from my shoulder was that Petey had shot from a distance. In the confusion of the smoke and the flames, his aim had been thrown off. Only part of the spray had hit me.

The wound throbbed. I had trouble moving that arm. But I had no trouble moving the rest of me. I was so primed with fear and adrenaline that I rolled toward a fallen tree, knowing that I didn't dare stay where I'd fallen. The fire again scorched my back. Its wind-driven smoke enveloped me. But it had to be enveloping Petey also. He wouldn't be able to see me.

I pulled the compass from my shirt and checked it again. Straining not to cough and let Petey know where I was, I aligned the compass on a northwest route and shifted forward through the fast-moving haze. I couldn't see more than five feet ahead of me. Prepared to shoot the instant I saw a threatening shadow, I worked farther through the forest, checking the compass frequently.

Blood dripped from my left shoulder. I felt light-headed. The fire was about to get ahead of me. Heat shoved me, urging me to move faster.

I was so busy watching the blowing smoke for a sign of Petey that I didn't pay attention to the ground. The slope to the stream was about six feet deep. I'd have fallen into it if a deer hadn't charged from the flames on my right. It startled me, crashing past me and down, splashing through water, then bounding up the opposite side.

I squirmed down to the water, feeling cool air. The stream was shallow. I crossed it, oblivious to my hiking boots and socks getting wet, concentrating on where Petey might be. On my right, farther along the stream, a shadow moved amid the smoke. I started to shoot but stifled the impulse, realizing that the shadow might belong to Kate as easily as to Petey.

I kept aiming. The smoke made my eyes water as I strained to see along the barrel. I stared at the smoke, waiting for the shadow to become more distinct.

The shadow disappeared. Whoever it was had climbed from the stream and continued through the forest. Keeping pace with it, I struggled up the slope and passed through smoky undergrowth, watching for the shadow to come into view again.

I kept thinking, If it was Kate, wouldn't I have seen a smaller shadow with her: Jason?

Not if he was on the other side of her.

I had to be certain before I pulled the trigger. Creeping farther through the trees, I blinked tears from my smoke-irritated eyes and stared toward the indistinct forest on my right. Something moved. For an instant, I caught a glimpse of Petey's beard. He raised his shotgun. I pulled the trigger.

Abruptly I was almost blinded as a gust of wind tossed flames overhead. Trees and bushes erupted into fire ahead of me. Feeling the explosion of heat singe my hair, I stumbled backward and this time did lose my balance. When I fell down the bank of the stream, I landed on my wounded shoulder. I strained not to cry out, rolling down to the water, coming to a painful stop.

It took all my effort to stand. I'd dropped my compass. I couldn't find it. Not that I could get any help from it now. With the fire ahead and behind me, with Petey possibly on my right, the only safe direction was to the left along the stream. I had no idea if I'd hit him. But if I hadn't, he'd need to take shelter in the stream, which meant that he'd stalk along it in my direction. All I had to do was find a curve in the stream, hide, and ambush him.

I couldn't remember how many times I'd shot. My pistol might have been almost empty. Trying to keep my hands steady, I pressed a button on the side, dropped the magazine, grabbed the fifteen-round spare from the pouch on my belt, and slammed it into the grip, ready to shoot again.

My vision grayed. As the smoke thickened, I fought for air, realizing that the fire was sucking away oxygen. The flames squeezed closer. Afraid that I'd pass out, I worked along the stream, trying to stay on the bank, to avoid making noise in the water. But loss of blood added to my dizziness. I couldn't control where my hiking boots landed, sometimes splashing in the water, sometimes slipping through mud.

Hot air seared my nostrils. I rounded a curve, its slope protecting me from the flames above me on my right. I lurched around another curve, and cool air struck my face. I'd reached a section of the stream that wasn't yet bounded by fire. The coolness was the most luxuriant thing I'd ever felt. I sucked it into my lungs, hoping to clear my thoughts, to get rid of the spots that wavered in my vision.

As the fresh air took the gray from in front of my eyes, I staggered to a halt at the sight of footprints in the mud. Two sets of them. An adult's. A child's. They were following the stream, as *I* was.

Kate. Jason.

I whirled toward urgent footsteps splashing through the stream behind me. But as I aimed, it wasn't Petey, but a panicked dog that scrambled into view. It raced out of sight along the stream. The air became hot again. The flames drew closer.

I ran in the direction of the footprints. A tree had fallen across the bank. I ducked under it, straightened on the other side, and groaned as something heavy walloped across my forehead. The blow sent me reeling back against the tree. Dazed, I sank to my knees in the water.

Blood trickled down my face. I tried to clear my blurred vision.

Her eyes frantic from the drugs, Kate stood over me, a clublike branch raised to hit me again. Jason cowered behind her.

"No, Kate." I was appalled by how distant my weakened voice sounded. "Don't. It's me."

"You bastard!"

I managed to raise my right arm before she struck me again. The club whacked below my elbow, deflecting the blow, but the pain that shot through my arm made me fear that she'd broken it.

My pistol thudded onto the bank.

"No, Kate, it's really me! Brad!"

"*Brad!*" Kate shrieked and struck again with the club.

I dove to the right, barely avoiding the blow. It smashed into the stream. She swung again. I rolled as she kept swinging.

She gaped at something behind me.

I followed her gaze.

Petey's face showed above the tree that spanned the stream. His forehead was covered with soot. His hair and beard were singed. His shirt was blackened by smoke. Blood flowed from his left shoulder, where I'd evidently hit him the last time I'd pulled the trigger.

His shotgun rested on the horizontal tree, its barrel facing us.

Jason backed away.

"If you know what's good for you, son, don't take another step," Petey told Jason.

I was on my back in the stream. My right arm was useless, probably broken from when Kate had struck it. My buckshot-punctured left arm was in similar agony, but at least it was mobile. Sweating from the effort, I groped for the knife on my belt.

Jason kept backing away.

"Listen to your father," Petey said. "Stay put."

Jason opened his mouth in a silent wail.

Then *Petey* wailed as I rolled under the tree and plunged the hunting knife into his thigh. The blade scraped bone. When he lurched back, his shotgun went off. The pellets whistled past my head. No! Afraid that the blast had hit Kate and Jason, I stabbed Petey's thigh again. As his blood spurted over me, I redirected my aim toward his side.

But he rammed down with the butt of his shotgun, hitting my wounded shoulder. I almost passed out, able to do only one thing, to throw my weight against his legs and bring him down with me into the stream. I crawled onto him, stabbing toward his face, but he pushed me to the side and grabbed my throat, choking me so hard that I feared my larynx would break.

Smoke reached us. The fire crackled nearer. I plunged the knife into his wounded shoulder. In agony, he fell back, landing where he'd dropped his shotgun. He grabbed it, pumped out an empty cartridge, and pulled the trigger.

I lurched back from the blast that would blow my chest apart, but the shotgun made only a clicking sound. It was empty. Roaring, Petey swung it like a club, but loss of blood weakened him. The blow glanced off my leg. My left arm was in greater agony, much less mobile, as I thrust with the knife and missed.

A shot kicked up dirt.

We spun toward it.

Kate had crawled beneath the trees. Wavering to her feet, she held the pistol that I'd dropped. Doing her best to keep it steady, she looked as if, throughout her ordeal, a small part of her mind had remained lucid enough to fantasize about getting even. Normally, at close range, there wasn't any trick to using the gun. Even though she knew nothing about pistols, all she had to do was look down the barrel and pull the trigger.

But she was drugged, and she'd already missed once, and now she mustered her concentration, her eyes dark above her hollow cheeks. The twin vision of her nightmare—two Peteys, two Brads—must have threatened the little sanity she had left.

"Help me," Petey said. "I came here to save you. Shoot him."

She hesitated, then turned the gun toward me.

"Please, Kate, don't," I said.

I watched her finger tighten on the trigger.

"Shoot him," Petey said.

"I love you, Kate."

"I'm your husband. Do what I tell you," Petey said.

She turned toward Petey and shot him in the face.

She took a step closer, pulled the trigger, and this time missed. So she stumbled closer, until she was on top of him. At point-blank range, she shot him in the chest. The next bullet burst his throat. She didn't aim at those parts. They just happened to be where the barrel wavered. She shot and kept shooting, too close not to hit him somewhere, his shoulder, his knees, his groin, riddling his body, until all fifteen bullets in the magazine had been expended and the slide on top of the pistol stayed back.

Tears rolled down her face.

I managed to stand.

But as I approached her, wanting to hold her, she staggered back in fright. She raised the pistol again and pulled the trigger repeatedly. Nothing happened. The gun was empty. But if there'd been any rounds left, she'd have killed me.

I tried to make a reassuring gesture. "It's okay. You're safe now. I'm not going to hurt you."

But the dark frenzy in her eyes told me that she didn't believe me.

"I won't touch you," I said. "But please let me help you. Please." I felt heat behind me. I heard a crackling roar and looked over my shoulder at the fire. "We have to get out of here."

I took another step forward. In response, she backed away toward the tree across the stream.

"Jason?" I asked. "Where's Jason? *My God, was he shot?*"

As I stared frantically under the tree toward where I'd last seen Jason, Kate scrambled under it, trying to get away from me. I lurched after her, rising on the other side. Fearful that I'd see Jason's body blown apart from Petey's last shotgun blast, I breathed out in relief when I found him standing next to the stream.

He threw a rock.

It struck my chest, but I was far beyond pain. All I wanted was to get him out of there.

"It's okay, Jason. You've got nothing to be afraid of now."

I took a step toward him. Covered with blood, singed

by the fire, I must have looked indistinguishable from Petey.

He scrambled up the bank and into the forest.

Off balance from my injuries, I struggled after him. Heat and smoke almost succeeded in pushing me back as I stumbled through the underbrush.

I saw bright flickers within the smoke. The heat intensified. A tree exploded into flames. A wall of fire reached bushes.

"Jason!" Smoke clogged my throat. I bent over, coughing, forced myself to straighten, and veered past more trees.

The wind cleared the smoke for an instant. Ahead, Jason was blocked by the approaching fire. He turned, desperate to run from it, then stopped when he saw me. I must have been more threatening than another wall of fire. He dodged to my left and raced toward an opening in the blaze. As I leapt, the wind hurled flames toward him. I knocked him down an instant before a fiery gust flashed above our sprawled bodies. With the remaining strength in my wounded arm, I dragged him back from the flames. He kicked and hit me. Then Kate was hitting me. "Let him go!" she screamed.

The three of us tumbled down the bank and landed in the water. They kept hitting and kicking, but I didn't resist. Their punches weakened. Finally, they collapsed, staring at me, their gaunt chests rising and falling.

"I love you," I said.

They stared.

Something slowly changed focus in their eyes, as if they dimly remembered a time when those words had been familiar.

"Stay here. There's something I have to do," I managed to say.

As the fire approached the top of the bank, I splashed water over me. Then I ducked under the tree that spanned the stream. I came to where Petey lay. His body was almost totally covered with blood from the number of times he'd been shot.

But that wasn't good enough. He'd come back once. I needed to be absolutely certain that he was dead, that he could never come back again, not even in my nightmares.

I grabbed his feet, but my injured arms had stiffened too much, causing too much pain for me to drag him up the bank. I tried as hard as I could but was about to give up, when Kate's hands came into view. I looked at her, startled, but she didn't say a word, just helped me tug Petey up the slope.

We threw him toward the fire. His corpse burst into flames. Only then did we stumble back down to the stream. At the bottom, Kate fell, but she wouldn't let me touch her to help her get up. Keeping a wary distance from me, she and Jason ran.

Epilogue

Epilogue

The three of us were in a hospital for quite a while. The police and the district attorney questioned me, demanding to know why I hadn't let the authorities go after Petey. I did my best to tell them that events had overtaken me. How could I explain that I was afraid the police would have gotten Kate and Jason killed instead of saving them? Despite my repeated denials, they insisted that my motive had been rage, that I'd been determined to get even with Petey.

So I had to appear before a grand jury, and the way my attorney explained it to me, I could have been charged with what amounted to taking the law into my own hands. But I doubt there was a person on the jury who, after looking at my broken arm in a sling and the burns on my face, didn't think that I'd gone through enough. Certainly Kate and Jason had gone through plenty. Their eyes had the haunted expression of war refugees.

It took three weeks before we were allowed to leave. I paid someone to drive the Volvo back to Denver while

Kate, Jason, and I flew home from Columbus. Our friends welcomed us back. They phoned. They visited. They had a party for us. We thanked them. But the truth was, we were too traumatized to be sociable. Smiles and small talk were difficult to manage, and as for "large talk," when we were asked details about what had happened, we weren't ready to discuss it yet. After a while, the newness of our return wore off. The phone calls, visits, and invitations declined. Finally, we were left to ourselves.

Jason remained so silent that the parents of his friends didn't feel comfortable having him around their children. For her part, Kate got nervous whenever she had to leave the house. She finally gave up trying to do so. The only good thing was, as soon as I shaved my beard, as soon as the drugs wore off and Kate and Jason distinguished me from Petey, they no longer considered me a threat, although I'm always careful to let them see when I'm going to touch them.

I've tried to be honest with myself. I've done my best to understand what happened, hoping to adjust to it. But sometimes I wonder if it's *possible* to adjust to what Petey . . . Lester . . . did to us. Odd how I struggled so hard to deny that Petey was Lester and now I accept that the two were the same. My brother died a long time ago. Because of *me*.

Sometimes when Kate and Jason aren't aware of it, I study them, trying to decide if they're getting better. Without being obvious, I try to see beyond their eyes. I look in the mirror and try to see beyond my own. Do we carry darkness in us?

Payne came over the other day, a welcome visitor.

I asked him about his wife. "Is she well? What was the result of the biopsy?"

"The lump on her breast turned out to be a cyst, thank God."

Only then did I realize that I'd been holding my breath. "I'm glad to hear good things can happen," I said.

In the backyard, Payne eased his weight onto the chaise lounge where Petey had sat the previous year, peering up at our bedroom window.

Kate brought us two glasses of iced tea.

We pretended not to notice that her hands shook and the ice rattled.

"Thanks," I said.

When I touched her shoulder, she actually smiled.

Payne watched her return to the house. "Has she been seeing anyone?"

"A psychiatrist? Yes," I said. "All three of us have."

"Is it doing any good?"

"My own guy has me writing a journal, describing what happened and how I feel about it. I talk to him about it once a week. Is it doing any good?" I shrugged. "He claims that it is but says that I don't have the objectivity to know it yet. He also says that because the trauma we went through lasted a long time, it isn't reasonable to expect to get over it quickly."

"Makes sense."

"Kate went into the supermarket all by herself today."

Payne looked puzzled.

"It's a big step," I explained. "She has trouble being near crowds and strangers."

"What about *you*? Do you plan to go back to work?"

"I'm going to have to soon," I answered. "Our insurance doesn't cover all the medical expenses. Certainly not the *legal* expenses."

"But how are you feeling? Are you *ready* to go back to work?"

I sipped my iced tea and didn't answer.

"When I was with the Bureau, I had to shoot somebody," Payne said.

"Kill him?"

He concentrated on his glass. "I got shot in the process. Three months medical leave. A lot of counseling. I think I told you that's when I put on all this weight and left the Bureau. It took me a long time to feel normal again."

"*Normal*'s a complicated word. I wonder if I *can* feel normal again. In my previous life, it's like I was blundering around in a world of hurt but was too stupid to realize it."

"And now?"

"I think Kate's right to be careful of what's going on around her. Anything can happen. One moment, I was standing on a ridge, admiring the scenery. The next moment, my brother shoved me into a gorge."

"Caution's a virtue."

"So I've learned. You asked me if I planned to go back to work. I *am* at work."

"Oh?" Payne studied me.

"Taking care of my family. It's my job to love Kate and Jason as hard as I can, to thank God for every moment I have with them, to hold them and cherish them and do my damnedest to keep them safe."

Payne's concentration was powerful. "You know what, Mr. Denning?"

"Please call me Brad."

"The more I get to know you, the better I like you."

More
David Morrell!

Please turn this page
for a preview of

THE PROTECTOR

available in
May 2003.

Cavanaugh got out of the taxi at Rockefeller Center, glanced down at the United Nations flags around the outdoor restaurant in the Lower Plaza, went through the front of Brookstone's, and exited through the back, glancing behind him to make sure no one had followed him through the store. Two indirectly taken, crowded blocks later, he reached Fifty-fourth Street and the Avenue of the Americas, entering the Warwick Hotel. The Manhattan landmark had recently been renovated, but its marble and dark wood lobby still evoked tradition and character.

Cavanaugh turned to the left and entered the hotel's quiet bar, where an attractive woman with green eyes and an intriguing expression sat with her back to the wall at a corner table. He approved of her choice of location: against an inside wall, away from the bar's numerous windows. Not that he believed she was in any danger. Even so, like the roundabout route he'd taken to get to the Warwick, it was always good to maintain precautions. If there'd been any risk, he wouldn't have let her appear in public in the first place.

Her name was Jamie Travers, and until recently, she'd lived in seclusion with him at a ranch in the mountains near Jackson Hole, Wyoming, from where he periodically set out on security assignments, taking care that her weapons training was up-to-date and that a few colleagues in need of R and R were there to watch over her when he had to go away. Two years earlier, she had testified about a gangland killing she'd witnessed. The mob boss who'd gone to prison had put out a contract against her. Twice, despite police protection, she'd nearly been killed, prompting Cavanaugh, who admired her determination, to step in and arrange for her to disappear. The contract had finally ended when the man who'd ordered it had choked to death while eating spaghetti and meat balls in a federal prison. Despite the seeming innocence of the mob boss's death, Jamie had been convinced that Cavanaugh had something to do with it, but he continued to deny any involvement, even though he'd once told her that the only way to stop the mob boss from being a threat was to kill him. "Kismet," was all Cavanaugh would say about the reportedly accidental death. Now they continued to base their lives in Wyoming, but for its beauty, not its seclusion.

Jamie had shoulder-length brunette hair that looked

as casual and comfortable as the attractive black slacks and turquoise blouse she wore. Admiring, Cavanaugh moved a chair so he could sit in the corner with her. The location allowed him to survey both entrances to the room as well as the people passing beyond the windows along Fifty-fourth Street and the Avenue of the Americas.

"What are you drinking?" he asked.

"Perrier and lime."

Cavanaugh tasted it, savoring the lime. "How was your afternoon? Enjoying being a tourist?"

"Love it. I haven't been to the Museum of Modern Art in years. It was like seeing an old friend. And how was your afternoon?"

Cavanaugh explained why Duncan had wanted to see him.

"You accepted another assignment?" Jamie looked surprised.

"We planned to head home the day after tomorrow, so this won't interfere with much, especially since you're getting together with your mother again tomorrow. I didn't think you'd mind going back to the ranch ahead of me. I'll join you in a week."

"But you're barely healed from the last job you did."

"This one's easy."

"That's what you said the last time."

"And the money's good."

"I've got more than enough money for both of us," Jamie said.

Cavanaugh nodded. His protective agent's income allowed them to stay at the Warwick, which was comfortable without being palatial. But if they'd used Jamie's money, which came from the sale of a promising dot-com company she'd founded during the Internet frenzy of the 1999s, they'd have stayed in a master suite at the Plaza or, at the very least, the St. Regis.

"Why don't you let me take care of you?" she asked.

"Foolish male pride."

"You said it—I didn't."

Cavanaugh shrugged. "People need protecting."

"And that's what you are—a protector. I shouldn't have bothered asking."

She hooked her arm around his. "So what makes this job so easy?"

"The client doesn't want anybody to shield him."

"Oh?" Jamie looked surprised again. "What does he want?"

"The same as *you* did. To disappear."

Cavanaugh got out of the car, a two-year-old Taurus that International Risk Management had supplied him. Apart from its special modifications, including a race-car engine and a suspension to match, it had been chosen because its dusty dark blue color and ubiquitous design made it nondescript. Sunday afternoon, however, it was the only vehicle in this abandoned industrial area of Newark, New Jersey. He scanned the graffiti-covered warehouse: a sprawling three-story structure that had most of its windows smashed.

Rust-streaked doors hung open, revealing what at first appeared to be garbage but turned out to be a city of the homeless. As far as Cavanaugh could see into the shadows, listing cardboard boxes provided shelter. Black plastic bags held whatever possessions the inhabitants treasured.

Dark clouds cast a cold shadow. On the river behind the warehouse, boat engines droned. A tug blew its horn. Thunder rumbled. Cavanaugh pressed his right elbow reassuringly against the 9 mm handgun holstered on his belt beneath his leather jacket. The Sig Sauer 225 held eight rounds in the magazine and one in the firing chamber. Not a massive amount of firepower, not the sixteen rounds that a Beretta was capable of holding, but Cavanaugh found that a pistol containing that much ammunition was slightly large for his hand, affecting the accuracy of his aim, nine well-placed shots being better than sixteen that went astray because of a poor grip. Plus, as the Federal Air Marshals had decided in the late 1980s, the Sig Sauer 225's lighter weight and thin compact design made it an ideal concealed-carry weapon. But just in case, Cavanaugh had two other eight-round magazines in a pouch on the left side of his belt beneath his leather jacket.

A chill wind strengthened, redolent of approaching

rain. At the gaping entrances to the warehouse, a few grizzled faces squinted out.

Cavanaugh took his cell phone from his jacket and pressed the good-for-today-only numbers Duncan had given to him.

As the phone rang on the other end, more grizzled faces squinted from the warehouse, some apprehensive, others assessing.

On the other end, the phone rang a second time.

"Yes?" a man's trembly voice asked, sounding like he was in an echo chamber.

Cavanaugh supplied his half of the recognition sequence. "I didn't realize the warehouse was closed."

"Ten years ago," came the other half of the sequence, the voice continuing to be unsteady. "Your name is . . ."

"Cavanaugh. And yours is . . ."

"Daniel Prescott. Daniel. Not Dan."

This exchange, too, was part of the sequence.

More haggard faces peered from the warehouse, an army of rags trying to decide if Cavanaugh was an enemy, a benefactor, or a target.

Isolated drops of rain struck the greasy pavement.

"Global Protective Services is supposed to be the best," the voice said. "I expected a fancier car."

"One of the reasons we're the best is we don't attract attention to ourselves and, more important, to our clients."

More drops struck the pavement.

"I assume you can see me," Cavanaugh said. "As you wanted, I came alone."

"Open the car doors."

Cavanaugh did.

"Open the trunk."

Cavanaugh did. The man evidently had a vantage point that allowed him to look into the vehicle.

The dark clouds thickened. A few more drops of rain struck around him.

Cavanaugh heard faint, echoing, metallic noises on the phone. "Hello?" he said into it.

No response.

"Hello?" he asked again.

More faint, echoing, metallic noises.

Thunder rumbled closer.

A few scarecrows of men stepped from the warehouse. Like the others, they were scruffy and beard-stubbled, but the desperation in their eyes contrasted with the blankness and resignation Cavanaugh sensed in the others.

Crack addicts, he assumed, so overdue for a fix they'd try taking on a stranger who was unwise enough to visit hell. "Hey, I came here to help you," Cavanaugh said into the phone, "not to get soaked."

More metallic noises.

"I think we both made a mistake." Cavanaugh shut the trunk and the passenger doors. About to get into the car, he heard the trembly voice say:

"Ahead of you. On the left. You see the door?"

"Yes."

It was the only door still intact. Closed.

"Come in," the unsteady voice said.

Cavanaugh got behind the steering wheel.

"I said 'come in,'" the voice told him.

"After I move the vehicle."

Cavanaugh drove along the weed-choked, cracked-concrete parking area. Near the door, he turned the car in a half circle so it faced the direction from which he'd come. He left sufficient room around it so that, when he returned, he'd be able to see if anyone was trying to hide near it.

"Entering," Cavanaugh said into his phone.

He shut off the engine, left the car, and locked it via remote control while he sprinted through the drizzle. Movement in his peripheral vision made him glance to his left along the warehouse toward where more crack addicts stepped into the increasing rain and watched him. Wary of what might be behind the door (more predators?), Cavanaugh put his cell phone into his jacket pocket and did something he hadn't planned: drew his pistol. As he turned the knob, he noted that, although the lock was coated with grit, there was a hint of shininess underneath—the lock was new. But it wasn't engaged. Pulling the heavy, creaking door open, he ducked inside.

As swiftly as the door's protesting hinges allowed, Cavanaugh closed it. No longer a silhouette, he shifted toward the deepest shadows and took account of where he was. At the bottom of a dusty concrete stairwell, metal steps led up. Cobwebs dangled from the railing. On the left, a motor rumbled behind an elevator door. The place smelled of must and gave off a chill.

Aiming his pistol toward the stairs and then toward the elevator, Cavanaugh reached behind him to turn the latch on the sturdy lock and secure the door. But before he could touch it, the lock's bolt rammed home, triggered electronically from a distance.

Cavanaugh concentrated to control his uneasiness. There wasn't any reason to suspect he was in danger. After all, Duncan had warned him that the potential client, although legitimate, had eccentricities. Prescott's merely being cautious, Cavanaugh tried to assure himself. Hell, if he's so nervous about his safety that he feels he needs protection, it's natural he'll make sure the door's locked. He's the one in danger, not me. Then why am I holding this gun?

Cavanaugh pulled the phone from his pocket and spoke into it. "Now what?"

His voice echoed.

As if in response, the elevator opened, revealing a brightly lit compartment.

Cavanaugh hated elevators: small sealed boxes that could easily become traps. God knew what might be on the other side when the door reopened.

"Thanks," he said into the phone, "but I need some exercise. I'll take the stairs."

As his eyes adjusted to the shadows, he noticed a small surveillance camera mounted discreetly under the stairs, facing the door. "I was told you wanted to disappear. It seems to me you've already done that."

"Not enough," the unsteady voice said. This time, it came not from the phone but from a speaker hidden in the wall.

Cavanaugh put away his phone. A vague pungent smell pinched his nostrils, as if something had died nearby. His heartbeat quickened.

No matter how softly he placed his shoes, the metal stairs echoed loudly as he climbed.

He came to a landing and reversed direction, shifting higher. The pungent smell became a little more noticeable. His stomach fidgeted as he faced a solid metal door. Hesitating, he reached for it.

"Not that one," the voice said from the wall.

Nerves inexplicably more on edge, Cavanaugh climbed higher and came to a door halfway up the stairs.

"Not that one, either," the voice said. "Incidentally, am I supposed to feel reassured that you're coming to me with a gun?"

"I don't know about you, but under the circumstances, it does a world of good for me."

The voice made a sound that might have been a bitter chuckle.

Heavy rain hit the building, sending vibrations through it.

Cavanaugh reached the top level, where, next to

the elevator, a final door awaited him. The door was open, inviting him into a brightly lit corridor, which had a closed door at the other end.

The same as stepping into an elevator, Cavanaugh decided. The pungent smell seemed a little stronger. His muscles tightening, he didn't understand what was happening to him. A visceral part of him warned him to leave the building. Abruptly, he wondered if he *could* leave. Even though he always carried lockpicks in his jacket's collar, he had the suspicion that they wouldn't be enough to open the downstairs door.

Breathing slightly faster, he had to keep telling himself that he wasn't the one in danger—Prescott was, which explained what Cavanaugh hoped were merely security precautions and not a trap that had been set for him.

He glanced up at a security camera in the corridor he was expected to enter. To hell with it, he thought, annoyed by the nervous moisture on his palms. If Prescott wanted me dead, he could have killed me before now.

Regardless of the insistent pounding of his heart, a strong intuition told Cavanaugh to surrender to the situation. Something else told him to run, which made no sense inasmuch as he had no reason to believe he was in danger. Impatient with himself, he came to a strong decision and holstered his weapon. It's not going to do me any good in that corridor anyhow.

Entering, he wasn't surprised that the door swung shut behind him, locking itself loudly.

After the gloom of the stairwell, the lights hurt his eyes, but at least the pungent smell was gone. Managing to feel less on edge, he walked to the door at the end of the corridor, turned the knob, pushed the door open, and found himself in a bright room filled with closed-circuit television monitors and electronic consoles. Across from him, bricks covered a window.

What captured his attention, however, was an overweight fortyish man who stood among the glowing electronic equipment. The man wore wrinkled slacks and an equally wrinkled white shirt that had sweat marks under the arms and clung to his ample stomach. His thick, sandy hair was uncombed. He needed a shave. The skin under his eyes was puffy from lack of sleep. The dark pupils of his eyes were large from tension.

The man aimed a Colt .45 semiautomatic pistol at Cavanaugh. Its barrel wavered.

Cavanaugh had no doubt that if he'd entered the room, carrying his weapon, the man would have fired. Doing his best to keep his breathing steady, he raised his hands in reassuring submission. Despite the big gun that was nervously aimed at him, the uneasiness Cavanaugh had felt coming up the stairs seemed of no importance compared to what this man must be feeling, for, outside of combat, Prescott was the most frightened man Cavanaugh had ever seen.

*   *   *

"Please remember you sent for me," Cavanaugh said. "I'm here to help you."

As Prescott continued to aim the Colt, his pupils got larger. The room became more sour with fear.

"I knew your one-time-only phone number and the recognition code," Cavanaugh said. "Only someone from Protective Services could have had that information."

"You could have forced those details from the person they were sending," Prescott said. As on the phone, his voice was unsteady, but now Cavanaugh understood that it wasn't an electronic effect— Prescott's voice shook because he was afraid.

The door behind Cavanaugh swung shut, its lock ramming electronically home. He managed not to flinch. "I don't know who or what you feel threatened by, but I hardly think one man coming here would be the smartest way to get at you, not the way you've got this place set up. Logic should tell you I'm not a threat."

"The unexpected is the most brilliant tactic." Prescott's grip on the .45 was as unsteady as his voice. "Besides, your logic works against you. If one man isn't much of a threat, how can one man provide adequate protection?"

"You didn't say you wanted protection. You said you wanted to disappear."

Sweat marks spreading under his arms, Prescott studied Cavanaugh warily.

"My initial interviews are always one-on-one," Cavanaugh said. "I have to ask questions to assess the threat level. Then I decide how much help the job requires."

"I was told you used to be in Delta Force." Prescott licked his dry puffy lips.

"That's right."

The classic special-operations physique involved strong-looking shoulders that trimmed down to solid, compact hips, upper-body strength being one of the goals of the arduous training.

"Lots of exercise," Prescott said. "Is that what you think qualifies you to protect somebody?"

Trying to put Prescott at ease, Cavanaugh chuckled. "You want my job stats?"

"If you want to convince me you're here to help. If you want to work for me."

"You've got this turned around. When I interview potential clients, it's not because I want to work for them. Most times, I don't want to work for them."

"You mean you have to like them?" Prescott asked with distaste.

"Most times, I don't like them, either," Cavanaugh said. "But that doesn't mean they don't have a right to live. I'm a protector, not a judge. But the man who taught me to do this did set minimum standards. No drug dealers, arms merchants, terrorists, mobsters, child molesters, wife beaters, members of militant hate groups, or anybody else who's an obvious monster. Are you any of those?"

Prescott had a look of incredulity. "Of course not."

"Then there's only one other standard that'll help me decide if I want to protect you."

"Which is?"

"Are you willing to be compliant?"

Prescott blinked sweat from his puffy eyes. "What?"

"I can't protect someone who won't take orders," Cavanaugh said. "That's the paradox of being a protector. Someone hires me. In theory, that person's the boss. But when it comes to protection, I'm the one who gives the orders. The employer has to react to me as if I'm the boss. Are you willing to be compliant?"

"Anything to keep me alive."

"You'll do what I say?"

Prescott thought fearfully and nodded.

"So, okay, here's your first order: Put that damned gun away before I ram it down your throat."

Prescott blinked several times, stepping back as if Cavanaugh had slapped him. He held the gun steadier, frowned, and slowly lowered it.

"An excellent start," Cavanaugh said.

"If you're not who you say you are, do it right now," Prescott said. "Kill me. I can't stand living this way."

"Relax. Whoever your enemies are, I'm not one of them." Cavanaugh surveyed the room. To the right, in a corner, past the electronics and the monitors, he saw a cot, a minifridge, a sink, and a small stove. Beyond was a toilet, a showerhead, and a drain. The type of food on a stack of shelves made clear Prescott didn't worry about being overweight: boxes of macaroni and cheese, cans of ravioli and lasagna, bags of chocolates, candy bars, and potato chips, cases of classic Coke.

"How long have you been here?"

"Three weeks."

Cavanaugh noticed books on a shelf below the food. Most were nonfiction, on subjects as various as geology and photography. The latter had a naked woman on the cover and seemed to be a sex book. In contrast, one volume was *The Collected Poems of Robinson Jeffers*, with a few books about Jeffers next to it. "You like poetry?" Cavanaugh asked.

"Soothes the soul." Prescott's tone was slightly defensive, as if he suspected that Cavanaugh might be mocking him.

Cavanaugh picked up the book and opened it, reading the first lines he came to. 'I built her a tower when I was young—/Sometime she will die—'."

Prescott looked more defensive.

"Knows how to grab my attention." Cavanaugh set down the book and continued scanning the place. Videotapes sat next to a small television. Prescott's taste had no consistency: a Clint Eastwood thriller, an old Troy Donahue-Sandra Dee teenage-romance tearjerker . . .

"I've seen worse places to go to ground." Cavanaugh thought about it. "Homeless people and crack addicts as your cover. Smart. How'd you know about this warehouse? How'd you set up this room?"

"I did it a long time ago," Prescott said.

"Whatever your trouble is, you saw it coming?"

"Not the trouble I have."

"Then why did you . . ."

"I always take precautions," Prescott said.

"You're not making sense."

"In case," Prescott told him.

"In case of what?" Movement on a TV monitor abruptly caught Cavanaugh's attention. "Wait a second."

"What's wrong?" Prescott spun toward the monitor.

On the screen, a gray image showed a dozen ragged men plodding through the rain, converging on Cavanaugh's car.

"Jesus," Prescott said.

"Crack addicts are amazing," Cavanaugh said. "No matter what it is, if it's left alone, they'll try to steal it. I once knew a guy who stole forty pounds of dog food from his father so he could buy crack. What's more amazing, the dealer he went to took the dog food rather than demanding money for the dope. For all I know, the dealer ate it."

On the screen, drenched with rain, the ragged men tugged at the side-view mirrors or used chunks of metal to pry at the hub caps.

"Have you got a way to hear what's going on outside?" Cavanaugh asked.

Prescott flipped a switch on a console. Immediately, the sound of rain came through an audio speaker.

Cavanaugh heard the distant scrape of metal as the ragged men worked in the downpour to try to disassemble his car. "Get a job, guys."

He took the car's remote control from his jacket pocket. It was more elaborate than was common, equipped with a half dozen buttons.

Prescott looked puzzled as Cavanaugh pressed one of the buttons. Suddenly, the audio speaker filled the room with an ear-torturing siren that came from the Taurus and made the ragged men drop their makeshift burglary tools, fleeing like drenched versions of the scarecrow in *The Wizard of Oz*.

Cavanaugh pressed the button again, and the siren stopped.

"Are you ready to get out of here?" he asked Prescott.

"To?" Prescott looked apprehensive.

"Somewhere safer than this, although Lord knows this place is safe enough. After my team arrives, after we get organized, we'll get you a new identity and relocate you. But first I need to know what kind of risk level we're talking about. Why are you so frightened?"